The Street of Four Winds

Andrew Lazarus

Copyright © 2002, Andrew Lazarus

All rights reserved. No part of this book may be used or reproduced,
in any manner whatsoever, without the written permission of the Publisher.

Printed in Canada

For information address:
Durban House Publishing Company, Inc.
7502 Greenville Avenue, Suite 500, Dallas, Texas 75231
214.890.4050

Library of Congress Cataloging-in-Publication Data
Andrew Lazarus, 1924

The Street of Four Winds / by Andrew Lazarus

Library of Congress Catalog Card Number: 00-2002103005

p. cm.

ISBN 1-930754-21-3

First Edition

10 9 8 7 6 5 4 3 2 1

Visit our Web site at
http://www.durbanhouse.com

Book design by:
Strasbourg-MOOF, GmBH

THIS BOOK IS DEDICATED
TO MY WIFE,
RAILI

Many thanks to:

Bob Middlemiss, a rare and invaluable editor; Rosemary Morgan for her patient transcribing of the text; Mary Kreimer, Gretchen Peterson and several others who provided helpful insights; Dagobert Scher, who tried to keep my French honest; my daughter Kris for her suggestions and to the city of my special love for just being there—

PARIS

The Street of Four Winds

PONT SAINT-MICHEL

ONE

Our blue Peugeot climbed a winding road into the Hudson Highlands, and I had to be careful of the hairpin turns. It was a fine October day with the leaves just beginning to turn. Another year was coming to an end, and new discoveries were merging with old memories.

Holding our landmark Columbia College class reunion at Arden House had an irony to it. At least I saw it that way. First, we checked in, then ascended an elaborate staircase to the library where a bar had been set up. While a drink warmed in my hand and unrecognized classmates and their wives moved around me, I studied the great expanse of the Harriman's Arden House, its spaciousness, ambiance and outmoded taste. The hilltop place was rife with a sense of the past. It was both reassuring and utterly free of concerns about the present. High ceilings and heavy drapery fabrics muffled drifts of conversation and the occasional too-loud laugh. It was odd how the free and easy but tentative conversations about old classmates made for a sense of adventure.

I had walked through the endless hallways and parlors, the grand rooms, libraries and dining facilities absorbed in the echoes of a bygone age. And now Ellen and I cavorted beneath bright crystal lighting that revealed the scars of time on faces once known for their youthful alertness and intense expectations. My thoughts were hard to pin down.

"A penny for them," Ellen said.

I looked at her. Like all of us, she was older now, the smile a bit slower, her breasts fuller, but there was still a brightness about

1

her that always fascinated me. Her blue eyes remained young and active, still probing as when I had first met her.

"I was thinking about this reunion and the irony of it all," I said.

"Irony?"

"Yes. Your love of horses, for instance. when you were a kid. Now here we are in the former home of Averell Harriman, a world class polo player and owner of fine racehorses."

"I didn't know that."

"And I was thinking of Irene in Paris. Funny that Harriman was our special envoy to Russia. What would our communist comrade, peddling her newspapers, think of this place?"

"Yes, Irene." Ellen said acidly, an old jealousy still running in her veins. "I have other memories of her." She spun her glass nervously. "Can we get another?"

"I'll catch a waiter when he comes around."

"Oh, my God!" she said in a hushed voice.

"What?"

"There're Norman and Betty. They're coming over."

They moved toward us. Norman Tunison and his still girlish Colorado wife Betty. She had been the prime mover in Norman's completion of a fine study of Rabelais, largely written while we were all together in Paris after the war. I'll never forget how excited he was when they first met. Norman had aged since, but that alertness, that quick movement in his trowel-shaped Jewish face, and his plump cheeks puffed up while his jaw moved up and down as he chattered—these were the same. Betty was in tow, his faithful and devoted research assistant, who in those days spoke the fluent French he had never been able to master but needed for his work.

"Hello, you two," Norman said. "Good to see you. By the way, Tom, nice piece in the Trib."

"Thanks. I was just going to freshen our drinks…"

"Here he comes, load up!"

We took new glasses. Ellen raised hers to me and then offered her own irony: "Happy days and lurid nights!" She had not wanted to come. Nor had I, thinking it would lead to trouble or sadness or great disappointment. And that crack about Irene didn't bode well.

Norman's glass came up. "To Paris nights, Tom. How the hell did you ever get me back to my lodgings those times?"

I smiled. "Pastis did have a way with you. Still, the rue de Tournon wasn't far."

He laughed. "Those were good days," he said, his prominent jaw clamping shut.

"Those were pompous days, Norman," Ellen said. "Maybe the trouble was that we really didn't give a damn…enough. We drank that pastis and exchanged endless clever insights on politics, France, the States. And we uttered windy observations regurgitated from artsy-fartsy textbooks. Frankly, I think everyone was more concerned with bedding each other."

"Not so," Betty said, her years of serious apprenticeship to Rabelais suddenly called into question.

"We were struggling, trying to make sense of things in that postwar ferment—"

"And screwing each other," Ellen said.

Norman grimaced. "This is it? After all the postwar intensity? What would Buck think?"

Everyone was suddenly still. An absent voice had been summoned. I missed its high pitch, its grandiose delivery of pretentious, universal ideas that once seemed so solid—and weren't.

"Let's not talk about Buck," Ellen said quietly, cutting things short.

"Or about Pam." I said. Now I was irritated, annoyed by Ellen's arbitrary arrogance in raising and just as suddenly dropping old ghosts.

"She's dead, too," she said.

Betty's voice was too bright: "Norman received an award last week in Early French Literature. Well deserved, I say." She always had a way of keeping things on an even keel, avoiding problems.

"Congratulations, Norman," Ellen said, raising her half empty glass.

In his humble way, Norman moved on: "What's with Bill Clinton, Tom? I can't figure out this man at all, except for his total lack of culture and style…maybe self-control—like the French."

"Are you still on that bit?" Ellen asked.

"Still on what?"

"The French," I said. "You used to say, 'Scratch a Frog and the glory of Napoleon shines through.'"

"And what do you get if you scratch Clinton?" Betty asked, relieved that the conversation had moved away from dark memories.

"Raw passion," Ellen said. "It's always passion."

"Remember the Relais Odéon?" I asked Norman, trying another tack.

"Those uncomfortable plastic seats…"

"And that fluorescent light," I said. "Jesus, no wonder we couldn't come up with any profound ideas. And that was the same time the Existentialists met in the same cafés as ourselves. Damn! We never had a clue."

"But seriously, Tom, the French have this damned pride in what they once were. That's why they hate us and our position in the world today."

"You said that in Paris as well," I said. "It was Buck who called you on it. Right?"

"He said I was full of shit."

"Yes, that was it."

Norman waggled his glass at me. "And he always got his way because he had the money. The rest of us were getting by on army savings or the GI Bill."

"…don't forget gas coupons and the high rate of Arab exchange," I said.

"I for one appreciated the handouts," Ellen said. "The best meals I ever had were when Buck was holding forth, leading his interminable discussions over the ragout."

"And he did that, didn't he, Ellen?" Norman's eyes brightened and his jaw jutted. "That half-assed seminar on the post-war generation, our generation."

"I hear Buck's family made some incredible grant to Columbia," I said.

Ellen nodded. "A professorship in political science."

"Well, we have to appreciate that," Norman said, "but one has to wonder at its origins—Buck and his idiosyncratic ways, perhaps. Then Buck and his grand design: Birnbaum's great chance to publish his own history of the postwar years? And all that AC/DC nonsense—a fine mind gone wrong, wrung out on some emotional rack."

"Norman!" Betty said.

I was relieved when Fred Furness showed up. Fred the poet looked relaxed. If our faces had registered with him as tense and uncomfortable, he did not show it. He had the poet's calm, and he now enjoyed some fame—not a bard of our time, but a good, solid poet for the anthologies.

"I saw some of your work in the New Yorker," I said.

"Ah, my Thomas Aquinas. Did you just see it or read it?"

"Of course I read it. I even caught a hint of some of the things you wrote in Paris—under the spell of Joyce."

"Really? She was in the wilder stanzas, the poems of memory. Bookends."

"You're getting cynical, Fred," Ellen said.

"No. Perhaps it's this reunion. Stuff bubbling up. Buck, Pam…" His tone broke. "The missing voices. Even Joyce." He looked a bit wistful at that moment.

"Joyce was a piece of poetry," Norman said.

"As a matter of fact, Fred," Ellen added. "We were just talking about Buck and the seminar, the conference,"

"Ah!" Fred said, staring at his glass. "The seminar. You know, Norman, you were wild in those days—those outrageous generalizations, the crazy capers on the Paris Metro, the Swiss mountains…"

"Oh-la-la…and the pastis."

"And that rotten French of yours with that brash American accent," I said. "How did you ever get into Rabelais?"

I watched Norman's face with interest. It ran the gamut of pleasure, excitement, lust and lost youth. Oddly, I remembered his black naval officer's raincoat, with his sloping shoulders stooped over, resembling the shape of a burgundy bottle. I mentioned it once to Ellen during our early married days, saying, 'He wears it like a medal, even though he stayed Stateside preparing sailors for Japan's occupation.' She had been cutting: 'And you with your war wound, Tom—carefully hidden away.' I never mentioned it again.

"You know, Ellen," I said, "There's another irony to this place."

"Oh?"

"Averell Harriman was lonely, cut off from his father… destined to accomplish great things but couldn't figure out what—as a nine year old kid, that is." Ellen's stare was like ice.

Fred was recalling some of those Paris scenes, the Rodin Museum. "Remember that place in 1948?"

"We were both mesmerized," I said. "La Porte d'Enfer…"

"God, I loved that," Norman chimed in. "The Gate of Hell." He seemed carried back. I wondered what Norman could possibly know about hell, the hell that Fred knew with the German tanks in the Ardennes. Joyce had told me he cried out in his nightmares. Just like me. Hidden wounds.

"The perpetual struggle of man," Norman was saying about the sculpture. "How well Rodin caught it!"

"Remember Lizette?" I said. Norman's jaw clamped shut. Betty looked questioningly; I was sure he hadn't told her.

"Lizette…?"

"Small, lithe, brash and sensual. Dark, knowing eyes."

"She didn't care about Rodin's sculpture," Ellen said. "I recall her disdain, her nodding at you, and making come-hither eyes."

Norman stared at her, incredulous. "What the hell's got into you?"

"Sorry, Norman."

"Lizette. I remember."

"It all comes back to screwing," Ellen said.

"No," I said, and everyone looked at me. "It really didn't."

"Well," said Ellen, "there was a lot of it going on."

"That there was."

The Street of Four Winds

Paris. City of Light. City of escape. The war had left her virtually unscathed, only a bit down on her luck. Hitler never got what he wanted—to burn her to the ground. For everyone she was always exciting. The small, winding streets of the core city—their suggestiveness. One had to get beyond clichés like the Eiffel Tower and move into the pastels of romantic buildings, the streets like the rue de Seine itself, past the hub-bub of the market stalls full of food in the Marché de Buci, the small hotels, the Beaux Arts school. And the curious book stores everywhere. Monumental St. Sulpice itself, up toward the Palais Luxembourg, St. Sulpice with her sharp bells orchestrating the life of the quarter, audible everywhere on the Left Bank. High, down-beaming lights painted the walls so beautifully. The quai along the welcoming walled riverside, its dark surface glittering now and again in the street lights from both sides of the Seine, Right and Left. Down from the Pont des Arts the Louvre squatted squarely at this crossroads of Paris. The Vert Galant, heart of my Paris at the tip of the Île de la Cité, was a separate world of peace and comfort in the midst of the teeming city and the smooth river flowing around the island. The graceful arches of the Pont Neuf. Notre Dame's stubby pair of towers and buttresses to the east. And the lovers strolling through paradise.

In 1948 a group of us were enjoying coffee and drinks at the Café de Flore, a popular bistro in our neighborhood of the 6th Arrondissement. Beside me was my girl of the moment, Irene Malakoff—sensual, exotic and grey-eyed, with a high-cheeked face that drove me mad. I held her dark, warm hand while I listened to the noise around us and Norman going on about Rodin. "He's quite classic, you know—Grecian. He alone revived a classic sense of the human body…"

At that I looked across at Bill Watson, a Negro from Chicago who was in Paris to work on his painting. More deeply, he wanted to resolve being black in a white world. I could always find Bill near me when he was in our group. I guess he felt comfortable with me. And British Joyce, of course. Joyce and her alabaster skin set up a special feeling between Bill and herself. It might have caused problems later, but so far the relationship was going fine. Right now I was trying to gauge Bill's reaction to Norman's preaching. He gave me that slow, confident smile…

"…like Maillol really," Norman said, shoving aside his naval officer's raincoat, "cutting out all that neo-classic crap of the 19th Century, which is why he's so important in the grand tradition." Norman looked around, waiting for support. But it was Buck Birnbaum who took the mood and carted it away.

"Nonsense! I find it more interesting to watch Bill and Irene," Buck said, both of them looking shy.

"Why?" Norman said.

"They're both savages." Irene and Bill grinned. Buck cleared his throat. "Of course, Joyce and Bill present fantastic possibilities, too. I can visualize the intimacies."

"You've got a dirty mind," Irene said, her fingertip, which had been circling my palm in boredom, now motionless.

"Notice the artist's eye," Buck went on, "how Bill picks up on her Russian and Moroccan blood, those fascinating grey eyes against that stunning skin. Can your palette capture that, Bill?"

"She hasn't got Moroccan blood; she's a pure-bred Tartar from southern Russia," I volunteered.

"I could try," Bill said. "A brush and one man's skill can do only so much."

Irene smiled across the table at him with her gypsy grin. "Better try Joyce," she said.

"But you haven't asked to paint them—Joyce or this leftist woman , this firebrand," Buck said.

"I am not a firebrand," Irene said simply. "I'm just a believer in the truth and I sell newspapers. I get out the truth."

"Those rotten capitalists, you mean?" Buck's voice went reed-thin. "Did you know that those rotten capitalists have pumped nine billion dollars into Europe so far since the war?"

"That is as it should be, Monsieur Birnbaum. After all, you plundered it from Europe…from us."

Buck grinned.

The Street of Four Winds

Arden House had known more elegant conversation than tonight's; had embraced far more eminent figures; indeed, it had participated in history, in the delicate utterances of difficult truths, of banks and bonds and war and havoc. But tonight it belonged to us, we five, a reunion within the Columbia reunion, harking back to those magic Paris days. That was when we dreamed of a better world after the war and hammered out the future with our insights and hopes, while our blood pumped hard and we lived our never-ending youth. So we drank our now warm drinks and talked around absent voices, not world diplomacy in these endowed but tasteless halls. For us, just cab rides to the past, the Paris past…

Norman looked at Ellen, a smile pulling his jaw wide. "I remember that night after the Relais Odéon, we had dinner, remember? I was making a mess out of myself about Rodin, and Buck challenged our resident negro: paint Irene , he said."

"But he never did. Not then, anyway."

"She always had her hand under the table."

"She liked to hold my hand, thank you very much," I said.

"If I may say so, Ellen, you were rather prim that night."

"That wasn't primness, Norman, that was my reaction to yet another of your lectures. "

"Ouch!" he said.

"Serves you right, Norman." Betty said.

Ellen put down her glass. "I remember the cab ride."

"Me, too," I said.

"You in the middle," Ellen said, her blue eyes, now faded, watched me. "And Irene on one side of you and me on the other."

"And the cab swayed," I said. "A nice pressing of thighs…"

"But before we left," Norman said, "those girls came, the Lycée girls? Pam, Sally and Faith."

"Smith, Incorporated—ah, yes. Pam," Ellen murmured. "Edna St. Vincent Millay—a light burning far too bright."

'"Knock it off," I said annoyed.

"And don't forget Fred's girl…"

Fred gave a theatrical groan. "Goodie Goodstein."

Betty smiled. "Those three midwestern girls, all peas in a pod, and Fred's Jewish princess."

Fred waved a dismissing hand. "And Joyce," he said. "What a bird! The English girl with the really white skin and the condescending attitude."

"No, she wasn't there," I said, remembering. I remembered almost everything, especially when it came to the women.

<hr />

The Café de Flore was now acrid with the smell of Gitanes. Smoke cushioned our gusts of laughter, the swiftly moving waiters, the buzz of the place. Goodie Goodstein, a colorless blonde, kept turning her gold ring on her left hand. She began a conversation in her faulty French with Lizette. More than language separated them—Goodie, the bland and blonde Jewish princess, constrained by inherited expectations from possessive parents, and Lizette, lithe, free and spontaneous, bemused by these Americans— including me, of course. I think I was judged more lightly because of Irene, a woman Lizette could understand. It was Lizette who suddenly broke out with, ""Je veux aller au dancing."

"What dancing?" Goodie asked into Lizette's widening eyes.

"That's a dance hall," Buck said in his superior way. "And that's not a bad idea."

"Aimez-vous danser?" Lizette turned to him with her husky voice.

"Non," Buck responded, "mais si tu veux."

I watched Ellen Cassidy. She had said nothing during the entire evening, and I found that odd.

Perhaps now she would. She was from Darien, Connecticut, and attending Swarthmore. She had come over for the summer with Buck, seemingly content to be his silent partner. There was something attractive but aloof about her—a lady of mystery, like they all were. Light blue eyes and regular features. Open to banter but keeping her distance. In front of her was a paper napkin with a butterfly doodled on it, a pictorial mystery, no easier to solve than her relationship with Buck. Ellen watched me from time to time while under the table Irene's hand made its fingertip circles in my palm.

"We could go to a boîte," Buck said.

"Why not?" Norman chimed in, grabbing his raincoat, and before we knew it Birnbaum had paid for all the drinks and hailed three taxis to take all of us to 'Le Chat Jaune,' a club in Montmartre. Lautrec's Paris of another time—but Paris all the same. And Van Gogh's and Renoir's Paris, a Paris best seen on an early Spring morning or a cold Autumn afternoon. Better still at night. But we, the supposed intelligentsia, were out slumming. Dutifully, we followed Buck, our leader, banker and host.

In my cab I enjoyed the thighs of Ellen and Irene pressed against mine. But frankly, I would have preferred to be alone with Irene. There was a strong physical tie between us, developing as soon as we met, which was just after she had broken up with a French boy (her "bijou," she once said), who failed to marry her. That had been her first, short, serious affair, the kind the French call a "fleur bleu." And she was looking for a sympathetic partner when I arrived. I had come to Europe to put behind me an impossible relationship in New York, so we had a lot in common. I favored her thigh as the taxi whirled through the Paris festival lights and over its dark, suggestive waters.

At the 'Chat Jaune' we spilled out of the cabs, babbling awkward French and very American English. Buck hurried over to pay the fares before anyone could object. Then we were inside the narrow door of the boîte, which was jumping to a lively tune played by a small orchestra. Black and white musicians. The lights were low and tempting—comfortable.

"Alors, on danse," Buck said to Norman's Lizette. He grabbed her around the waist with a flourish, like a matador doing a veronica in the dark, smoky club. She squealed in delight. The rest of us drifted to a nearby table. The three Smith girls were tittering about something "sooo-French," and I leaned back in my chair and relaxed. Then suddenly I felt a hand taking mine and squeezing. It wasn't Irene's. I looked over into the warm bespectacled eyes of Pam Batterford. Her grip was firm, a commitment of sorts, maybe a promise. So, puzzled, I asked her to dance. Candlelight flashed on her glasses. The drinks were too strong, and I didn't give a damn. I excused myself to Irene with a look she seemed to understand: American solidarity. Only Ellen's glance was unreadable, but then I plunged into the pungent Armagnac and the woman who had taken hold of me. Pam said nothing during our brief turn on the small dance floor, but her pelvis seriously nudged mine. It was a bit out of character for a Smith girl. Sitting down again on a ripple of chromed trumpet, I was soon holding hands with two women: Irene on one side and Pam on the other. It was, as the French say, très amusant, an evening of sensual body parts: thighs in taxis, and pelvises, and secret hand-holding. Ellen watched through the blue smoke, then went back to her doodling.

"Picasso!" Buck said out of nowhere. "Mere production!" As tobacco smoke rose in blue whorls, I watched Irene light up for the first time since I had known her. When the match flared, her grey eyes were almost opaque against her dark skin and high, dark cheekbones. She looked like the gypsy she wanted to be.

Pam's hand squeezed around mine. "You were in Scandinavia?"

"Yes."

Fingers palpated and pressed. "Something cool, it must have been," she went on, "not like this."

"Very."

Then she began to tell me about her junior Smith year at Geneva with Sally and Faith, and I became interested. But an interruption came.

Buck was on his one-note of artistic outrage: "Picasso's so overrated."

"Damn right," said Norman.

The Street of Four Winds

Then, across the room from our group, I heard raucous voices and saw that a fight had broken out. A smartly dressed woman began to scream. She cursed, stopping the sudden anger. Then as quickly as it had started the incident was over. Two hands again found mine. I was confused but amused, and when I looked at each woman they offered identical smiles. A feminine universal, I thought. A sheltered midwestern Smithie and a worldly wise Irene, a Russian from Odessa whose family had left the Soviet Union before the war and settled in Rabat, Morocco, with other old "white" Russian sympathizers. Women had always been a mystery to me, and no more than right then.

A disjointed evening gently resolved itself when Norman started humming Noel Coward's "The Party's Over". Goodie Goodstein joined in, then the Smithies, Sally and Faith. Both Norman and Goodie were quite drunk, and no one was feeling any pain. Two hours passed with the singing of old songs, then a reprise of "The Party's Over."

Buck said, "Very nice," although he had not joined in the singing. Maybe because of his high-pitched voice. "But it isn't over. Let's go get some onion soup."

"Where?" someone asked.

"Over on the rue Dauphine, that upstairs place, where they serve big bowls of the stuff with gobs of rich, stringy cheese that can strangle you if you don't watch out…"

"And you can burn your tongue…"

Quickly we broke camp and took the late Metro to the Odéon Carrefour, while Norman did his impression of Maurice Chevalier singing, "Don't Fence Me In." Norman's fractured French had Fred in stitches as we skipped along down to the river. From the Odéon we walked deep into the softly lit streets of the quarter north of the Boulevard St. Germain where in a few years Sartre, Camus, and de Beauvoir would replace Gide, Éluard and André Bretton in the cafés. Then, while Bill Watson's baritone carried us along on "Alouette," we were on Dauphine.

"If the oils and canvas fail, Bill, sing!" Buck called out.

Bill looked across at Irene. "I'll sing of your gypsy charms," he said. Irene turned her smiling face in the stage-lit street.

We climbed the stairs of the "salle de soup," as we called it. Many a night we ended up here, carrying on our flow of quasi-intellectual conversation as we feasted on the thick, marvelous soup and fretted about our world. A big topic in those days was the House Un-American Activities Committee and the conservatives at home. It was Irene who caught a *Combat* newspaper headline shouting about the newest French government, a premier with the funny, impossible-for-Americans-to-pronounce name of Henri Queuille. He was a Radical Socialist, who was about to fall. "Merde!" she said. And far away in America an Agence France Presse article predicted Dewey's victory in the upcoming Presidential election.

"No comment, Irene, besides merde?" as Buck went into his shopworn speech about the "descending state of our morality in the States."

"C'est suffisant. I have newspapers to distribute, Tom. It's quite late." She was adamant, her grey eyes flashing.

"The big Sunday edition."

"Oui."

Nothing would deter her from leaving, so the next day she could sell the Communist newspaper *L'Humanité* on our neighborhood streets. She was devoted to it, so we were the first to break away. Before we did I made a point of kissing every woman with us in the French manner on both cheeks, especially Pam Batterford, who said softly, "That was nice—let's continue," in farewell. Irene, who had heard Pam, lifted her critical gaze to mine without comment. Ellen simply held up her right cheek for my quick kiss but then stared coldly at me. Then Irene and I went down the stairs and began our walk to the Odéon.

Irene said in French, "What a life you have. You Americans!"

At the hotel we went to bed exhausted. But she still had time for words.

"You must be careful with that woman," she said.

"Woman? Ellen?"

Grey eyes searched mine. "Ellen the nature artist, the arrogant one? Don't be silly. No—Pam the school girl." Her identification was severe.

"Why?"

"I've known girls like that. In Morocco and here in Paris. Watch yourself, mon chéri."

"Watch for what?"

Irene shrugged beside me. "I'm tired," she said. "There's work to be done tomorrow."

"Watch out for what?" I insisted.

"How you are with her. Like me, you live in the moment, Tomas. I will lose you one day; you will leave. That's all right. I expect it. After all, you're nothing but a visiting American. But this one does not live in the moment."

In bed I spooned myself around her. Tentatively I found her firm, small breasts and caressed a nipple.

"Don't be silly."

We slept like that until she left me to go to her sister's room upstairs, then on out to her self-imposed political chores. I was dead to the world when the sun began to break through the shutters of my room.

Overhead the jumbo jets vectored for New York's airports on quiet engines; they looked like huge dragonflies in the late afternoon. We got into our Peugeot, but for some contrary reason I thought about the war and the Germans—just a flash—and our Paris band and resident poet Fred Furness who had a Nazi tank roll over his foxhole in the Ardennes. Then Jack McCormick, our class president, on the first wave at Okinawa. We moved out of the Arden House parking lot on squealing tires and headed back to the city. The silence between us was unnerving.

"What really happened tonight?" Ellen asked.

"A reunion, what else?"

"Not a Columbia reunion. Just Paris. Ourselves."

"True. We never got to Switzerland, but that was coming."

"And Buck. After all these years," she sighed. "He might have been there."

"He was, in spirit. Just like Pam was. And, speaking of what happened, what was bothering you?"

"I hadn't planned on Irene and Lizette, even that promiscuous Joyce Frost, the English mattress."

"That's not fair. Besides, you said all Paris was screwing."

Ellen pushed me with a penetrating look. "Yes, I shouldn't have said that."

"Not once, either—'twas a damned refrain."

"I said I'm sorry."

"Bill Watson cared deeply for Joyce."

"Ah, our resident negro. He never really belonged, did he?"

"And you don't think he didn't know that? He needed us."

I pulled the Peugeot around a slow truck, then nestled into the slow lane again. "He told me once we were pretentious and phonies, and he was the worst for wanting to be part of us. Joyce gave him her honesty, at least. Did you know when he painted that nude of her he made love to her? At each sitting he made love to her."

"It was a matter of contrasting skins, we all knew that. A fascination in black and white."

"Deeper than that, Ellen, far deeper. Joyce acknowledged his equality, both with her body and her open spirit."

"Spirit?"

"You make it sound dirty."

"And painting Joyce in those red tones and hues."

"For Bill that was her passion and honesty hidden within. Way beyond the matter of black and white, Ellen."

Ellen sighed. "Whatever."

We drove on over the Palisades Parkway in silence. Then I said, "If Buck were hovering over us tonight, it would have hurt him."

"Do you really think so?" she said. "Oh, the seminar."

"Yes, we took shots at it. Norman did, anyway. Maybe Fred in his laid-back way."

"Buck's seminar was everything to him," Ellen agreed. "When we were coming over to Paris he had the first notions about it. He always was after the grand scheme of things, always wanting to imprint order and cohesion through his intellect. He had a hell of a lot of integrity, Tom. You know that. And he felt so guilty about missing the war. We should be flattered, really, that he invited all of us."

I nodded. "You were right about Pam though. A light burning too bright. And I over-reacted that day. I must have been out of my mind…"

"True."

I saw her grimace next to me in the growing darkness. It was a strained, hard smile, because we were older now. Life had had its way with us. People we once thought were so tremendous had fizzled out. Others, almost ignored, had peaked. Or became renowned, like Norman with his book. Memory is such a bitch, especially when you're only an actor in the play.

Ellen said, "At the 'Chat Jaune.' Pam was so desperately naïve, pushing her pelvis at you, grinding away. Was she trying to get a good rise out of you?"

"Quit it, Ellen. It doesn't become you."

"Oh, Christ, Tom. We all did crazy things then. Get away from her death, for God's sake. That night was the start of so much. Fred was mentally composing a poem and Buck envied your focused bonding on that dance floor, so different from his own. Didn't you once tell me that high-school definition of dancing? A navel engagement fought at close range? Your and Pam's mutual infatuation that night was so damned obvious."

"You think Pam would've rubbed up against Bill Watson? Or would that primal rape thing have gotten in the way? How about you, Ellen? Was Bill ever worth a thought—one of your pennies?"

"He talked about us?"

"Of course. He was so lost in Paris, he only thought of possibilities. Even Pam, when she…"

Ellen let it go. I looked down at the dashboard and its dull glow. There had been screeching tires that night… Then Buck was gone. "We're going to need gas and an oil change soon."

"I'll take it in tomorrow. Tom, dear, what are you frowning at?"

"Nothing," I said.

"There's something."

"Yes, there is. Those ghosts from the past."

She said nothing.

We drove on into the night under the necklace of lights on the George Washington Bridge, and all of Manhattan spread out like a jewel box for a big party. But I wasn't in New York. I was in Paris and then in Switzerland at the seminar. And Fred wasn't composing a poem, he was kicking my ribs in. And Pam's trusting face was looking up at me in supplication, as if I were worth a try, and Buck was…

How deceptive memory is. So much happened when I lived so long ago on the rue des Quatre Vents. Change came from all directions, and the people came from everywhere. And then departed. Les vents frivolants. When we were young, fresh from the wars, nothing seemed frivolous. Now…

All of those months and hours on the rue des Quatre Vents were haunting me—and at Caux. But I would recover. It would stop. We drove into the city.

"What are you frowning at?"

"Damn." I said.

TWO

Sunlight poured mercilessly through the shutters when I was roused out of bed by the concierge. It was too fast a reveille, like an Army wake-up call. In any event, Dan Vorst and Belinda, his young sister, were waiting downstairs. I hadn't seen Dan in more than a year, and our relationship at Cornell had been tenuous. Yet here he was, apparently, with his sister in tow. Irene's presence was still in the room, a musky fragrance of heat and passion. Tonight, maybe…If she had had a good day. I savoured a wisp of her garlicy breath and the memory of her dark, snaky body. Well, the hell with it. I straightened the bed, opened the shutters, let the strong sunlight burn out the mood and spoor of her, the very mystery of her.

Dressing quickly I went downstairs to join Dan and Belinda.

"Hello, Tom. Good to see you again," Dan said. "Hope we're not interrupting anything. You remember Belinda, of course." I remembered the abandon of this bright, curvaceous and enthusiastic young girl.

They were far too perky, he in his crisp shirt and Belinda trying to contain her adolescent joy. It was Paris, after all. "Of course, I remember. How are you, Belinda? Still rehashing the Spanish Civil War?"

She grinned at me. "And still good for a chorus of 'Los Cuatros Generales' when the singing starts. I still hate that Fascist Franco!"

I looked at her anew. More mature than that night in the Vorst home in Connecticut. Her eyes were more determined, her jaw more set, and possibly a cause of some parental worry.

"Let's go upstairs. My room's a bit of a mess, but we can get comfortable. So what brings you here?"

My room was a mistake. Even with sunlight scorching it, it still held the sweet odor of Paris, a permeating sultriness that combined with traces of Irene. I found myself looking at Belinda. Her eyes were bright and roving, her brows raised a bit, and her nostrils flared with the awareness of another woman's mystery.

"My parents are in town, Tom," Dan said, tossing aside a discarded pair of socks and sitting in my one good chair. Belinda crossed her legs as she sat on my bed cover.

"Really?" I said. "So the whole clan's here." I smiled at Belinda, who was now really inspecting me with a curious gaze, half child, half woman. I found it erotic, feeling rather predatory, and then ashamed. "Well…"

"They want us all to have dinner tonight, over at the Ambassadeurs."

"Sounds pretty swish. A bit out of my class."

"So, we'll enjoy a scrumptious meal," Belinda said.

"The word is out about that place, they still use powdered eggs in their sauces," I said.

Dan winced. "For God's sake, don't tell mother."

"I'll have to rustle up a tie and jacket."

Belinda giggled. "Don't you have a tie?"

"Yes, but it got sauced a few nights ago." Irene had scolded me for being such a 'cochon.' I smiled at Belinda. "Don't worry. I'll get one for this special occasion. As I say, the Ambassadeurs is up there. Very de rigueur."

"Will you have to buy clothes, then?"

"God, no. I'll impose on my good friend Norm Tunison."

Her smile was innocent, and sweet with that yearning to be sophisticated. Whatever had brought Dan to my hotel and the laid-on soirée with the Vorsts, Belinda was clearly going to be at the center of it.

Late that afternoon I tied on Norman's garish tie and shrugged into one of his jackets. It was a bit loose around the shoulders but otherwise I could get by. All was illusion: powdered eggs and borrowed clothes. I left a note for Irene. It was impassioned and out of character for me. I wrote of her lovely eyes in candlelight, her fetching smile, the tantalizing musk of her. Tonight, maybe… I slipped the note under her sister's door and wondered what Belinda would think of such a note. Her eyes would roll at the foreign sentiment, something definitely Paris. And I wondered what the hell Dan was doing, getting me out of bed before my creative juices were flowing, and lining me up with his imperious parents. The Ambassadeurs was no accident, of course. This was all part of a carefully wrought plan.

I hunched the jacket shoulders one last time and left my room.

The Ambassadeurs, now in the opulent Hotel Crillon, was an even more fantastic place in those days, set in a grove of trees down toward the Place de la Concorde. It had large crystal chandeliers, mirrors, stylish furniture and heavy draperies. Some, including me, found it oppressive and stuffy. But still impressive. One didn't question food or service here without raising a native eyebrow. The first and only time I had been there was to interview one of Andrew Malraux's cultural sidekicks about how France could afford to restore her landmark monuments. The wine list was a treasure; the veal, certainly obtained on the black market, was marvelous. Tonight I settled on potato pancake topped with caviar-flecked smoked salmon, scallops wrapped in bacon with tomato and basil, and baby roast lamb—followed by sorbet aux fraises. I shuffled around in my new shoulders and smiled at my hosts. Mrs. Vorst, if anything, had become more of the dowager, her full figure girt in an expensive lamé dress, with a discreet touch of jewelry. She was a woman of class—good American class, too, nothing gauche. She kept her eyes on me, as did Mr. Vorst, a diminutive man with a menacing look. He was a typical American alley fighter, like Joe Kennedy or Jesse James, now concealed behind his money.

Belinda was chattering.

"This is really a woman's city," she said.

"Why do you say that?"

"Because it's so warm and inviting."

I wondered about that. "It can be cold and lonely," I said.

"We understand the war's done that," Mrs. Vorst said. "I noticed big beams holding up some of the buildings all over the city."

"But it's still delicious and wonderful," Belinda said, glowing.

Mrs. Vorst traced a hand over her brooch that was in the shape of a fleur de lis.

"We all have our points of view," I moderated.

Mrs. Vorst looked at me and tapped my arm, indicating she wanted to say something in private. "A moment of your time, Tom."

"The first course will be here soon," Belinda said.

Mrs. Vorst murmured something and Belinda relaxed. I assisted Mrs. Vorst with her chair, then found myself with her in the bar. We sat at a small table, while she waved off the waiter.

"Charles and I are somewhat concerned about Belinda going off to Spain. She plans to travel there soon with a friend."

"Yes?"

"Well. You know how she is, Tom. A head full of romantic notions about the Spanish Civil War, largely based on Hollywood films, not even Hemingway, and we think she could get into trouble."

"I see. Well…"

"Charles and I want you to go with them, be an escort. Goodness, Tom, she's young, she dislikes Franco, she could get into a world of trouble."

I watched her fondle her brooch again, as if it were some sort of talisman. Perhaps she had a different one for different dresses. Did I fondle Irene like that, her soft skin, her dusky heat, a gypsy presence? I snapped out of it. "But surely Dan could escort them—he's here, he's family…"

"Dan's got to go back to the States in a couple of days."

"I see."

"Look, Tom. You have your work, we know that. We will pay you, of course, and perhaps this could bring about an interesting writing assignment."

"Yes, possibly." Her eyes looked strained. Staying ahead of their daughter took its toll. How much simpler just to borrow a jacket and tie.

"Being responsible for two girls would put constraints on working a news story," I said. Beyond that, I fantasized, maybe being in bed with two girls would be provocative. It was an idea. It was a rotten idea.

She leaned forward, her heavy and brooched breast on the table. "Please, Tom. I can't tell you how worried we are. She's so headstrong."

"I'll consider it, of course, Mrs. Vorst. But please give me time to think about it. I'm in the middle of things, and there are other problems…"

"Yes, I do understand. Please think about it."

"Just a couple of days."

"Certainly."

Beyond the bar area light music coated the already opulent atmosphere. So far removed from the 'Chat Jaune' and Pam's pulsing pelvis. "Would you care to dance, Mrs. Vorst? We have time before that first course."

She smiled. "I'd like that. It'll make Belinda grind her teeth a bit while she waits."

I was getting an interesting little insight into two generations, mother and daughter. We moved sedately around the small dance floor. Mrs. Vorst's breath touched my ear. "It's so important to us, Tom."

Back at the dinner table Charles Vorst inspected me like a customs official.

After dinner and an immense amount of small talk, I excused myself. I needed to think it over. I rode the Metro and got off at the Odéon station. Across the five-way intersection on the Boulevard St. Germain was the relais where I was sure to find a compatriot sooner or later. A waiter came and I ordered pastis. At a nearby table an older couple were talking with vigor over coffee cups. I sat there and tried to think under the harsh fluorescent light. The pastis tasted good, and it cleared out the debris of the dinner with people who had little meaning to me. A second pastis helped me shape my response to the Vorsts: sorry, no can do. And yet…and yet…Belinda offered some lascivious attraction, and I had to admit it was there. Women were always a mystery to me, and she was an unexplored vessel en route to understanding. Irene would sneer, of course. Don't be silly, she would say. Joyce might understand, the playful Englishwoman who was exploring mysteries of her own. Like Bill Watson, a struggling but talented artist, and ebony to her alabaster.

But when Joyce was with you she was yours. Just don't get too serious, darling, and spoil it. That skin, cool and hot by turns, her exuberant spirit, her unaffected freedom. How she gave her body to you and demanded yours! And she was sincere, having a childlike innocence, as when she found the wound on my thigh. That time she stopped her lunging and pulled my legs apart, running her electric fingertips over the criss-cross scar. Soft mewing sounds, as she stared at it and kissed it.

"It was the war, wasn't it, Tom?"

"Yes. I try not to think about it."

"Then, darling, we won't, will we?" she said, mounting me again and resuming her rapid lunges, which, to her delight, turned me inside out. Her joyous smile down on me banished all the bad memories.

I finished my pastis and looked across at the old couple. They were discussing the astronomical prices of food and rent, the franc's inflation. The American dollar kept our own costs low.

When they turned to look at me I averted my gaze, casting around for something other than stray cats at night and loose women and gypsies.

I thought about Buck Birnbaum. Buck of the high voice and deep thoughts. Who bit his nails, which perhaps said more than his words. We had met recently in a bistro some place. He was worried about the wandering souls lost after the war: American souls, English language souls.

"Look at Jack McCormick," Buck said, picking at the remains of a fingernail.

"You keep chewing and picking on those nails and you'll get something infected," I said.

"McCormick—our old class president," Buck said, overriding me. "He fought at Okinawa and survived. Many didn't, you know. Now he's screwing around with class politics, just as if nothing serious happened to him during the war. Even landing in the first wave on Okinawa was no picnic, I hear. He's a charming guy and could do so much."

"He obviously doesn't fathom the seriousness of the situation."

"You baiting me, Tom?"

"No, I'm not. I just happen to know that those who were in hard action prefer not to talk about it. Those who only read about it or had Stateside jobs talk so knowingly about it."

"I'm not after talk about war. I'm after what he learned from it, this searing crucible he was in, how he came out of it."

"Unscathed, as far as I know."

Buck stood up. I grabbed his arm and said, "Sorry. Sit down. Tell me what you're thinking."

Part of it was my irritation with Buck's high-pitched voice, which jibed so much with the homosexual stereotype. I had never been comfortable, ever since I had that experience as a young kid at that trolley stop with the too kind man enticing me to go along with him. I had run away, thank God. At best Buck was AC/DC, and, judging by the way he related to Ellen and openly embraced Bob Kemperman, he was more flit than anything. Thoughts of

Ellen drifted. The 'Chat Jaune' and her primly offered cheek, her unreadable look.

I remember Buck sitting down, his driving energy, something more than New York Jewish aggressiveness. "I'll say this, Buck, I envy you."

"Envy me?"

"Your drive, your athletic achievements, your intelligence, your sense of purpose. You're a missionary. I don't have that."

"Well, thanks at least for that. Forget the athletic stuff. That's only a coverup for my personal deficiencies. But I do have the drive, and I'm no damned missionary. What I don't have is a direction, a goal, a clear objective. My God, there's got to be more around than the garbage the Leftists are dishing up, or what the World Government people are offering. Or even the Democrats."

I grinned at that.

"In some ways it's got to come from outside of us individually. We've got to help shape that future, Tom. We, us, 'we band of brothers.'"

"And shape it how?"

"With the highest cultural and societal concern for Mankind."

Across from us a cleaning woman wiped trash into a tray. Garters held up her frayed stockings.

"Shit! What's the answer?" Buck said.

Then he shifted into gear with history: America's great liberal traditions…Emerson, Roger Williams, Jefferson…the very moral basis of World War II. He bunched his fist, struck the table, then sat back and chewed at a nail.

"Frankly, Buck, I'm more selfish and concerned with microcosmic man."

"Concerned how?" Buck's eyes were beady with surprise and sudden interest.

"Women—aesthetics—peace of mind—pleasure. Deep inside, though, I wonder where I'm going."

"You have your writing."

"Yes."

"And there's no answer there?"

"Nothing final. There's got to be something else."

Buck smiled at me then in genuine warmth. "My God, Tom, your problem isn't much different from mine."

"Except one thing: I don't want to lead a great cultural crusade. I just want to know about me…and what the war was really all about on a fully personal level. Was it just beating the shit out of the Germans and Japanese, who represented the cellars of this world, the evil in this world?"

"Ah-hah!" That's all he said. He seemed to cope better with universals, with multitudes in the abstract than one character sitting across from him wondering what his life was about. That's what the war had done to me. It had isolated me, surrounding me with questions.

"Want to hear more?" Buck looked a little uneasy but he nodded. "Let's get another round."

"We were pretty certain about things," I began. "We were on the side of justice, whatever that was, and finally we prevailed over something morally evil. The message was always clear, like FDR triumphing over the polio he had: bridging all needs, hearing all voices, somehow apportioning equality. There were no Sergeant Yorks. But the best of it was, we had something worth dying for."

"A faith, then."

"Faith, you call it? More than that, Buck. The war gave us that purest of faiths, a faith in freedom. Nothing like it in history. More than any one church or synagogue or mosque could offer."

"Then why are you drifting now? You have your women, your aesthetics, your pleasure, as you said before. That's a foothold."

I shook my head. "It's not that easy, I'm afraid."

"You see America as a dream, but you're having a nightmare."

"A good piece of ass helps."

At that he smiled. It was genuine, free of artifice.

"You know that's not my cup of tea, but I'm sure Irene and Pam help you a lot. Breaking up the logjam."

"Can't Ellen allay your own anxieties?"

"I need something else," he said, " something truly worthwhile beyond myself—something we used to say, in the best sense, Christian. And don't take that the wrong way."

For an instant, he froze me with his glassy stare, then smiled: "You mean enlightenment."

I'll always remember that last word. I don't think Buck ever had what for most of us would be a good lay. It always got tangled up with identity and guilt. He was Jewish and flitty that way, flitting from Kemperman back to Ellen perhaps. The poor bastard! I felt sorry for him at a time he was agonizing with me. Damn! But that conversation was in the past…though well remembered… Enlightenment was the word.

In the Relais Odéon that night, after the extravagant dinner with the Vorsts, something happened. I was thinking about the idea of the war itself, and what I figured would happen afterwards. It was so simple: Go back to college, resume my studies, get a job and a wife and a house with a white picket fence. But that wasn't going to happen, and I knew it. Behind the reason why was my trip to Europe and the new impression I had of America. Because America as I thought about it when I was fighting was more than a nation; it was an attitude and an idea. Now it wasn't any longer. Because the war was really a watershed, and America would never go back to what it was before. That's how I thought in the French café. All of my plans wouldn't pan out. That would have been far too easy.

And that's when it happened. I had several drinks of pastis, and all of the previous conversation with Buck, the new world after the war and everything else, became jumbled. I became disoriented.

I gradually became aware that I was being stared at. The stare came directly at me from someone looking at me through the window out on the Boulevard St. Germain. With my disorientation,

I had no idea who was behind the stare. Then, after several moments, the person came into focus. It was Pam Batterford.

She was alone, looking with amusement at me, but somehow appearing vulnerable. Her soft, bespectacled eyes gazed into mine. Then she moved into the relais and its harsh light, squinting in her surprised way, as if she were trying to be sure it was me or someone she knew. I got up and offered her a seat and drink.

Any woman who had held my hand the night before was certainly worth a drink.

"Don't mind if I do," came through in her flat, dead-center, low midwestern voice that sounded so formal. "Thanks. I was wondering what you were so concentrated on, all by yourself here at this hour." She had a good smile—open, with real warmth. There was something soft and attractive about her. And I liked the direct, declarative way she talked. Her lower register was irresistible. She had done me a favor, getting me out of myself. "What's on your mind?" she said.

"I wondered that about you, mademoiselle—at this hour, alone on the boulevard, mysterious. One's liable to get ideas about people."

"Don't make any assumptions. I was just going home from a late dinner with Sally and Faith."

"Northampton, Incorporated. Did they like last night at the Chat Jaune?"

Light winked from her lenses. "Not as much as I did." Her hand was warm under mine. "Aha!" she said softly, surprised but not displeased.

"No struggle? I didn't think Smith girls were so forward."

"Especially Smith girls like me. But there are times," she said, feigning a laugh. "Tell me, what were you thinking about when I came by? Tell me."

"You."

"Be serious, what was it?"

"Do you really want to know?"

Her gaze was riveting. "Yes, I guess you do." She smiled in triumph.

29

"Someone's trying to proposition me," I said.

"Are you propositionable?"

"That leaves an opening for me, but the answer is sometimes, not now." "Oh."

"I've been asked to chaperone two girls to Spain."

She laughed. "You? My God! Well, anyway, Spain's an exciting place, especially with two women. Not a bad deal."

"Pam, you have a promiscuous mind. It's unbecoming a Seven Sisters' girl."

She giggled. "There are parts of me that are promiscuous, but not my mind. So, are they attractive?"

"A bit, I guess."

" I see. Well, I guess it's your affair to sort out." There was a time of silence. Her hand was still under mine, and her fingers moved a bit now and then. "May I please have a cigarette?" she asked, pulling her hand away. I lit her cigarette and admired the way the match flared out to reveal her smooth throat. "Think you'll do it?"

"I honestly don't know."

"Spain's a good place." She had a restraint about her, not at all like Joyce or Irene. It piqued my curiosity. She shook her head nervously, her thick, short hair trembling. "Lost my light," she announced.

I held the match to her face, and her hand took mine to steady it.

"I like the way the match highlights your throat."

She brought my hand down to the table and I clasped hers again. "Come-come," she said.

"That was nice last night."

"What was nice last night?"

"I think you know."

"What? Buck and Ellen—Irene—Bill Watson—me?"

"Not the conversation, lady. You and me. The dancing."

"Yes, it was nice. I was a-venturing." She looked away.

"Pam?"

"Yes?"

"Will you stay the night with me?"

She smiled, but again hesitating. She pulled her hand away just a bit. "Maybe. If you don't misconstrue the whole thing. I don't like being taken for granted."

"I won't misconstrue and I don't take any woman for granted."

"You're more sure of yourself than that."

"I'm never sure."

She opened her eyes wide at that. "Tell me about Irene."

"No."

"Why not?"

"Because I'm with you."

"She's awfully attractive. She's got that exotic look, and her eyes are challenging. She's not afraid of much."

"Are you?"

"Yes. Yes, I am."

"What in particular?"

"Everything in particular. The way I approach things, a midwestern neophyte viewing the world through funny glasses. Goggle-eyed." She leaned forward.

"You've got great eyes. Take your glasses off."

"I'm blind without them." She removed them.

"You hide behind them. I like the eyes…and you."

"Tom, I'm a virgin. Did you know that?"

I stared and clasped her hand.

"That dancing was harmless, innocent. My pushing at you, like a young animal."

"I loved holding you, the way you moved to the music. You were all I could think of."

"I'm not your Communist zealot—Irene."

"I don't want you to be."

"Obviously, I can't match her, Tom. I may be free but I'm vulnerable."

"Will you forget about her? I'm quite sure she's not thinking about us."

Her hand found mine. "Now, tell me, what were you pondering when I saw you through the window?"

"You are persistent."

"So are you. Now, tell me."

"I was thinking about myself and America and where I was going, if you must know."

"Any luck?"

"No. Except maybe it doesn't pay to think too much about yourself, like you're doing now. The only important thing is to think about others, like I'm concerned about you—right now."

"Don't bother. I'm just a girl from Park Forest, Illinois—an idealist—in love with the possibilities of Europe—half scared to get involved, like now…"

"Could that be because you, like most of us, don't understand or trust yourself?"

"Maybe, but I don't think so. Perhaps it's because my hopes are too high."

"Then, why do I rate a maybe? I'm not to be trusted, you know."

"You're so obvious, looking for compliments, Tom. Why?"

"Bad toilet training…"

"But you are thoughtful. You seem to care. And I think you have a lot to give that you try to cover up by being clever."

"Okay. Now, tit for tat. I've made myself plain, been honest with you. I want you tonight. But you never told me something that night at the Chat Jaune…and that was, what did or didn't happen in Geneva."

"If you're interested in my European sex life, forget it. I answered that a few minutes ago anyway."

"OK. We're making progress. Just so you know about the cast of characters, people like Lizette and Fred and Bill Watson…"

"What for?"

"You're being clued in on how sexy this group is."

"Is this by way of preparation for my entry into a bordello?"

"No, but this is a racy crowd. Do you know Joyce?"

"I don't know her well."

"She's white on white. Bill's black on black. Potential connection."

"That's actually quite lovely," she said, "and enormously erotic."

"You have an active mind."

"Like you?" she asked.

"Oh, yes."

"Is it time to go and get on with it?" she asked in a strange voice. "I'm scared."

"Don't worry, I'm a gentle beast."

"Yes, you are, I hope."

I'll always remember her eyes, the sudden fragile quality magnified in her lenses. Her look, her quick switches in emotion. I'll remember too my brief fear about that fragility and also hearing Irene's word: 'I've known girls like that. In Morocco and here in Paris. Watch yourself, mon chéri.'

We walked arm in arm across the boulevard and turned right at my street, the rue des Quatre Vents, one of the city's shortest. The old buildings around us and the streetlights hitting their grey sides suddenly seemed romantic to me. The light washed them and fell down on them dramatically, as it does on a stage.

Just then, two bicycle-riding policemen flew by, their dark capes flying behind them.

"Les hirondelles, they call them." I said.

"What's that?" she asked.

"Swallows."

"Oh."

I kissed her gently on the mouth. She clung to me, her lips tentative against mine. A bit reluctant.

"Let's take a walk around here," I said, gently letting her go.

"Around here?"

"Yes. I want to show you the Odéon theater at night so you can see the Left Bank Théâtre Française…"

"Molière's there. 'Les Femmes Savantes' is playing now."

"Have you read it?"

"My dear, I went to Smith. Of course, I read it." She seemed more relaxed now, her womanly secret a secret no more. She would soon share her mystery, and I felt confident that she was comfortable with it.

"Like the theater arcade?"

"Yes." She kissed me impulsively in the sudden darkness.

"And there are the Luxembourg Gardens—all locked up for the night."

"Les Jardins du Luxembourg," she sighed.

"That's a good Smith girl for you. The right accent. A Vassar girl wouldn't have said it that way. Not even a Wellesley type." She pinched me. She was loosening up. I kissed her again, softly, making her feel safe in my arms. In a few minutes we had walked down de Tournon and were back on the rue des Quatre Vents.

Once inside the hotel, we passed the sleeping concierge. I reached over his bowed head and took the heavy key to my room. We climbed up to the top floor. We kissed again, this time more seriously, and unlocked the door. Without any overtures, we stripped down, except for her glasses. I watched her take them off and carefully place them by the bed. When she turned to me, she had that fuzzy, myopic look. Her body was calm and full. Then I could see why she had said she was free—and vulnerable. I went to the sink, took a heavy towel and placed it on the sheets beneath us, giving her my washcloth to help her clean herself. We lay down.

"Oh, Tom," she breathed as I looked down on her. She turned her head aside for an instant. I asked her why, saying it couldn't be more natural. "Are you sure?" she asked. "Everything's new..."

"Positive." I kissed her forehead and nuzzled her reassuringly, rolling over her a bit to kiss her breasts and thighs. She looked away for a moment, then said "Oh, my Tom."

She looked at me pleadingly, trustingly. I hadn't noticed before, but her body was more voluptuous than I had imagined, and I caressed and kissed her everywhere until my lips were dry. Her skin responded and she purred. She was ready, and I moved over her.

She touched my nose affectionately and winced, biting her lip, as I entered.

Outside a man yelled in raucous street French. Something crashed on the sidewalk. Another voice grumbled in German. Then it quieted down, and St. Sulpice struck twice.

Her pelvis moved under me, awkwardly finding itself around me, pulling me in. "Now you," she said. "Now you."

We danced a sinewy dance, so different for me and so entirely new for her. When I came she laughed and pulled me down on her in a victory celebration, a newly found confidence, wrapping her legs around me, holding me inside.

"Tom."

"Yes."

"Tom…"

We held fast and fell asleep.

IN THE TUILERIES GARDENS

THREE

Bill Watson, the black Chicago artist, stood there in the Orangerie Museum. Holding himself stiff and erect like a soldier on dress parade, he admired the series of Monet oil paintings of Rouen Cathedral. He was enthralled. The artist's subtle shades of color on the building moved him with the sun's changing position in the sky. He had been there for two hours, wholly absorbed in the wonders of France's Impressionistic painters. Just outside, the frantic Place de la Concorde and the relaxed Tuileries Gardens coexisted in war and peace. It was all familiar in a way, for it gave him confirmation of a feeling he used to experience at the Chicago Art Institute when he was a student there: wonder and total absorption in the joys of color.

People speaking the world's languages drifted past. They bobbed forward occasionally to view the labels on the frames, then pulled back to get a wider perspective, often blocking his view. But Bill Watson didn't see them. He remained focused on the Monet group of paintings, occasionally muttering, "Marvelous."

Then he thought: "What's a nice colored boy from Chicago doing here in Paris?" He looked about furtively, almost expectantly, and finally a woman came to his side.

It was Joyce Frost, her pure white skin and dark hair radiant as they held hands shyly. "Here's the person from the Black Country," she announced to the coal black American.

"I'm a black from a white country."

"You are? You could fool me."

"Well, sometimes yes, sometimes no. I'm ambivalent. Still, it's not a matter of choice for me."

"It is for me," she said. "And I choose you, black inside and out."

"Ah, that's another thing." He laughed at the game they had begun to play the other day when they first met. "Freedom."

"Freedom now?"

"Nonsense," he said.

"It's all too deep for me, darling," she added.

He bent to kiss her quickly.

"How are the children?" he asked.

Joyce laughed. "Glad to be on an outing with their parents and away from my charge."

He touched her cheek, sampling its whiteness. "You called me darling."

"Just keep it within bounds, darling Bill. Not too serious now—keep that artist's profundity at bay."

He smiled, wondering if she would consent to his request, needing her but not getting it into words.

They drifted out of the gallery into the sunlit gardens and sat down on a bench in the shade of the protecting trees. She looked straight ahead and smiled, almost to herself. They had met only a week before at a dinner with the group of Americans and Irene, and they had become intensely curious about each other. Now they held hands, his dark skin around hers.

"It's so neutral here," he said, "being away from that group of phony intellectuals—except Tom, who shakes hands with me like he means it."

"You like Tom," Joyce said.

"Yes, he's sincere. A bit lost but sincere. An artist picks up on that sort of thing."

"A good bloke," Joyce said, smiling. "What does your artist intuition tell you about Fred?"

"That he's drifting from Goodie—disenchanted, perhaps. She's no longer fertile ground for his poetry." He touched her arm. "And he's interested in you. Are you interested in him?"

The Street of Four Winds

"Now, Bill," Joyce chided. "Stay within bounds."

"Are you interested in him?"

"I'm interested in knowing who I am and celebrating who I am."

"So you will sleep with him"

"Perhaps. But when I'm with you, Bill, there is only you."

"Are there any others?" he asked.

"Yes, why shouldn't there be? How's the painting going?" she said, ending it.

"Slowly. Very slow."

"You need more inspiration."

"The very thing," he agreed. "Maybe you can supply that. You know I want to paint you." His heart was in his throat in anticipation. "Joyce, what would it take for you to model for me?" She said nothing immediately, considering his request. She held her silence, almost to titillate him.

"Why me?"

"Because you're beautiful and I want to," he said cautiously. "You are, you know."

She flushed, tinting white with pink.

He sensed her hesitation and hastened to reassure her. "You don't need to be concerned. I'll behave myself. Honestly.

"As I am?" she asked, "or nude?"

"Probably both. Does it make any difference?"

"Probably not really." A young couple strolled by in front of their bench, pausing to kiss now and then. Bill watched them and noticed the girl was a dark-cast Oriental, he probably French. Joyce smiled as she took them in. "Where? And when?" He turned to her impulsively, reached for her small hand, then kissed it.

◎◎

Across the river from them on the quai Malaquais, I was drinking by myself. I was waiting for Buck Birnbaum, who continued wanting my support for his grand project. I was also

39

contemplating what would be the next bit of sightseeing I would conduct for Pam. We were taking in all the sights together, the point being to spend as much time together as possible…

Now here was Buck. We ordered drinks. I felt comfortable with him. I admired an ambitious person like Buck Birnbaum, despite his quixotic hopes and deviate quirks. And I had requested the meeting to settle something in my own mind about my friend.

"Buck, can you be frank with me?"

"Always have been, old sport…"

"You sound like Gatsby and a bit out of sync. But I need to know something."

"What's that?" His eyes were bright.

"I don't want this to be out of order, understand."

"Don't be coy," Buck said. "My life's an open book, you know."

"Really?" I said. "OK. Can I ask about Ellen?"

"Sure—what about her?"

"Are you two a real couple? Are you in love?"

"Why do you ask?"

"Look," I said. "I was somewhat familiar with your social life back in school, so I'm a bit puzzled."

"You probably remember that laughing bitch at the dance after the football game, and what she suggested about me and my sex life," Buck said. "Well, it's not that simple, friend. And about Ellen—does she appeal to you?"

"It would be weird if she didn't appeal to any man. The question is, does she appeal to you? If I'm probing too much, stop me, please."

"You've always been diplomatic." Buck paused longer than necessary, looked past Tom over towards the Louvre for several seconds, then said deliberately, "She, like many others of either sex, does appeal to me. I know a lot about her…and her problems."

"We all have those."

"Yes, but hers are special—and frankly I've no right to discuss her confidences."

"Fair enough. Forget them. I'm only asking about you two. Over here you're always together. Almost always. Still I don't sense the fire between you…"

Buck Birnbaum stared off into space. Finally, he said: "Tom, she's my traveling companion. I asked her to join me in Europe because I feel a bit responsible for her. She's also a form of insulation for me. You can take that any way your want, sir. Besides, she needed to get away, and it all worked out conveniently for both of us. How's that?"

"It helps. Thanks."

"She's a really fine person, Tom—highly intelligent and lovely and sensitive, almost too much at times. And I care for her very much. Now let's talk about something else."

"Okay, but love?"

"Let's just say this," Buck said. "If she were to get hurt by anything or anyone, I'd be damned mad." With that and a few pleasantries, I excused myself to rejoin Pamela Batterford.

⊙⊙

…I was very much drawn to Pam. There was something exciting about her, her quick mind, her infectious, innocent laugh, her soft, responsive body that turned me on—how much I loved to touch and handle it—her "vulnerability," as she put it that first night we spent together, and that one other thing: her deep need for a great deal of affection.

And then the paradox, after making love. She would be under me, a sparkle of sweat between her breasts, and her head would be to one side, away from me, her weak eyes gazing into some hidden landscape. At these moments she was gone from me, even as I held her tightly, buried deep inside her. Whatever insatiable need she had—and it was insatiable, I knew—I could but touch its edges, not the primal flow. Sometimes it frightened me, but I loved her, either as challenge or some strange solace for my own needs.

Pam and I went everywhere, even to parts of the city I scarcely knew: wonderful parks, obscure museums, specialized bookstores, fascinating art galleries, that vital River Seine running through southwest Paris, enticing international restaurants, historic landmarks in undiscovered parts of town, compelling smells and colors, even the racetrack at Auteuil where we won a few francs. And the local swimming pool along St. Germain. Then there were the other lovers who seemed to be everywhere.

"One can't be totally unhappy in Paris, Tom," she said once. "It's too beautiful for that."

We once walked through the Luxembourg Gardens and noticed Fred Furness and Joyce Frost lying next to each other on a lawn, a violation of the park's rules. Fortunately, they did not notice us. He was reading to her, and once she interrupted his persevering efforts to put her arms around him.

"Nice," Pam said, rising on her tiptoes. "Like us…happiness. Oh, I've never been more so, Tom." I pulled her along to watch the children leaning earnestly over the shallow pool behind the Palais, pushing their toy boats along. It was where I had met Irene. Then we would walk through the visual adventures of the quarter, our quarter—the 6th Arrondissement—to see surprises like the Place Furstemberg with its white-globed lampposts just off the rue Jacob and the miniature ancient St. Julien-le-Pauvre church built at the same time as the giant cathedral facing it, and the intricate streets near the Institute just by the river.

Then there was "our" bridge—the Pont des Arts. We would walk it or just stand, gazing out at both banks of the Seine. We liked being just downstream from our favorite spot, the Vert Galant.

I recall one day in particular. Pam took off her glasses as she looked out across the Seine, her sensitive eyes straining, sometimes squinting for focus.

"You'll see more with them on," I said, nudging her playfully.

"It's not always so, Tom. Sometimes I see more without them, a tuning in on other worlds, other ways of seeing." She turned to me seriously, a light breeze ruffling her short hair. "Don't you stand between two worlds—or more?"

"I'm having enough trouble understanding this one." I said.

But she would have none of it. "Clean my glasses, will you?" I took out my handkerchief and wiped the lenses, noting how the world moved in deep refraction through their prisms. I handed them back to her and kissed her lightly on the cheek.

She put them on and smiled at me. "Now I am blind again," she said.

"I sometimes wonder how we see—and why we don't see things the same way. Take Buck, for example, and how he wants to make the world conform to his personal vision."

"Yes, that's true. All my life, Tom, I've had my narrow view of things. But now I see something new. Besides you, my charming prince, and with the help of Paris, I have a new focus on peace. I've never had so much peace of mind before…"

"That's the beauty of the place you talk about…" Just in front of them a low-slung barge struggled upstream against the current. To the side of the embankment, traffic moved briskly.

"But it's more than that—maybe the time and place and how I see them all in some kind of grand design. Or maybe it's just a happy concurrence that doesn't happen very often. Like the cards in bridge partners' hands and how every once in a while, they let you make a bid of seven spades or something fantastic like that…"

Above them a flock of swallows wheeled over the Tuileries. Beyond stood the stolid Louvre buildings, massive like a Sphinx transplanted into the Seine Valley.

"You have to know what you're doing to make seven spades, and often we don't know what we're doing at all."

"Do you know what you're doing, right now?"

"I'm in love with you," I said, and she immediately rebuked me with:

"That's not doing anything at all."

"Okay, touché," I said, grabbing her around the waist. "God, you're an armful! Let's just say, then, that I'm engaged in making you happy. That's enough for me."

"But it's limited. Where is it going?"

"I wish I knew, but now it's super."

"I want more than now," she said and looked away. I heard a slight gasp, then she turned full face and hugged me with as much force as she could muster.

Then there were the restaurants, especially the student eaterie near the Marché de Buci and its festive atmosphere. It was called the Bouillon, the domain of a high priestess cook who prepared our omelets with a finger that scooped out the cracked eggs and allowed the reigning cat to lick it before she spat in the frying pan to be sure it was the right temperature. They were the best omelets I ever ate. And the views from Sacré Coeur on the north side and the Eiffel Tower in the southwest, where we saw the whole panorama of the city thinning out across the Seine Valley towards Burgundy, Aquitaine, Flanders and Normandy in the far distance, the directions from which came the four winds that named "our" little street in Paris and made the city what it was. The Hôtel des Quatre Vents clicked in my mind. We had come from the ends of the earth where the winds began, skittering across the oceans, to mingle our lives. And all the winds collected there on the shortest street in Paris, compressing our cast of characters and the aimless actions that occupied our lives.

It was glorious for me to display this female city, my urban mistress, to my other urban mistress, Pamela, who absorbed it all. We would eat when we wanted, relax or make love on the spur of the moment, and luxuriate in the pure joy of being there in our heaven on earth. Moreover, all of this happened to us at the lowest possible cost, thanks to the dollar's rate of exchange on the Arab-run black market, our gasoline coupons and our other survival tricks.

But money can never be equated with paradise and our days there were numbered. Pamela—or more accurately, I—was running out of gas, Fred and Goodie were breaking up, and no one save

Buck had any real sense of purpose. We were all playing the field, and then too, I did feel the compulsion to get back to work…

⊚⊙

Pamela had a habit of recording her emotional experiences and observations in a diary. She was good about keeping it up to date, and during this period she was quite assiduous about the diary.

Just once chance allowed me to glance at it. I shouldn't have read it, of course. But I found myself with things I needed to know, like the turn of her head away from me after we had made love, the weak but beautiful eyes searching wild landscapes out at the end of the world.

'For the first time in my life,' one entry stated, 'I am in love and proud of myself. How it all came together in Tom! Sharing myself with him at the height of my womanhood, then capturing and entrapping him between my legs—where did that come from inside me, that celebration…?'

Then another excerpt caught my eye: 'We were on our bridge today, and I took off my glasses to commune, to search my visions. Tom was a bit nonplussed, and perhaps I need to be careful with what I share. In love or not, I don't want him confused by my moods. I need his practical approach so much, this teacher, confessor who sees a world I don't know. But I love him so, need him so…'

At that point I wanted to put it down, escape from it. But earlier pages rippled by and drew me in.

'Strange, it's a coherent life that began back in Park Forest when both mother and father thought I was so independent, even after the time at the Cranbrook Academy in Michigan and college at Smith. One thing it never covered up, a feeling of insufficiency that summer when father touched me once too often out on the lake, and brother Alex noticed it.

'Then that cute young clarinet instructor at Interlochen music camp who said I had a dreamy look, after years of being kidded about my glasses. He took no action, in a way confirming what a girlfriend reported Dorothy Parker once said: 'Guys rarely make passes at girls who wear glasses.' Not funny for me. Moon-face, starry eyes, a song went, but no action for moon-face Pam.

'Depression, they called it, when I visited a psychologist on my own in Boston as a sophomore at Smith. But with the excitement of that junior year in Geneva with Sally and Faith and the others, I didn't pay any attention. If you were a girl from the Mid-West and had the chance to go to Europe—that never-never land—anyone would forget any problems, even feeling lonely and different from others…that handsome Swiss boy who invited me to come meet his parents at Vevey down the Lake of Geneva one weekend turned chicken and canceled within the hour of our departure. Moon-face, starry eyes struck out again. How confident in yourself can you get? Gloom again.

'Back for senior year in Northampton, and what a bust of depression that was. I just didn't know what to do—until Sally and Faith talked me into returning to Europe for a return engagement, this time in Paris after graduation. Hope does spring eternal. And now it's sprung: Tom Cortell, my darling Tom. He's so perfect for me, despite those European women like Irene and Joyce I know he sleeps with. They don't have any sense of shame. But he taught me how to make love…so tender…I could die of it.

'Only one thing, when he sometimes wakes up screaming in the night from that battle experience in Italy. He almost gets convulsive about it, a chill running through him, and I have to hold him close to stop it. We all need support, not just me. I guess we all have our own separate ghosts, our hidden moments of horror. But I have him now and it will last. I know it will last…'

I put the diary back where chance had offered it.

FOUR

From the brasserie we could see the Pantheon, which was a peculiar backdrop to our conversation. For a group of displaced Americans cutting their way through post-war Europe, the building was an anomaly. An unformed idea that could never coalesce—an egotistical fixation of Louis XV that became through the years a church, the grave of Voltaire and Rousseau, home of a Commune and later a lay temple. Under the tasteful dome its windows were closed up by the French Revolution, so that the streets around it, next to the University and the Law Faculty, could no longer be viewed. Now they were blind, purposeless. And for the many students running about the quarter it became a symbol of nothing at all. They were there now, smoking and yelling.

"I feel like that crazy building," I said. "Useless."

"It's like a de Chirico painting," Buck laughed. "Big, sad, and pointless."

"Yes, something time forgot, which is the fix I'm in."

"How so?"

"Well, this bloody trip to Spain with the girls. Should I chaperone them or not...?"

"I don't see why you need to," Buck said. "After all, you hardly know them. Unless, of course, you've got some obligation. Why not tell this Dan fellow to scrub his trip home and watch out for the family chick himself."

"He's got a job to get back to," I said.

"But if it's so damned important, let the first team take over—not you, who's being seduced into it. If I were you, I'd forget it.

47

Besides, you've got to stay. I have plans for you. And I want your enthusiasm."

"Oh, the conference you talked about?"

"Yes," Buck said as they ordered another drink. " I want you there. In fact, without you it won't be what I want."

"So what's it all about?"

Buck chewed at his right thumb. "It's a discussion group, but more than that…"

"Yes?"

"It's going to have major repercussions, if it comes out the way I hope. I need a few days to iron out more details, Tom. But when I do, I know you'll be pleased."

Faith Carlson and Sally Satterwaite began to walk past the brasserie, and I noticed that two French boys were following them. The four of them marched like an Army platoon, oblivious to the Pantheon and the busy sidewalk around them.

"Sally," I yelled.

"Hi, there! Say, what are you up to with our roomy, Pam?"

"Have no idea what you're talking about."

"Tom, she's transported." Faith Carlson grinned, grabbing the hand of her French student. Then the four of them were gone in the crowd of students rushing towards the Law Faculty building.

"What's that all about?" Buck asked. I said I didn't know, but Buck didn't believe me. "Are you making a play for one of them?"

"Perish the thought," I said. "Just had a date with Pam Batterford. Nothing critical."

"The moon-faced girl with glasses? The one you danced with at the boîte? I remember. That was quite sexy, the way you two moved together. Irene was vexed, to say the least. Tom, you should be careful with these American women, especially that one. They take men so seriously…"

"Now tell me about the discussion group," I said

"I'd prefer you be patient and serious about what I'm going to propose to the group…more patient than you are with the ladies, obviously."

"Well, it sounds like an earlier talk we had: Emerson, Roger Williams, Jefferson, I think it was. Your concern about the post-war period."

Buck pushed his jaw at me. "In a way, I suppose. We're going to discover some truths. Truths for our generation, before we get bypassed by that crowd." He jerked his thumb at the passing students. "We're going to shape a future for all of us."

"And who's the hidden genius of the group? Besides you, of course."

"It's a bit premature to discuss that, and there are several of us, I hope…"

"What's the big secret?"

"I want to talk to Norman and Fred…"

"Sounds like Columbia inbreeding."

He smiled at that. "There'll be others, including women." The talk stopped there for the moment and we sat back to watch the passing scene.

"I'm a bit concerned about Fred, Buck," I said. "Fred and his poetry, I mean. No growth there."

"That happens to everyone. He'll be OK. He's obviously got problems with Goodie, but…"

"We had a beer awhile back—Norman, Fred and I."

"Why do you bring that up?" Buck asked.

"Because it involved our old Columbia days. They brought it up, and it might have something to do with what you're planning. Do you remember Professor Macey?"

"Oh, the man in social psychology. He was a kind of nut, I heard."

"No, he wasn't. In a way, he was a new backboard for us to bounce off developments in government and history. He made us sensitive to the whole problem of stereotypes, the way we used to make judgments about what we learned at school. I can't reconstruct it now, but he was one of the great teachers we had—and everyone laughed at him."

"Why are you bringing it up now?"

I chose my words carefully. "Basically I just want your grand discussion to avoid the pitfalls of the usual inane discussions about war, peace, society, and peoples' feelings about what's going on in our world."

"And if I do offer inane discussions, I'll be laughed at. Is that it?"

"That's not it. You won't be inane…"

"Glad to hear it…"

"It's just that when I think of Macey, I kind of wonder how we're ever going to reconstruct the world."

"Well, I'll try not to disappoint," Buck said, his eyes glittering. "So what else did you discuss?"

I knew it was coming, and I felt I had to go into the matter.

"They talked about other things at Columbia—for example, that dance when the girl laughed at you and literally stopped the band playing."

Buck shifted uneasily in his brasserie chair. "You had no right to talk about me like that."

"We all talk about each other. At a bar everything's fair game."

"That bitch was trying to embarrass me about some of my hangups—about men and women. So what was next on your Buck Birnbaum agenda?"

"Buck, you weren't the star."

"But there was more; I can see it on your face. What?"

"Your name—Edward. Then the football at which you were so good, and how it was a compensation and probably why you were so successful at it…"

"Compensation for what?" He was bridling.

"Come on, Buck."

"My voice…my preference for men?"

"Sure, if you must know."

Buck gnawed a nail. "I can hear the whole damned thing, including your dissection of Ellen. Well, mind your own fucking business!"

His timing was excellent, for that was when Ellen appeared. I hadn't seen her since the soirée at the Chat Jaune and the onion soup place. I thought she was cool and lovely in blue, an unusual shade that matched her eyes. She seemed highly controlled compared to Pamela, and when she sat down I noted her good legs, slim and muscular. She even wore a small white hat that set off her proudly held head. I watched her accept the cigarette that Buck held up for her. We all leaned back in our plastic chairs, three Americans on separate personal quests in the city.

"Just remember, Tom," Buck finished up authoritatively. "It's vital you bear something in mind, whatever the personal flaws involved. I've always been looking for something to do that has large dimensions, something of significance. Ellen knows that—at least she's heard me talk about it a lot…"

Ellen exhaled smoke and nodded dutifully. I watched her carefully, particularly the way she went along with what he had to say. At the nearby corner, traffic rumbled by on the Boulevard St. Michel. Buck cleared his throat, on the verge of a major announcement.

"God, it's hot!" Ellen said, adjusting her hat.

"Just give me a few days, Tom, and I'm going to surprise all of you," Buck said.

Just then the waiter came to our table, motioning to me. "You have a telephone call, monsieur." Buck looked up, surprised, and Ellen let a slight smirk touch her face.

"Who is it this time?" she asked, flicking ash from her cigarette. "Irene from *L'Humanité* headquarters…or Pam, your great dance partner?"

"I expect a call from an editor, if you must know."

She continued to smile. It turned out to be Joyce Frost, my English lady, though some would hesitate to call her that.

"Well, my love. What's kept you away?" Her voice was insistent, a bit tense.

"How did you know I was here, sweet?"

"You have a short memory for some vital things, love. We had aperitifs there…"

"And I promised to call you," I said.

"Yes, you did—me and all the other girls. An honest girl has to get on the queue…"

I let that go, being more preoccupied with her tension. That was unusual. "Something wrong?"

She was silent a moment, which disturbed me. "It's Bill and the painting. We had a row."

"I'm sorry to hear it. What about?"

"Oh, I was tired, and it was another sitting, and he insisted on having me. You know the routine. I asked him which was more important to him, me or the canvas."

"You were tired…"

"I'm not that way with you. You refresh me…"

"I'm glad."

"It's true. This was so stupid. I threatened to destroy the portrait. But I really love it. I really do, Tom. He's captured something in me that even I don't recognize. But then there were his bloody questions—like the Gestapo—about my pose, the skin tones, which are odd because they're red—all in the red spectrum. He insists it's the real me. He's, as you say, pissed off at people saying we're just a sexy black/white relationship. A cliché, he says. That way, he finds our relationship an affront. Then he got after you and Buck and the others in the band, that we merely tolerate him as a token black. Finally, he blames himself for falling into our token trap. Oh God, Tom. What do I do?"

"Want me to come over?"

"Desperately, darling."

I said I'd come right away, giving an excuse to Buck and Ellen that I had a deadline to meet.

Ellen picked it up right away. Her smirk returned. "Tight journalism," she observed. Her eyes held that critical look I had felt in the boîte and later over the onion soup. Buck didn't miss his chance, either. Not that I could blame him for his reactions to the roasting by Fred, Norman and myself. I cursed myself for having brought it up.

"Tom's a lusty soul. That's his success with women."

Ellen skewered me at that, and I left.

☙❧

The Metro shot me from the heady barricades of the student quarter to the neat, calm and orderly atmosphere of the 16th Arrondissement. After the car doors snapped open, I took the steps two at a time from the underground exit up into the bright sunlight of that wealthy district on the Right Bank of the Seine. Its focal point was the Arc de Triomphe where France's Unknown Soldier from World War I is buried. I thought about Jack McCormick, home without a scratch from Okinawa, and myself wounded in Italy. And Fred Furness, haunted by German tanks in the Ardennes and the Battle of the Bulge, and then all the others who didn't make it, the new unknown soldiers of the latest war. And I wondered what all the unknown soldiers of the world would think of Buck's plan to create a cultural interpretation for Mankind. Probably not much.

I came to the building entrance of Joyce's rue Pergolèse apartment with its Duhamel family and pressed the button. Her clipped British voice answered on the speaker promptly, a bit scratchy in the static. The entry buzzer sounded and I went inside to the lift.

Upstairs I stepped out of the cagelike door and found her there, pale and waiting. She looked a little tentative; not the effusive Joyce I had become used to. I kissed her lightly on the cheek. "You look upset. What's the matter?"

"I've felt better. Come in. When they left with the children I just couldn't tolerate the loneliness, that and Bill's ravings."

I handed her a box of the chocolates she liked. "Now, do you have any wine?"

"Some. A bottle of St. Estèphe."

"Great. Hunt up a couple of glasses, will you?"

She hesitated. "Tom, could we just go to bed? I want your arms around me. I feel, I feel cold. I'm full of sharing today with someone I don't have to worry about."

In bed she fit her body around mine. We re-explored ourselves, yet this afternoon we stopped to relish our slow motions for some deeper communion. I licked her eyelids, kissed her ears, talking to her and stroking her the way I would a cat. She clung to me in bliss.

"Ummm," she purred in my ear as she held me tightly. "It's so lovely making love with you. No one like you, darling, and never any strings attached. But, of course, we'll end it some day, as though it never happened at all. And no regrets, no sorrow, only good memories, like, if you'll pardon the joke, a good ball game."

"Yes or maybe cricket," I said, kissing her ear and the tear on her cheek.

She pressed against me. "I'm not red, Tom, am I?"

"Hey, come on…"

"Bill paints me red, but that's only his interpretation of me, and I suppose it's flattering—but I'm not red!" Anger now, and salt from her tears. "I'm white, Tom. I have what is often described as a typical English complexion. I've always prided myself on it…I…"

I got up to ease open the shutters for the blinding sunlight. I looked back at her on the bed, admiringly, at the youthful body with its alabaster skin, the curly dark hair. She stared back at me and I went to her then, murmuring a reminder to her of what she was, her essence, her luster, and she responded to the words and touches. I kissed her again and again, knowing she needed my support then, and rolled her over to reach every part of her.

There was no frenetic loving, just a quiet assertion of who we both were, a gentle entwining that had everything to do with knowing each other, of stopping time and knowing why. Afterwards she lay quietly in my arms, and I waited for her to come around.

"That was nice, Tom," she said.

"Yes, it was."

"Have you helped anyone like that before?"

"No."

"There's a surprising gentleness to you—when you release it."

I nuzzled her hair, which was damp with sweat. "Feel better about Bill now?"

"Yes, I'll straighten it out."

"Know what Groucho Marx said when he first saw Gainsborough's 'Blue Boy'?"

"No. What?"

"Got it in red?"

She hit my arm, and it stung. "True—that's what he said."

"Silly, he was just being funny. Bill isn't trying to be funny."

"Bill's an artist."

"That covers a multitude of sins."

"Yes, I suppose it does."

Her hand moved down to my thigh where the war wound was, then pressed it with her fingers and looked up at me. "Was it bad, the war, I mean?"

"Not all the time. But at times I was terrified."

"When you got this?"

"Yes. It was a German grenade; it landed near me at Monte Cassino. I was desperate to crawl into the ground. It was an eternity."

"Then what?"

"It went off. But I was lucky. Other men close by weren't."

"God, Tom, how awful. And here I am going on about a stupid painting."

"It's not a stupid painting. Things will straighten out with Bill."

She took my hand and placed it on her breast. "Am I lovely, Tom?"

"You are lovely and white as milk."

"Lovelier than that Moroccan girl, Irene?"

"Joyce—"

"She's flat chested…nothing up top."

"That's not quite true. And let's change the subject."

"All right."

"Fred's not too happy about you and Bill—his being a Negro, a rival as a painter."

55

Joyce pressed her hand over mine on her breast "Fred has an anger in him. I can feel it when we're together. But it's not about Bill being black. It's the art and the competition in that, I suppose. Did you know that Fred has nightmares?"

"Nightmares?"

"He talked about it only once, when he woke up in a sweat and pushed me away. Then he realized he was in bed and calmed down. Do you have nightmares?"

"Sometimes." I remembered Pam's diary, my own terrors caught in her few words. "What did he say?"

"He was in the Battle of the Bulge, and a German tank ran over his foxhole. Other things."

Joyce propped herself up on an elbow. "You know, I think part of his dislike for Bill is that he senses Bill is too creative. Fred even admits he emulates other poets now and then. Poets like Sassoon from the First World War…" Her hand came down on mine. "Tom, promise me you'll never tell Fred about our love-making."

I smiled. "That's fine with me, but would it be such a bad thing if he knew? After all, he's already putting up with a black painter."

"You won't say anything—please. He gets terribly angry sometimes. Possessive."

"Why should I, sweet? I've got enough to keep me busy for now."

"Promise?"

"I promise."

"If you really promise…and cross your heart." I did.

"Now, let's continue what we started so you have something to keep you busy," she said, pushing me down. But before we began again, she bent down, slid backward to my knees and kissed the place where I had been wounded. "It must have been awful," she whispered.

FIVE

"You'll need these later," Buck was saying to people as we trickled into the Auberge Bretonne, the restaurant he had engaged for the "Grand Plenary" planning meeting. Here he would reveal his ideas for the great project he had talked about for days to his friends. "These" were pencils and paper for the participants. He was all business.

The restaurant was one we all knew quite well, and Buck had selected it for that reason. Its artificial ceiling beams created an ambiance of old Brittany, and its regional food was what we liked.

"This is really important to Buck, and Switzerland's got something for all of us to share, you'll hear," Ellen said, her blue eyes probing each of us over pencils and paper. "It's going to be a genuine interdisciplinary conference, and each one of us will take more than one chance at leading the discussions. But it's interdisciplinary in style…"

"Rabelais to the fore!" Norman said.

"I'm sure you're not limited to Rabelais, Norman," she said. "The coverage will be large, beyond what you might expect. Buck wants each of us to cover our wartime experiences, whether in the U.S. or overseas. It all applies to what he's after…"

"I think we ought to focus on the postwar period, especially the political side," Sally Satterwaite was saying.

"Very current things, of course—the Marshall Plan, European and Japanese recovery, the power vacuum in the Pacific." People were milling about, waiting for things to get started.

"It's got to be focused on news," I said.

"And changing male-female relationships," Faith Carlson said.

"Just so long as we end up in bed," Norman said.

"Sounds good," I added.

"You both are naughty boys," Ellen said.

"Just adventurers," Norman said. Buck scowled when he heard this while he organized his papers and looked around the room.

Henriette, daughter of the restaurant owner, stood next to Buck, exchanging pleasantries. At one point she thanked him for selecting the restaurant for his meeting. The entire second floor had been taken.

"Vous êtes très gentil, Monsieur Birnbaum," she said, to which he responded in a whisper:

"Merci, but I'm really Jewish."

"Quelle blague!" I said.

"No kidding. Who's blague?" Norman said.

"You are—forget it," I said.

Buck got ready to begin his talk when everyone quieted down. Pam sat down next to me, Norman and Sally Satterwaite.

"You are probably curious about this meeting," Buck said. "So first off, let me say how gratifying it is to me personally that you all could make it. This session is the precursor of something that lies close to my heart…"

"You see. I told you," Ellen said at the next table.

"Now Utopia, as you know, is derived from the ancient Greek and means no place…"

I knew right then that it was going to be heavy going in the Birnbaum manner, and delivered in the high-pitched voice we had become accustomed to. I looked at Ellen nearby, studiously prim next to Buck, holding her straight, classic nose high, like a spaniel on the hunt, her blonde hair falling away neatly over her forehead and partially concealing her intensely blue eyes. Pam squeezed my arm as she listened, but my thoughts were elsewhere.

My gaze shifted from Buck to Ellen and back; a question in my mind. I wondered if Pam sensed it.

"...We live in an historical era...and this group represents something special in terms of its familiarity with the war, the aftermath. Your grades, my research shows, are the highest in your respective undergraduate classes..."

Finally he got to it. "I propose a special seminar in a utopian environment—Switzerland—where we'll discuss and record our findings...produce a document for our times, reflecting our common and varying views about our post-war world...It will be an organized discussion...and I've made preliminary arrangements to have it published by one of the university presses..."

He explained that he would underwrite the event, supplying everything but the group's transportation and food while at Caux, "down at the east end of Lake Geneva, a mile or so above Montreux—an idyllic location."

"Now, topics will be assigned to individuals according to their academic backgrounds. At the end we'll organize the results into formal proceedings for publication.

"Question." Norman said. "Can I use Rabelais?" Ellen groaned.

"If you can fit him in. Why not?" Buck said, grinning. "Now who's next? Goodie—psychology, right?"

"Absolutely."

"Bill, you're an artist. We need you to contribute something from the graphic arts."

Bill Watson smiled and looked at me. I smiled back.

"And you, Tom. Journalism, of course...your observations on communism in postwar Europe—the inside story...things you picked up on that trip to Czechoslovakia, etcetera..."

I nodded, while he turned to Fred Furness across the room. "Fred, literature, no?"

"I'm already preparing a saga for you to read, Buck."

Everyone laughed.

"I'll count on that, Fred. We'll serialize it in the *Nation*..."

I was enjoying this view of Buck. He was in his element—at the same time trying to overcome his natural stuffiness, at least to give the appearance of going with the drift of things. To make his project a success he really needed us, and he was going all out. He needed us in more ways than one. Certainly he needed the validation of his friends. He always had, and he couldn't stand failure of any kind. That was his nature.

Pam spoke up. "I'm equipped to take over social studies, Buck."

"Indeed you are, Pamela. I have you down for that, maybe with a bit of emphasis on America's fundamental economic change and its effect on our society after the war. Anyone else got a comment?"

At my side, Norman was discussing the conference and Buck's plans for publishing the results.

"It's what you'd expect from Buck—academic as hell."

"When he concentrates on something, it's well thought out," Fred said.

I watched Ellen, still wondering about her and Buck. What a strange relationship. What had brought them together? How had they managed it? Despite what Buck had said the other day, I still didn't get it.

Fred and Goodie talked about Switzerland. It would be new to them. "I can't wait," Goodie said. "Maybe it will solve some of our problems. Maybe the mountains will make us lose ourselves, sweet."

Fred looked at her, surprised and curious.

"Don't stare at her, Tom," Pam said, about my glances at Ellen. Her fingers dug deep into my arm.

"Pay attention, you people." Faith Carlson said.

I thought more about Ellen. She was too controlled, too confident, too stunning. It doesn't add up. And why did she keep drawing those butterflies?

Buck kept talking. "The conference will be conducted along the lines of our Columbia College colloquia courses. Those not familiar will be informed about that. You might be interested in this list," he said, shuffling through some papers.

He distributed it to us. It consisted of names and areas of academic and professional expertise. And as Henriette and Dominique brought around the café filtre cups, their bright metal tops glittering and jiggling, the noise level of discussion rose in the room. Buck looked around with a grin of pride.

"I'm purposely withholding my tentative list of subjects," he said imperiously, "because everything should be fresh and spontaneous. No homework preparation." Each of the group members would be responsible for leading his or her session. Buck discussed some general areas for study. "And if you have some ideas right now, please jot them down on the sheets I passed out—with your names, please. That'll constitute your desire to attend. I'll have the precise dates as soon as possible."

What was Ellen thinking right now? I asked myself, and what were the butterflies all about? She would tell me before we went to Caux. That meeting occurred secretively, and I asked her specifically about them.

We had met and were walking along the banks of the Seine, casually checking out the boquinistes' book displays. I got an inspiration and took her across the quai to one of the street cafes to have a drink. We ordered, and I thought it a good time to probe. She seemed relaxed and was full of smiles.

"Tom, you really make me feel relaxed."

"I was just thinking that. And I really want to. I like women…"

"…as well as love them a bit, I gather."

"Don't believe Buck," I said. "What the hell would he know about love?"

"That's cruel and ugly." Her eyes flashed an anger.

"Sorry."

"What is it you want to ask me, Tom?"

"Am I that obvious?"

She sipped her drink.

"What's with the butterflies and your doodling?"

She laughed, but her voice had lost its mellifluous tone.

"Oh, that. It's no big secret. I doodle all the time."

"So why butterflies? It's always butterflies." I offered her another drink, but she refused. Instead, she reached over the table and took mine, watching me over the rim.

"It began with a rotten day at school when I almost flunked a major exam in my senior year. That put my chances for Swarthmore at risk." She sipped my drink. "It was a bad day all around. Mother and Dad had a terrible row. You know the kind?"

"When you think the world is coming apart? No firm footing and everything going wrong?"

"Yes, exactly."

"What did you do?"

"I took the bull by the horns. I went out to the barn behind the house and bridled up my horse. I always felt strongly about that horse. I took him out in the woods where I used to ride when I wanted to get away from things. It was so peaceful there."

"You like to ride?"

"Love it. All girls do, I think. Anyway, off we went at a quick trot, and soon my tears had dried and I was feeling better. That's when we saw them."

I waited.

"Butterflies, Tom. They were in the middle of a muddy puddle, dozens of them fluttering, their lovely wings clapping in the air. Clapping at what a wonderful sunny day it was. Yellow and black monarch butterflies. They're a good size, you know."

"They must have been beautiful."

Her blue eyes watched me. "They were dancing in the sunbeams, utterly beautiful above the mud- puddle."

I chose my words carefully. "No offense to the butterflies, but I hope you have more beauty in your life than them."

Her glass came down onto the table and she made wet rings with it. Then she smeared them. "Tom, I'm glad you didn't phrase that as a question."

"Why?"

"Because I wouldn't have answered it."

"Sounds serious."

"And now is not the time," Ellen said.

I waited, watching the blue eyes get wet.

"Damn you," she sighed.

"I'm doing nothing."

Her smile was ironic. "You're doing everything, dear Tom, and you know it."

I smiled back. "I've been accused of being like a priest."

"Like a priest, but not one. Just extracting confessions." She looked at me, her face a frieze of calm that was disturbing. Then her voice dropped:

"It was an uncle. He took advantage of me. I was thirteen."

I waited.

"It's hard to describe the casual violence of it, Tom. Not the taking of my virginity, which he did, while I shivered. It was in my home, you see. Where one is supposed to be safe…"

In the restaurant Buck was percolating with his metronomic delivery. "This is my dream, something dear to my heart. I say this perhaps to emphasize how serious I am about my confidence in you and the validity of this project. It's unique and full of promise. And it's terribly important…" His voice rose even higher than usual as he said this.

Then the room broke into applause…ideas for the conference flew about…things like the changing role of women in society, how a third world war would be impossible as business grew to be more international, a loss of the old moralities, growth of the cold war between the USSR and the USA, so many subjects…It became contagious and built a lot of enthusiasm. Buck said he would give them a schedule soon.

If my table were any indication of the general reaction, Buck's idea already was a great success. I did think about how the conference might restrict my article writing; then I figured what a special opportunity this man's generosity would provide all of us—and the very idea of imposing a discipline on such an ambitious venture became highly attractive.

63

"Who knows what marvelous things might happen at Caux?" Sally Satterwaite said to Norman Tunison. "I'm ready for anything."

"Honey, I'm prepared for everything!—including you," Norm said, grabbing her arm and squeezing.

"Well, almost anything," she cautioned.

On the way out afterwards Buck came up to Pam and me, suggesting that the four of us have a private drink together. I was anxious to return to the hotel for some telephone interviews and to arrange to meet Irene for dinner so that we could plan our bicycle trip to Chartres; so I didn't accept at first. But Pam urged me to "be polite."

We strolled over to the Boul' Miche and the familiar brasserie on the rue Soufflot and ordered drinks. Buck Birnbaum fixed me with that focused look, asking, "Now, come clean, Cortell. What do you really think? Your opinion is important to me. Ellen thinks I'm off my rocker." He nodded towards her. Her eyes were on mine.

"That's not quite true," she said, extracting a pencil from her handbag and reaching for the paper tablemat to make a note.

"Well," Buck went on, "you do think I'm crazy in a way."

"I never said that. I said it was highly ambitious and that you were expecting too much from your friends. But, then again, you always do." She glanced quickly at me, expectantly.

"Well, as you didn't say, Buck, it should require lots of homework," I said, observing Ellen beginning a sketch of her butterflies. "There's no doubt you've got an interesting bunch of smart people—excepting me—but I hope they can pull it off for you. A lot depends on you as the group leader. You realize, our opinions are cheap…"

"Opinions don't matter; it's the reactions of aware and gifted people I'm after. And don't be so damned modest, Tom. You fought in one of the toughest campaigns during the war. You got wounded. You've been published in important newspapers and magazines. You've had a superb education. You do count. We all do. Our generation isn't a bunch of deluded fools like the World War I people who led us directly to the last war."

He then turned to Pam, who appeared stimulated by the day. She removed her glasses, and he saw the excitement in her shining eyes. "Certain things are obvious," she said slowly. "Number one: it's a flattering thing to be included, Buck. Behind it all, however, is something you didn't mention at all. That's because the whole thing has a lot to do with why we're all in Europe now, whether we admit it or not. We're all looking for answers. I know Tom's been questioning a lot lately…"

"Tom questions everything," Buck said. "He even did back at school."

"That's what doubting Thomas is all about, no?" Ellen volunteered, again fixing her eyes on me.

"It's also the mark of a scholar, whether he sees himself as one or not" Buck said, sniffing. "Besides, he's not so much doubting—rather cantankerous."

"Thanks for the public dissection, people, I love you to death," I said.

Pam was strangely quiet and watching Ellen, noting my long attention on her. There would be diary entries tonight.

"You love a lot, it seems," Ellen suddenly said.

"Yes, indeed," Pam said softly.

"But if the truth be known, he loves himself least of all," Buck said, his penetrating voice taking on an edge.

I was annoyed. "Did you all set up this group analysis in advance?"

Ellen said quickly, "I'm really glad you're coming, Tom."

"Thanks," I said.

"Buck believes you're essential, but he forgot to mention why. Your love is another matter." She paused, filling in the wings on her napkin, adding delicacy and depth to her sketch. "I'm expecting a lot…"

Why was Ellen glad I was coming? More revelations about uncles and innocence?

"Seriously, Tom," Buck was saying, "in your view is this whole thing just my vanity?"

"You've got a lot of that," I said. "But one thing's for sure: your heart's in the right place—and the idea is excellent. I was only wondering just what we'll all think of the whole thing twenty, thirty years from now. What presumption! But it's sure worth a try. Who the hell else would do it but you?"

Then I got to my feet and excused myself. I wondered what Buck had learned from my questions. Ellen had finished her sketch. Pam raised a question of her own looking first at me, then Ellen. "What's going on?" she said.

☙❧

For the moment they had made up. Bill Watson and Joyce Frost lay entwined on his bed that afternoon after the conference luncheon. His black arms held her tenderly, the white girl under him, his rough cheek rubbing against hers. At first, they talked quietly about the American group and their tensions. But they were guarded, sticking mainly with Fred Furness and Goodie Goodstein. Joyce avoided any reference to Tom, and Bill to any of his abortive French liaisons.

She held his bent head between her hands, a black bowl between marble fingers. She kissed his neck hungrily and cautiously at the same time. It had been her first connection with a Negro and it was still new for her.

"What do you think of Buck's seminar, that Swiss thing?" he asked.

"Why can't they behave themselves?" she smiled.

"I don't know. I wish I did. It's embarrassing." He kissed her breast.

"Will you join them, Bill?"

"How can I be so rude as to refuse?"

"Were they rude to you?"

"No, it was the usual noblesse oblige." As he caressed her, she sucked in her breath.

"They're just white, they don't understand."

"What's there to understand? We're all humans."

"There's a lot to understand. Mainly my skin, my race. Maybe the answer lies with you, Joyce. Why are you different?"

"Don't know that I am—just a beast of a person. And I'm British, clear through—adding empire all the time." She laughed. "As a new colony, you make me feel so good."

"If we were in England, would you make love with me?"

"Don't know. But I'm here. Bill, this isn't noblesse oblige. It's loving."

"Does that make a difference to you, that you're here in Paris?"

"No. Nothing matters, except the man I'm with. Only him." She pinched him. "You're not pink, are you?"

"Yeah. Yeah. I'm pinky and slinky, and if you assault me again, I won't get to finish that painting."

"Is it so important? Is it your conquest, just holding me here for a bloody painting?"

"Interesting use of bloody: like the painting, like your passions. It's your color, Lady Alabaster. You're not really white or pink either," he said, getting to his feet.

She laughed at him. "But, darling, it bothers me that I'm red in the painting. Really does, you know." He stepped toward the bed and picked her up almost without effort, licking her. "What are you up to now?"

"You're coming with me—to that chair. I want you to sit on it and look remorseful. No. Look proud, look very proud of our lovemaking. Hold you head high and smile like a conqueress. Proud, like that." He began to mix the paints.

"You want to capture that?"

"Yes, just like that."

The brush moved over the canvas with authority and grace. "You know," Bill said "you and Tom are the only two who accept me as an equal."

"Oh, come on, Bill. It's not that bad."

"Keep your head up. Yes, it is that bad. Most of them are too smart-assed."

"I love those Americanisms. Smart-assed. Doesn't it work just as well with my accent—smart assed?"

'Will you please keep still?"

"Sorry."

The brush worked the canvas. "I think they're scared of me," he said at last.

"They don't know you, like I do. But you're right."

"They are a little scared of you," she said. "So are the French."

The brush stopped on the canvas. "How do you know?"

"I've seen you blacks with them. Not nice French girls, I can tell."

"That hurt," he said.

"Sorry."

"But it's true. I once met a nurse here named Josette," he said. "Up—up—up." He waggled the brush at her.

He told her about the time before he left for Europe, how his mother in South Chicago told him the French would accept him…

"And Josette?"

He paused and walked around her, observing her body critically. "I thought it might go, but her parents stopped it. She was apologetic, of course…"

"For what it's worth , I'm crazy about you."

"Even though I see you red?"

"I'm over that now. You care. I need that."

He resumed painting, then stopped. "Whose world is this, Joyce?" He led her down from her perch and kissed her. "Their's or mine?"

"Ours," she said, kissing his mouth hard. "And the way we make love."

"What's the matter with Tom, Joyce?"

"There's a problem," she said, closing her eyes.

"Tell me."

"I can't. It's got nothing to do with you."

"I know that. Open your eyes."

She touched his forearm, patting it softly. As they curled their bodies into bed again and held each other closely, she said:

"It was the war. It's done something to him that won't leave him. He's frightened. He's lost."

"He's lost what?" Bill asked, leaning over her with his eclipsing darkness.

"Maybe himself." She leaned back, stared at the ceiling and sighed. "I don't know what it is, nor do you." She turned away from him with her eyes closed, and he did not notice a tear falling down her pale cheek.

"You sound like you know him quite well," he said.

She looked back at him from her pillow. "Oh Bill, just love me. Okay?"

"Okay."

SIX

"Why do I go with you?" Irene asked. Her wide-open grey eyes gazed into mine.

"Because we go well together," I said. We had kept the door to my room open, just for appearances.

"I must be crazy. We are incompatible politically. And to go to a cathedral. I must be tout á fait folle."

"That's why I like you. Your politics only go so far…"

"You are wrong, chéri."

"Well, anyway, let me tell you a little bit about the church, which isn't much."

She waited attentively, and whenever she did that, her eyes became wider than usual, and, almost automatically, I found it hard to control myself. She was so stunning when that happened. Women's eyes were always my undoing. They inevitably suggested more than they delivered.

We had been planning the bicycle trip for months, and I was concerned how she would take to it. The cathedral had become an obsession of mine. I had studied several books about it, as though I were embarked on a cultural crusade. I didn't know why, but I sensed that I would learn something from the 12th Century church.

"Today's Katya's birthday," she announced. Katya, the beautiful three-year-old daughter of her sister, Tamara. It was a sad tale, Tamara and her child. And it became permanently sad for Tamara after she learned the truth about her American soldier. The Moroccan affair had been brief and stopped as soon as she discovered he was married. But the sadder Tamara became, the more lovely grew Katya.

"Let's buy a birthday cake and have a little celebration," I said.

"Now I know why I go with you, but I'll probably suffer the same fate as Tamara."

"Just control me with your gypsy eyes."

She grinned at me.

The birthday went well, and Tamara was beginning to accept me. She had never fully approved of her sister's relationship with me. But that night she made a point of kissing me in thanks for Katya's birthday cake, which I produced miraculously from the local bakery. Afterwards, the tutorial session with Irene continued until I left to see Pam to say goodbye for a few days.

"Don't ask me where I'm going…"

"I wouldn't have the nerve. She must be fabulous."

"She's quite fabulous, since her name is the Virgin Mary. I'm going to Chartres. Never seen it."

"I always thought there was something cloistered about you, darling. Have fun."

But her eyes were brooding.

The next day Irene and I rented bicycles and pedaled southwest out of Paris. We stuffed our saddlebags with clothes, food and wine and moved out with high hopes. The route to Chartres went past Sceaux and the hunting residence of the French President at Rambouillet. In those days the city thinned out rapidly, its suburbs still undeveloped, and the roads relatively free of traffic. Irene frequently led on the bicycle piste, because she was eager and in excellent physical shape. It was typical of her to lead anyway with her independent nature. How pleasant it was to be behind her and to observe her tight, round buttocks swaying from side to side ahead, always just out of reach. She led me from the front and behind, and drove me out of my mind.

As we pedaled along at a good speed, we moved into a more rustic setting. The land was flat and peaceful. Automobiles and trucks were few and far between, and we pretty well had the road to ourselves. Except when French cyclists, leaning over their handlebars, passed us in a rush. It was hard work for both of us, even on the featherweight French bikes.

By noon when we passed Breteuil, hunger caught up with us. We spotted a wheat field and pulled off the road. After being tantalized by her swaying motion, the first thing I did was to put my arms around her and kiss her, holding her close. She looked at me, first with a scold in that penetrating gaze. Then she hugged me. We laughed and took the ham and cheese from the saddle bags, cut the bâtard-size bread, poured the cheap wine and ate ravenously.

We found a secluded location at the edge of a field and stretched out to relax on a piece of canvas I had brought along. She laughed at my obvious fatigue.

"Paresseux! So lazy." she accused me. "Quel…Américain paresseux! How did you win the war?"

Then she leaned back on the tarp amid the wheat, and with her tight yellow chemise, she appeared to me as some kind of modern earth mother. Completely bushed, I lay down beside her, cupping her small breasts and rubbing my nose against her belly.

"You like that, no?"

"I like—I love you." I pushed back from her to stare her down.

"Oh, that's not true," she said.

"Really? Why do you deny my love?"

"You are a little pig. That's it—a little bête."

"Why do you deny it?"

"Because I know you will leave one day. And I want to be ready for that. You are not ready for one woman."

Then she laughed openly at me. Her slim, supple body lay slack on the ground, and once I bent down to kiss her cheek, at which point her arms enclosed us as she sighed in pleasure. Then she laughed aloud again when I told her how keen she looked, and she clasped both hands around my neck. I had never told her I loved her, but I did, at least at that moment, and before we realized it, we fell asleep for an hour or so, two innocent babes in the field holding fast to each other. It was wonderful, and when I stirred now and then I inhaled the hint of garlic on her breath. Once, when I kissed her on her open mouth, she blinked at me, those large grey eyes wide. On guard, she was.

In the afternoon we had cycled as far as Ablis, an unattractive, tiny hamlet where the sky was beginning to cloud over. We decided to stay the night. Our evening meal wasn't very good, but we always enjoyed being together. The beefsteak was tough, the beans underdone and the local wine kind of thin. Over the table, we talked and enjoyed ourselves, even the crème caramel, which was excellent.

"No politics now," I cautioned.

"But certainly not," she said. "Do you remember Maurice Thorez speaking at the Palais de la Mutualité?"

"Sure. It was like visiting the Papacy in Rome—Thorez, head of the French Communist Party. Quelle éminence! He was so anti-American."

"Not at all. Just realistic," she said.

"I see we are not talking politics. How feminine you are."

"You Americans are such exploiters," she insisted. "How can you be so naïve and exploit at the same time?"

"That's why we split for a week—because of this kind of nonsense. Let's avoid it. Remember our agreement never to discuss politics."

"How can we avoid it? We enjoy it, chéri. Besides, I am always right."

"Merde!" I said.

"Merde—merde! Alors."

"Speaking of that, this food is terrible."

"Yes. Now, I want to discuss something serious. I want you to meet my brother-in-law, the husband of Sylva."

"Why?"

"Parce que. He's a good Communist. You need the education."

"I'd rather learn from you."

"You give me too much credit. Besides, he's working on a housing project for the Polish government. He's an architect, you know, and it's his contribution to the communist government there. His drawings are striking, chéri. Really striking. You must see them. And you must remember that Edouard is more than a doctrinaire Communist."

"I figured that was the top rating in your world."

"Silly," she said, "he's an idealist, too."

"Ah, that makes him human. I guess that's why his drawings are striking and not drab like Communist thinking."

"Don't be naughty. Edouard is a militant but also an idealist."

"You can't be both, sweetheart. But I'd like to meet him anyway."

"Good," she beamed. "I like that word 'sweetheart.' It's like that other word, hothead, you use about my arguments on communism. But I am not a hothead! You will enjoy Edouard."

"But only if you will protect me." I pinched her arm lightly.

"Cesse ça! You will have to guard yourself."

A storm was in the making when we went upstairs to bed. As tired as we were from the ride, she kept talking in my arms.

"Chéri, one thing."

"Yes, gypsy."

"Your American friends, I don't think I talk well to them. I never went to university. I feel strange with them sometimes."

"Schooling," I said, "has nothing to do with intelligence or sociability. It's supposed to put you in touch with knowledge, not with a feeling of superiority over others…"

"Still, I'd like to be able to talk intelligently…with your friends."

"They're only my friends by accident, Irene…"

"Mais," she pushed on, "They seem so intelligent."

"They aren't, some of them. They just think they are."

"But I stopped my schooling."

"No, you didn't. You're alive; that's enough." She hugged me, then caressed my thigh, exploring it.

"Remember how we met in the Luxembourg Gardens, at the children's pool?"

"We were attracted," she said. "Good things happen by accident. But I miss something with your educated friends. You all went to university together. I didn't. I'm serious, Thomas. It bothers me. I'm very serious"

"So am I—about you."

"No you are not. You just like to make love, a little cochon."

"That, too, with you," I said.

"With several. I'm just a bad habit," she said putting one hand between my legs. "Oh, there it is: what the fascists did to you. That gets me angry. Oh, Thomas." The storm began outside—lightning and thunder and wind.

"Irene, you are a good habit." I pulled her close, and we lay that way when the rain came down hard. Every time the thunder sounded she clutched me, and in the sudden illuminations I saw a frown creasing her forehead. I pulled her close again.

Finally, she fell asleep, and I lay there her prisoner, thinking about her and her self-imposed inferiority. She once spoke to me about how she detested her office job, and how she felt uncomfortable about it but needed the income. She wouldn't accept any help. She had to work out her own destiny. When I fell asleep her fingers were still on my leg.

"Bonjour, chéri," she said, fresh and bright beside me in the morning. My nose touched her wide cheeks.

"Attention!" she warned. "Attention aux pommettes."

"I love them. They make your eyes exciting."

"Assez, monsieur. You are always making love."

The grim bistro with its zinc bar next to the hotel was the only handy place for breakfast. Strong roasted coffee with milk and croissants bolstered us, but we said little. We were just happy to be together, as we were yesterday in the wheat field.

Then we were en route to our mother church, pedaling along. Our bicycle wheels revolved smoothly in a rhythm of anticipation. The pilgrimage took us southwest again along the old road, and that was something to think about, the tradition of a pilgrimage that had brought so many before us. One didn't make pilgrimages any more. That was for the old times, I thought. Faith was needed for that, and we had lost it.

Once we stopped for a drink of water by the roadside and noticed some butterflies swarming. Something clicked inside. It was as if Ellen and Buck were there, Ellen and her unknown aspirations and Buck's plans for his conference. Moving along again, the sprockets flashed and chains turned our wheels as we bent over the handlebars, staring transfixed at the road rushing by. A rhythm took over and an old memory came back. It was a song from the past, a motion, a regular beat. Ezekiel and his wheel turning. Old Negro spirituals from before the war. At prep school I had heard them singing out—a small, gyrating group of black singers from Tuskegee, Alabama, who serenaded us in our school auditorium. A treble voice rose like a bird taking off, up high over a baritone counterpoint pumping under it. They slapped their thighs, beating out the old church songs. Cries of Negroes reverberated in syncopated rhythm:

> Ezekiel saw the wheel—turning—way up in the middle o' the air
> Ezekiel saw the wheel—turning…

Bicycle wheels, turning. Their sprockets flashed in the sun, turning…

> Way in the middle o' the air…the big wheel moved by faith,

The Street of Four Winds

> The little wheel moved by the Grace o' God, a wheel in a wheel,
> Way in the middle o' the air…

Another melody rolled along with us.

> "Jubah this—Jubah that—Jubah killed a yellow cat; to make his wife a Sunday hat, hey-down Jubah."

I could hear the old soft Negro voices of the Hampton Quartet.

Ahead Irene's tight buttocks pressed against her shorts, her dark olive skin lustrous in the sun.

She was turning our ride into a kind of pilgrimage of her own. Around us spread the sweet rolling landscape of the Beauce. We moved through the light waves of corn, past the wheat fields, and plowed forward on this traditional journey across the land to the holy church of Mary. Others had done it on foot eight hundred or more years ago. Now we ourselves.

Why was I doing this? Pedaling on tired muscles to a church. If the mission were based on faith—a turning wheel, a spiritual outcry, whatever—what was my connection with it? They had adored the Virgin Mary in a lofty way I couldn't fathom.

I watched Irene's firm round derrière in my own profane, adoring way…The Virgin and Irene. Where was I going? Maybe this pilgrimage would help me find an answer. Wheatland wheeled by as our bicycles moved along. Our wheels kept turning. Irene suddenly yelled: "Alors, Tom!"—breaking me out of my spell just in time to avoid a ditch.

I wondered where the cathedral was. It couldn't be far. I scanned the horizon. Nothing but corn and wheat fields, farm houses, cattle beside the road, and above: an intensely blue sky full of white clouds.

We saw an old castle at Gallardon. It was lovely country, full of farms. Occasionally a stream ran through it, and our wheels turned and turned.

Then the object of our journey greeted us. First just the tip of something grey on the horizon. We pedaled on.

"C'est vraiment beau…"

"Tais-toi!" she yelled, smiling back with her light eyes. Our wheels turned and suddenly she pointed ahead to the two spires. They looked like stout masts of an old frigate ship, boldly jutting above the wheat and corn. Then, as if by magic, the whole ship appeared. And we were rowing on the sea of green and yellow towards this great and merciful vessel. Irene and I were plowing past waves of ripening wheat to complete our pilgrimage. The church dominated the western skyline of the town, majestic for all to see.

Now we could make out the city's buildings shuffled up like cards against the great hull of the protecting grey cathedral. Its sharp spires, the stout one on the left, the higher, thinner, decorated one on the right were built centuries apart. They pierced ever higher the closer we came. Flying buttresses turned their great stone arcs to support the thick walls. The building was in motion and so were we. Then we were upon it in the square by the main west entrance.

We had lunch under the great towers and walls of the church. Its massive presence subdued us. Irene sat across from me in the sidewalk restaurant, her smile serene, glad to have arrived at the end of our pilgrimage. We ordered Cinzano and Campari. And the sun was warm as we ate our cheese omelets and took the fresh vin de pays. Finally, I said, "I believe I love you. I'm not sure, but I think so."

"No," she said. "It must be the apéritif."

"And your pommettes."

"Maybe something else."

"Your derrière."

"Méchant."

"Perhaps," I said. Pamela crossed my mind. How different from Irene…and Joyce. All three: different forms of adoration. Perhaps celebrations of myself. It was an unpleasant thought.

We walked hand in hand toward the great dark stone cave of Chartres Cathedral. Before us were the thin statues around the

Royal Portal entryway, where time and ignorant people had damaged the sculptured figures. There something stopped me—a look. It was the beatific face of a princess figure whose arms had been broken off. It stunned me. Her simple smile held me, suggesting women of all time: my mystery. Irene felt me stop and tried to pull me along. I continued to stare at the woman's face. Irene continued to pull, then she stopped. She waited, watching me with her wide, raised eyebrows.

Once through the inner swinging door and into the dark cave itself, our hands fell apart. We looked up. Around. We were dumbstruck before the soaring stone, the stretching blue windows. Just then the resounding bells in the north tower broke into extravagant booming music. At our feet the design of a labyrinth flowed around us. The penitents of older days had made their way around it on their knees. I was tempted to do the same, but before I could Irene pulled me along again, the heavy, deep bells clanging above us.

We passed dozens of deeply set, bright stained glass windows, gigantic columns holding the walls and windows together with pointed arches and courses of stone.

"It draws you into eternity, doesn't it?" I said.

"So old, Tom. And so beautiful. It touches me."

"Think of Edouard, what he would think. Architects of Egypt, Athens, and Rome have all this same stone."

"And the glass, Thomas. The blood and sky of centuries."

"Are you glad we are here?" I said.

Her grey eyes took in the sweep of stone and glass. "Incroyable," she breathed.

We moved down the nave, stopping at every new perspective and window, wondering. Then out to the aisles to check the choir sculptures, joining our hands, then separating to sit and admire. Once I noticed that she had moved to a wooden seat to look more carefully. Then we were in the middle of the church looking up at the west front windows, their kaleidoscope of colored glass, mainly blue, under the great broken moon of the high rose window. I had never been moved by any such sight in my life. She placed her weightless hand on my shoulder. "Incroyable," she said again.

I wondered how Bill Watson would react to all of this. It was a diversionary thought, but it came to me nonetheless. Suddenly the orange, red and yellow of the Solomon window were above me as we moved back to the east end of the transept. Light streaming through these colors bathed Irene. Had Bill Watson used his reds on Joyce in this way? And here was Irene in the refracted glory of the sun. She became a princess of the Orient, dark skinned, her soft lips gently parted as she studied the windows' messages.

Then we were in the nave again, looking up at the high stone arches. Then the window of the Virgin was behind us, her compassionate countenance shadowed from the sun.

"She looks so serene, Thomas."

I nodded. "A woman for all the ages."

"Can any ordinary woman look like that?"

"I think so; perhaps after giving birth, then taking her babe into her arms, like she is doing in that window…"

"Or giving oneself to a man in deepest love."

"Yes," I said.

"But that is not us."

"No." I looked into her eyes. "But I cherish what we have."

Her hand found mine, and we stood there, staring at each other. Later we rested a bit in the congregation's chairs under the three blue lancet windows. At one point a tinkling bell sounded somewhere in the building, reminding me that everything had been here for a long time, and would be long after we left.

"You are very quiet, Thomas."

"You, too."

"I—I had not expected to be so moved."

"I know."

"I deliver papers, chéri. Each Sunday I take out papers with all the latest news, the passions and ugliness of today. Mais…"

"Mais, quoi?"

"Well, here there is this calm of great achievement, an emotional connection with the eternal." She pulled a face. "I'm not educated enough to put it into words."

"You put it very well, Irène." It was odd, for I had used her French name for some reason.

"And you—what is all this for you?"

I hesitated.

"Come. Tell me."

"All right. I can tell you in here, this sanctified place. But it stays here, n'est ce pas?"

"Oui."

"I look at the Virgin, her serenity. Yet, she has always been with me, holding me in a spell. I use her as a prism to understand the women I—and the others."

"The Virgin is the perfect woman?" she asked.

I smiled. "That would be too easy. I don't know. I just know that being here in Chartres, in this fantastic place, in her silent embrace—it's touching me. A very spiritual thing."

"Which is good, Thomas."

"Yes. Yes it is. And I feel humble."

"Here," I whispered to Irene, offering her my hand. She closed her fingers over it. She was standing in a bath of blue light under the Virgin's window. For a brief instant she looked down on me, like the Virgin herself, with an angelic smile of utter satisfaction.

It was time to get back to Paris and the living. The overwhelming encounter with the past had diminished us. It was too much. So when we left Chartres on the road back to Paris, neither of us looked back to the Virgin's church. We didn't dare.

SEVEN

The day we returned from Chartres there was some mail waiting for me at the hotel. Irene watched me shuffle through the letters, her brow rising when I frowned at one envelope.

"Problems?" she asked, then caught herself. "Pardon, ce n'est pas mon affaire."

"Merci." It was from Pamela. It could wait.

When Irene passed the concierge's desk on the way upstairs, she watched me again. But I knew that would be the end of it. She had a fine feeling for privacy…

@@

Upstairs she entered Tamara's room; no one was there. She sat down on her bed, staring at the floor pensively. Then she saw the note her sister had left; she and young Katya had gone to Belleville where Edouard, Sylva and and their child lived. A sigh escaped her as she looked into the mirror. "Gypsy," she said, "gypsy face. Certainly not a Virgin face." She coiled her short dark hair and lifted her gaze slowly to herself. Then she rose and walked around the small room, opened a drawer to find a scarf, and put her hand tentatively on the door knob. She carefully opened the door, walked down a flight of stairs, and knocked on Tom's door gingerly…

"Yes?"

"C'est moi," she said.

"Oh, please come in." When she entered she noticed his taut expression.

"You needed more time?"

"No, thanks." One of the letters was opened on his night table. She regarded him for a moment. Then she put a hand on his slumped shoulders. She looked directly into his eyes, holding his in a steady, probing look.

"Thomas, I just wanted to say this to you, you crazy American…"

"Yes? Anything wrong? What's up?"

"Up?" she asked with a lift of her dark brows.

"Yes. Up. That means what's happening?"

"Oh, rien. Rien. Nothing special. I just wanted to thank you for Chartres."

"Thank me?" he said.

"You asked me to go with you."

"Irene, I wouldn't have gone without you. I needed you, if only to watch you enjoy it."

She smiled broadly, and impulsively kissed him full on the lips.

"Merci beaucoup," she said and, as quickly as she had come, pulled the door closed behind her…

∞

I sat down and shook my head for a minute, wondering about her. Then I poured a drink and read Pam's letter. Her perfume touched my nostrils, an uncomfortable presence.

> "Dear Thomas:
>
> Here I stand on our favorite bridge, thinking about us. How do I say these things to you, my teacher? I know I really don't need to say anything, but I have to tell you what you have done for me. First off, I'm grateful, and you hate to hear that, I know. Yet, it's not easy for me to say this. I'm dancing with joy, and that's an awful confession, I know.

You must know this instinctively, but you're the first person in this world who has demonstrably cared for me and my crazy feelings. I shouldn't admit this, but it's true. You must remember: I'm from a very conventional middle American background in Illinois. I'm not so sure you exactly know what that means. Back home, even thinking about Paris is suspect. Conventional conduct is de rigueur where I come from. It's not that way in the East, certainly not New York.

The nub of it is that I'm in love with you. You've never said anything like this to me, ever since we began our intimacies, but the fact is I do love you, knowing at the same time that you don't return it. Weeks ago when we first slept together it was my initiation, and you were wonderful—and it wasn't easy for you, I know. My God, how bored you must have been with a virgin at the wrong time of month!

Outside of admitting all of this to you, the other reason I'm writing now is that I don't want you to feel any sense of obligation to me. I told you once, I'm just a girl from Park Forest, so I accept my limitations…"

I held the letter up to the light, as if I hadn't seen it all and missed something. I didn't know how to take this confession, and, in a way, it bothered me. I hadn't even considered her inexperience. I had taken advantage of her, something I never did with women. But I had enjoyed showing her Paris. She was such a good study, and it was her newness to it all that made it fun. The concern now was that this letter had convinced me that I had taken on a responsibility. The thought suffocated me.

I poured another drink, not knowing what else to do. Then I began sorting the other mail and papers. Work was piling up, and I needed the money from the articles to stay on in Paris.

Why should I feel obligated to her, especially when she had let me off the hook in that letter? Why couldn't I accept this affair in the way I did sleeping with Irene and Joyce: simply having a good time? Why not? I drained the glass and thought: conscience.

But why think of it at all? I felt rotten, but unexpectedly, relief came knocking at the door.

Fred Furness was there. He urged me to get ready for dinner and a session at the Café de Flore with Birnbaum and the rest of the group. That didn't thrill me—but it was better than worrying about obligations. I knew beforehand it would be one of those late nights of anti-American talk, and I didn't need that after Chartres and Pam's letter. I was still under the spell of the cathedral. A thought came: I need my rosary beads.

"Don't brood," Fred was saying.

"What's that?"

"Forget it—but let's get to a bar for a drink…you look like you need one or two…and then dinner," Fred said. "I'm famished."

The dinner turned out to be another "obligation." Fred began to complain about Goodie, and that carried on interminably about how they were "nearing the end of the road."

"She's really getting to me, Tom, and I don't know how to handle it. And it comes at a time when I'm getting into some serious work. I've really got a great idea, a kind of saga about the war…"

"I thought it was Joyce you were getting into."

"Oh, that!" he said sheepisly. "That's a reaction to Goodie. Joyce is wonderful, but in a way I don't trust the whole thing. She seems so matter of fact about everything."

"Really? What the hell do you expect, a great romantic affair? She seems like a good antidote to your poetic anguish."

"Anyway, I've really flipped for her. It's a deep thing. I really care for her. She's wonderful. I've never known anyone like her. And all the time Goodie keeps nagging and wanting to tie me down."

"What do you expect of a Jewish girl who's beginning to get past her prime? She's working on first things first."

"I'm half-Jewish, you know." There was a hint of complaint in Fred's voice. It was news to me.

"So what?" I said. "You're not a woman. Jewish girls always keep their eyes on number one, themselves."

"You've noticed that, eh?"

"She's just street-wise," Tom said. "That's all."

"She's sure persistent."

"Then again, maybe you're not being too prudent about Joyce," I felt odd about this, being confident that Fred knew nothing about myself and Joyce. "Maybe you take sex too seriously."

"A poet's curse," he said.

Dinner went on this way for more than an hour, and we were due to meet the others shortly. It was like a fencing match with lots of ripostes and parries. Fred finally admitted he took sex too seriously.

"I've always taken a lot of things in life too seriously." I appraised him from across the table In college his verse was incredibly personal, strongly felt, derivative but powerfully expressed. He wasn't bad. Not everyone can get run over by a tank, I thought. But I really didn't care. I had had my own moment of truth in Italy and wanted to forget it. You've got to be tough.

"Well," I said, "just tough it out. Goodie will get the message. And I've had some bad days myself."

"How so?"

"Irene and I went down to Chartres."

"That must have been something," Fred said.

"It was a drag," I lied. It was none of his damned business.

"Really?"

"Yes, a total drag." With that I dropped it.

We were walking down the Boulevard St. Germain towards the Flore, and Fred was still complaining about Goodie. I asked him to change the subject. The café came into view, and it appeared complaining wasn't confined to Fred.

Buck was in the middle of a big bitch about America with Norman Tunison, the Smith girls, and some others. They were noisy. Norman was on stage. It was U.S. foreign policy.

"They just try to impose their system on others, especially in the Far East," he said. "We want every southeast Asian to be a capitalist, when all they want is to be good Buddhists."

"Right," said Buck. "Precisely—we always miss the point, don't we?"

"Why is it that every fascist dictator in the world gets our support—Battista in Cuba, Somoza in Nicaragua, Chiang Kai-Shek in China, you name it." I remembered these names later.

"We don't learn anything from history," Fred said. But Norman wasn't finished.

"…and DeGaulle, here in France, tries to stand up for his country, so he's in our doghouse…"

"U.S. foreign policy stinks!" Buck said. "We're never going to enter the modern world by carrying on strictly with an anti-Soviet line."

"As long as you're anti-Communist, you're okay," Norman said.

I decided to stay out of it, watching them like a foreign observer. Even though I agreed to some extent. I noted that the more they drank, the more anti-American they became. But every one of them kept his or her passport at the ready. They weren't about to give that up. All expatriates found it fashionable to trash their home country. It wasn't terribly intelligent.

Pam Batterford and her friends from Smith strolled into the café. She winked at me, but I sensed something behind her eyes, some distancing, perhaps fear. I readied a chair for her. "I can't take too much more of this," I whispered to her.

"What's the problem?"

"Aside from the usual story line here of bashing the U.S., your letter is the problem. But that's not for now."

"My letter?" she asked.

"Yes, you forgot something."

"I did?"

Norman was ranting on about Central American policy.

"Why don't we go now?" I said, touching her elbow.

"Tom, what's wrong?"

"Where are you going?" Buck asked surprised. "The talk's just getting good."

"I don't think so," I said. "My priorities are elsewhere."

"What in God's name is getting into you?" Norman said.

"See you later," I said.

Pam took my arm, and we walked away down the boulevard. She looked concerned. I pulled her along.

It was a warm night, the air unusually dry for summer in the Seine Valley. The cafés were all full of tourists and the French. The conversations were at their usual feverish pitch with people arriving and leaving on their secret missions. She continued to stare at me from time to time as we moved down the rue de Seine towards the river. We passed the closed bookshops and walked under the arch of the Institute, crossed the quai and then out over the wooden Pont des Arts bridge.

We knew it well. It had become "our" bridge. We relished its views of the Seine, sharing our intimacies and dreams there out over the river. But I could remember an earlier visit, of Pam taking off her glasses to explore hidden vistas, then putting them back on, only to pronounce herself blind. It had been an odd and disturbing display. And now there was her letter…

"I come here often, Tom," she said. Her voice had that throaty quality that had attracted me when I first met her. But now there was a suggestion of loneliness about it, some imploding around private thoughts.

Directly in front of us upriver floated the Île de la Cité where Notre Dame crouched in its display of magic light. Closer, at the near end of the island, glided the Vert Galant, another favorite haunt we first visited together during our recent tour.

"We both come here," I said.

"No, I mean alone…to think and dream."

"Ah." I reached out. "Perhaps I should come here alone, to think and dream."

"And would those dreams include me?" she asked quickly.

"Pam…"

"I see…"

"No, you don't, and that's part of the problem. You can't accept my genuine affections for you. You must always close in on me"—lack of sleep got the better of me—"sucking me dry."

"Ah..." I cast around desperately to repair the damage, and found some solace for us both in Apollinaire when he wrote about another bridge:

> Sous le pont Mirabeau coule la Seine
> Et nos amours
> Faut-il qu'il m'en souvienne
> La joie venait toujours après la peine.

"Every educated Frenchman of the Twenties and Thirties knew that," I said. "Today it's a Paris that is passing."

She took my hand. "Odd you should say that. We read Apollinaire at Smith. I never got that out of it. My loss." She squeezed my hand hard. Then, almost irrationally, she added: "So what did I forget in my letter?"

"This," I said, pulling her close like every other lover on the bridge that night, kissing her.

"And what's that supposed to mean?"

"You know damned well, mademoiselle."

"I do?"

"You know I love you, as much as I hate to admit it."

"That's a left-handed compliment, if I ever heard one. Tom, what are you hiding from?"

"Nothing. I just take each day at a time."

"That sounds like Irene, the lover I can't compete against."

"Let's drop it."

"Why have you never said that to me before—that you love me?"

"Because..."

"Yes?"

"Forget it. I simply don't want to be tied down. We have fun, don't we?" It sounded dreadfully thin in the brisk river air.

"Yes, but we could have something else."

"Well, it's that something else I want to avoid just now."

She let go of my hand. Tears were in her eyes as she stood there stiffly, expectantly. Then she rose on her toes and began to dance distractedly into the center of the bridge all by herself, first to her left, then to her right and finally around me, whirling in mad abandon. I didn't know what to do. She continued for a while and then, with a grin, she stopped suddenly and asked: "Do you want to make love now…to have fun?"

"What were you doing just now?"

"Laying a trap for you."

I was nervous. There was a wild glint in her eye when she dramatically removed her glasses. "Now I can see," she said, standing there, now rising on her toes and then falling back down to the wooden floor of the bridge. "What's your pleasure, sir?"

I wanted to respond to her, but couldn't. She had succeeded in extracting the confession from me but not the commitment. It was the commitment she desperately wanted, and she was whirling in its vortex.

She saw my confusion and quickly turned things around when she took my hand clumsily and led me like a dog on a leash back across the bridge to the Left Bank.

I asked where we were going.

"To our mutual pleasure, sir," she said, pulling me along.

EIGHT

We started walking south of the river, she pulling me along towards the Boulevard St. Germain.

"I've got to stop," I said, looking back to the river. "I want to remember this."

"Wouldn't you rather make love?" There was a vulnerable quality in her voice, as if she were ready for a rebuff and it would all shrivel like a flower petal.

"Not yet. Look at this." I gestured behind to the river and its lights. The city was all there. "All of it."

Night in Paris, the great illuminator. There was no city in the world like it. It was the wild illusion of my dreams. Irene was right. You can cry over its beauty.

"Look at this river, Pam. People moving about, holding on to their secrets. Like Pirandello and his theater."

"Theater?"

"It resonates with it—Paname and Old Lutèce…or Pantagruel or Mélisande…even Abélard and Héloïse—a whole cast of characters that have made this the great illuminator."

"Yes," she said, joining me across her intellect and sense of romance. "And what about Rameau and his nephew…or Cyrano… or Poulenc and his nostalgic tunes…" Her tone of voice was odd but with me in spirit. "Romantic, n'est-ce pas?"

"It flows, Pam. Like the river. The old buildings and zealous ideals. Nothing like Paris. Anywhere. It's such a symbol of excitement, endurance, emotion—the epitomy of the word culture…" I felt her touch, her returning warmth. "It was so right that we came here."

"To our bridge?"

"To Paris. To make our escape into something richer than America…to adapt as foreigners in this passionate place. We owe a debt to people like Buck for alerting us, for forging our intellects, for giving life a new meaning. Here. Just here and no place else."

But this time Pam wasn't in tune. She was only going through the motions. Paris and its singular light were reflected from her lenses and distancing her from me. She resisted holding hands, unable to accept my good will, my peculiar ability to step back and look at us objectively in the flow of all this history around us. So we walked on through the Latin Quarter and its stagelike streets until…

There on the curb, apparently unconscious, was a body slumped outside the Relais Odéon. Just another drunk, I thought. But then I saw the face and recognized it. It was the familiar trowel shaped pale face with puffy cheeks and the short-cropped hair with the long-lashed eyes shutting out the world. It was Norman Tunison sprawled in the gutter. He was completely out of it, and it wasn't the first time I had seen him succumb to his pastis. That was his inevitable downfall.

Pam looked at me puzzled and alarmed. She was suddenly lovely, desperately fragile with a new coldness to her, a cold that came from retreat within herself. But something had to be done about Norman. He couldn't be left there. On several previous occasions I had literally dragged him through the streets of the Latin Quarter back to his hotel room, stripped him down and tucked him into bed. Now it had happened again. He was blotto in the gutter. Years ago I had been there myself—at Cornell during a party weekend without a date and feeling sorry for myself, drinking too much and out of control. My parents did that once in a while, baptizing their unhappy marriage.

Pam looked helplessly at Norman crumpled in the street and then at me. "We can't leave him here."

"Of course not. Can you help me?"

"Sure," she said. Between the two of us we hoisted his deadweight body over my shoulders in a fireman's carry and lugged him slowly over the boulevard. Pam held his flopping arms and asked where we were going. I indicated his hotel on rue de Tournon. When we finally got there I explained the situation to Norman's concierge, and he immediately understood. While I held the heavy body, the concierge handed Pam the key to Norman's room. It was an old story for him and me. In no time we had Norman on his scarlet bedspread in front of the bank of outlandish mirrors. I removed his coat, jacket and pants, and he began to snore. Then we left, and, without a reason, I was holding Pam's hand again down on the sidewalk.

"Please don't mention this to him tomorrow," I said. "He's really ashamed of his drinking."

"Don't worry. I'm a good girl."

"From Illinois, I understand."

"Very funny. Now, where do we go from here?"

"That's up to you and your conventional background," I said.

"My letter," she said. "You read it?"

"Of course. You assumed a hell of a lot in that note."

"For example…"

"That I don't return things in kind."

"Like love?"

"Yes, which isn't true, Pamela," I insisted. "How do you want me to demonstrate it? Our first night and all the others? What do you want?"

"Tom, if you can't figure it out, I don't know. You have such a condescending way, as if…"

All I could do was hold her close and say nothing. She pulled away, and I reached for her again. This time she came forward.

We walked together arm in arm in the night towards my hotel on the rue des Quatre Vents. In a few minutes we were upstairs in bed, holding each other close, saying nothing, arms intertwined, pressing hard against each other. Nothing happening.

Just a lot of pressure. All night long it went on, no lovemaking, just proximity, occasionally kissing, sleeping, and kissing again, trying to prove something to each other. For a long time after she turned away we lay curled together like spoons.

I thought of the cathedral at Chartres and Irene. It was so illogical, being in bed with Pam, clutching the delicate girl and thinking about the church. I couldn't sleep, slung between such contrary thoughts. What it was I didn't know then. Only later. All I could think of was that the cathedral had taken me out of myself and my personal preoccupations. It had been a spiritual experience, removing me from time. Yet, here was this soft human being in my arms, a being who was more than a sex object, and for us, like Héloïse with Abelard, an old French story. I held her from the rear, my arms tightly around her waist, and she kept them firmly around her like a protective cage. Once she groaned and relaxed, and before I fell into a deep sleep, I heard her whisper, "Dear Tom, I love him…he loves me not…"

⁂

When I awakened early in the morning she was gone. The sweet smell of her remained, like the perfume on her letter. So different from Irene's. It was close to first light outside, the city still quiet. Where was she? I was worried and figured she couldn't have left too long ago. I remembered that she, Sally and Faith shared an apartment near the Observatoire on the south side of the Luxembourg Gardens. So I threw on some clothes, ran downstairs, and headed up the rue de Tournon. The Gardens were open now, and I cut across the big park to shorten the trip. I was moving sluggishly at the early hour, and few people were about. Then she appeared.

Pam was again dancing her wild dervish of the night before on the Pont des Arts. Now she was prancing on a set of steps. She seemed more out of control, whirling in a senseless, uncoordinated dance. She spun and turned, her contorted, bespectacled face half-smiling and strained. Her hair was undone and streaming behind her. All I could guess was that she had lost complete control. She seemed mad, and I could hear jumbled show tune lyrics as she turned and bowed and squirmed. "I'll follow my secret heart till I find you…" It was a Noel Coward song like the other one—"The Party's Over"—everyone had sung a few nights before on the streets.

Her body swayed back and forth, then stiffened, and turned again and again. I decided to shock her out of it and yelled her name as loud as I could. She whirled and whirled. So I bounded up the steps. Her clothes were pulled awry, twisted around her body. She had ripped her blouse open. Her bra was askew and other underclothes were loose. I shouted again, and she stopped suddenly. Then she began to cry.

"Pam, what are you doing?" I said as I put my arms around her. Her tears were gentle, soft and salty.

"He loves me not," she said.

I was not sure what I could do to bring her around, and when she repeated "He loves me not," she shuddered in the warm air and began to lose her balance, I impulsively picked her up in my arms. Moving south towards her apartment, I began to feel her weight and stumbled a bit. I couldn't help recalling how she had helped me with Norman a few hours earlier. Now we passed the rear gate on the way out of the Gardens.

I soon located the Beaudelocq Hospital near her apartment, fumbled in her purse for the street door keys and opened it. Pressing the minuterie button for light, I then struggled up the stairs, where Faith was waiting wide-eyed. She saw Pam in my arms and said: "Dear God!"

I quickly explained. "She's in a bad way."

"You're not kidding."

In a minute we had undressed her and carried her to her bed. Sally was still asleep and had missed the revelation. Faith covered her body with a nightgown, looking askance at me while she did it. Pam's head flopped to one side and she breathed quite deeply. It was almost a gasp. Her forehead was split with a frown and she groaned. Then she cried gently to herself and shook her head back and forth.

Faith looked at me helplessly. "Tom, this is terrible."

"Just let her sleep it off. " I said and decided to leave. "I've never seen her this way before except briefly last night. I can't figure it out. I think you ought to get some medical attention. Here." I scribbled a note with my phone number and a doctor's name and number.

"Tom, this must be terrible for you. But I can tell you this isn't the first time she's lost control. It's upsetting to have it recur now."

"Yes, and I feel a bit responsible. Let's see if she recovers later today. Call me. I care a lot about her, and I know this behavior has something to do with me. Please keep me informed." I stood nonplussed and put my arm around Faith. When I did she clasped me tight.

"It's not the first time, you say?"

"No. Fairly often."

"Recently?" I felt her body shiver.

"Ever since Smith." She wiped her eyes.

She sensed what I was driving at. "But not since she's known you. I think you've been good for her. She started a diary, did you know? Girls do that when deeply involved. Every time you two have been together she's been happy about herself."

"Faith, did anything happen to her when you all spent that college year in Europe?"

"Nothing special—except maybe one problem, but she got over it. What's happening now never happened before, as far as I know."

"Then how do you account for her performance last night and this morning?"

"Last night?"

"Yes, her weird dancing on the Pont des Arts bridge."

"Oh, God! What triggered it?"

"I have no idea."

She studied me. "Tom, do you love her?"

"Yes, I do, but that doesn't seem enough…"

"She's been let down before, you know. Or maybe you don't. She's a one man woman. And there's something else, which I'd rather not discuss now…"

"Why not? We're baring it all."

"Well," she said, eyeing me cautiously for effect. "It has something to do with her family, I think. I believe a long time ago her father once got a little interested in her…"

"Oh, Christ!" I blurted out. "Faith, has she ever had any psychoanalytical treatment—ever?"

"Yes. It was quite abortive, but at Smith she once went off to Boston where she had a consultation. She wasn't pleased with that visit, however." Faith tried to smile, lighten things. "Tom, she's a wonderful, caring, person. You know that."

"Yes, I do—and I care very much for her."

"But do you love her? And not just her sexy body?"

"I care for her, but I don't think I can give her the permanent commitment she wants. Not now anyway, because I'm pretty screwed up myself…"

"God, Tom, don't play with her, offer words too easily misinterpreted—"

I'm not, dammit." But I had said I loved her. "I'd rather not go into that now. I'm pretty exhausted."

"But do you love her?" she repeated.

"I care a lot for her, maybe more than ever now."

She regarded me questioningly.

"You're her first real man, and I hope you remember that."

"Yes."

"Tom, be careful. She's a delicate commodity…"

I wanted to end the discussion and get home to rest. The past two days had been upsetting, even for a selfish bastard like myself. Even Faith was asking for a commitment.

"Will you please let me know what's happening to her, Faith? I mean it."

She said she would. I kissed her cheeks. For a brief instant she held on to me. "Tom, you need to love her."

"I know." She finally let me go. Then I left.

Two rescues in a day were too much for me. I walked north through the Gardens to the Palais. I paused at the steps where Pam had first appeared that morning looking so disheveled. I walked slowly, past the children's pool and the Palais. Then down Tournon to the hotel. I lay down confused. I smelled the rumpled sheets that still carried a trace of Pam's presence. Just for a moment I thought about two things: what Faith had said about Pam's father, and her repeated question to me. I remember being angry—at both her father and myself.

☉☉

I couldn't sleep and lay there unhappy:

The magic of Chartres is gone. Pam's breakdown alarms me. And I can't rest. I'm the subject now—not even Pam's lecherous old man, the son of a bitch.

And now you, doubting Thomas, as Ellen said, you've gone and done something, too. You're a son of a bitch yourself.

What was all that garbage about the Cortell name being dimly related to Andrew Jackson—another pirate? Fine old American WASP stock. And going to a prep school near New York where more than half my friends were Jews from well-to-do (like me) professional families of only the second generation (not like me). There's the contradiction. What are you, really?

Sisters Martha and Anne didn't help me a bit, except when I needed them. And the old man was screwing everything in the neighborhood during his real estate "expeditions" in Westchester. He wasn't any more help than mother and her addiction to Scotch whisky. A lousy marriage.

At least I come by it honestly. From the first time when I was left alone at age twelve and maid Dorothy introduced me to the joys of sex. Not at all like my first honest crush on Mary Lou, that innocent dark Irish girl from Brooklyn. I met her at fourteen on the Conte di Savoia when mother took me and Martha away to Europe—to keep her sanity. Sex had nothing to do with the young girl. She was pure and lovely, a face I haven't seen until that princess' face carved on the front of Chartres. I might never find it again, that loveliness and innocence. Even Pam has a bit of the same quality.

Certainly not the one at Cornell, who drowned me in bed; or later, after the war, at Columbia. Until I came here to Europe, thanks to Martha's advice about getting away from that lady who dropped me: "Get away," my sister said, "and learn something—about yourself. Not just women. You can't win the female wars, Thomas, any more than you could win World War II—which is why, my dear brother, you were wounded. Almost served you right."

What made me a casualty at Monte Cassino wasn't the physical damage. More spiritual, I guess. I really believe in nothing but ass and, oddly enough, beauty. Objectively, they're both the same, I think. Chartres, for example, and Irene's derrière on the bicycle. Strange how it's all held together by the Virgin Mary.

How can I get away from Pam's love? It will kill me, like Fred Furness will be strangled by Goodie, who actually does have her fine points. She's no fool, either. But Pamela—burning bright—yet not giving a lovely light. What she wants won't happen. I've gone too far with her. The way her father…

I hear St. Sulpice's sharp bells ring 3 a.m.

LUXEMBOURG GARDENS

NINE

In the morning I picked up some roses and sweets on the way out to see Pamela at the Observatoire. Just outside the store Buck and Ellen appeared with Bill Watson. They were discussing an exhibit of oils at a rue St. André des Arts gallery, and Buck was holding forth with strong opinions about a new French artist, André Minaux.

"He's so obviously derivative of Bonnard, I can hardly believe it. But his colors and forms are excellent…"

"I like his work and wish I could see more of it," Bill said.

"Well. I met Hélène and André at a party recently, and I think we can arrange that. She runs a book shop in the Marais. It can be arranged…"

"Particularly I want Joyce to see the colors. She's got a thing about color."

"So have you, Bill," I said. He grinned.

"You don't look too good today," Ellen commented coldly, staring at me.

"I'm not. I think I heard the bells of St. Sulpice strike every hour."

"That must be rare for you," she said. "The ladies don't like that form of interruption."

"You have me all figured out."

"We do," Buck said. "Just like you have us figured out."

"Those are nice flowers and chocolates anyway," Ellen said. "You must be off to a jousting."

"I've won it already, but it's too late."

Ellen stared at me questioningly, while Buck was extending his art criticism of Minaux with Bill, who winked at me.

It was a sunny day, and the Luxembourg Gardens were beginning to fill with children and adults. I had always enjoyed watching the kids launching their toy boats across the big pool behind the Palais. Walking past the pastoral scene, I watched them kneel on the raised sides of the pool and excitedly prod their little sailing vessels along. The sailboats could be impressive with their decorations. Eager hands launched them into the great toy regatta. Here and there vessels collided, eliciting cries of shock or glee, depending on whose boat was hit. Parents or nannies would suffer these confrontations dutifully, sometimes disciplining a child who became too aggressive.

It was a relief to shed Pam and watch the children. The Gardens were my oasis of peace and brightness in a city that had grown dark and grimy from neglect during the war years. Even the people had the light squeezed out of them. But a certain beauty was there for all of us, Europeans and Americans—the weaving river, the parks, the gardens and the old monuments.

In the Gardens I walked past the white stairs Pam had used for her dancing madness. Only now there were enthusiastic pétanque players tossing their hollow metal balls. The bald or bereted men took it all seriously, clinking their balls down the course. Elsewhere, children scrambled through their jungle-gyms, and white-haired men and women read their newspapers and magazines to pass the time. In the distance the old guignol puppet-show drew children's squeals and applause. When the afternoon light faded every day, everyone knew that the gates would shut, and life would stop. Trees and grass would grow overnight without human interference. Then somewhere near dawn the Gardens would rouse themselves. Gates would reopen, and the carousel would begin again.

I thought about Pam and how she would look. And then, when I arrived at the apartment, there she was, looking wonderful. No suggestion of the apparent breakdown. The night before had moved from the tension between Goodie and Norman to a wild, mad dance on the Pont des Arts, to Pam's collapse in the Gardens.

I would never forget her dancing, and I wondered if Bill Watson could paint it: her lithe, ethereal figure, the old bridge, and, below it, the darkling waters…But why try to recapture it?

Pam and I had passed our peak. It always happened in my love affairs. I presented Pam with the flowers and chocolates. Yet I wanted her love, some sign of her feeling for me. I did not realize at the time how cruel that was.

"Thanks for coming, Tom," she said, "I guess I made a fool of myself."

Her smile told me nothing. She wore a white summer dress with flowers embroidered around her high, prim neckline, and when I moved forward to kiss her she reached out a bit tentatively, not sure of either of us.

"No, you didn't. Your reactions were just a little strong…probably my fault."

I felt her tight clutch. "Can I do anything?" I asked, knowing I could by telling her what she wanted to hear. She brightened.

"Yes, you can. Come to Switzerland with me."

"I was planning to. Buck said last night it would be in two weeks or so. Is that all right?"

"Of course, you must come. Faith and Sally are, too."

"I know. The whole troop." We sat down on a couch and leaned back. I took her hand.

"Pam, I think I know what you want," I began. She sat there listening. "In the first place, I've been worried about you for days. You can't underestimate my feelings for you. You must know…"

"But what?"

"I'm not reliable. And I'm probably not good for you, not now at least…And…"

"Yes?"

"I'm probably not good for myself just now, too confused. I never expected to meet anyone like you in Paris."

"That, I suppose, depends on what you might have counted on."

"For one thing: not an American girl. One reason I came here was to get away from American girls."

"You wanted to try the foreign ones, then. How they are. Irene, for instance. What are her eyes like in the dark?"

"Pam..."

"Pam what?"

"Her eyes are expressive and she takes one day at a time."

"Not blind like mine. Sounds like she's a bit eager for bed."

"There's no need for this, Pam. Look, I'm in love with you." A second time. I said it a second time. I could feel Faith's anger. "If I weren't, I wouldn't be here."

"They call that pity where I come from,"

"You know, your saying that means to me you don't understand yourself...or me. You've got to know that I've never cared for any woman like I do you." I reached out my hand, and she took it half-heartedly. Then I pulled her to me, caressing her and kissing her neck. All of a sudden her body relaxed, and I began to kiss her cheeks and nose, saying, "Pam, why can't you work this thing out with me? I know it isn't easy and it's come on me fast."

She looked up, smiled and said, "You're the person of experience—not I."

"I have no experience in this. It started on our first night together and it's driving me nuts."

"Does Irene drive you nuts, too?"

"Only in a physical sense. We make love and talk about Communism."

"We've both got the same equipment, you know. We take and give the same sort of pleasure..."

"Don't be so analytical. You sound like a mechanic."

"Tom, that's me. I am analytical. I like to know where I stand with you. Can't you understand that?"

"Frankly, no. I'm not keeping score. When you're in love you don't keep score."

"Tom, have you ever really been in love?"

"That's not an easy one. "

"I know it isn't. I've come to depend on you too much, Tom."

"You have to be careful about me or anyone else…"

"You're not just anyone else."

"I see, but there are others in my life."

"Being in love, you don't keep score. How European you've become," she said. "As you said about Irene, you only live for the moment."

"And right now, you're the moment, my passion."

"It's not enough."

"I'm sorry. I enjoy the present, the now."

"That's a male point of view and for exotic political gypsies."

"So that's what they taught you at Smith! What did Geneva teach you?"

"Well, if you must know, not much. There was a Swiss boy I was interested in. Like you, he said he loved me. But nothing ever happened between us, really. It was all in my head. Maybe I was in love with love."

"Perhaps."

"Anyway," she resumed, "there's been no one since…until you…"

"And you don't want to get hurt again. And you're worrying about Irene or any others who might pre-empt your position. Why not focus on us?"

"Our physical pleasure, you mean…"

"That, too, but more important, the joy of us. Like that first night…discovering each other…all this time we've shared together…the sense of satisfaction you've given me on our ramblings about this town. And, more important, the joy I've had just being with you and watching you enjoy us. Pam, I do love you. Do you understand that…?" I declared my love a third time. How casual. And after Chartres and the cathedral experience.

She had reached for my hand and held it in her lap. As I talked, she held tighter. I babbled on, and she warmed to my words. I wanted her to get out of herself.

We left it that way. Unresolved. But I had the feeling that she might now understand how I felt, and that I wasn't ready to commit myself to any one or any thing.

To encourage her, all I could say was: "Aren't you glad we've got Switzerland together?"

※

When I returned to the hotel on the rue des Quatre Vents that Sunday morning I was tired from all the conversation and introspection. I stretched out on my bed. What little peace I found was interrupted by a knocking at my door. When I got up to open it I found Irene. She had returned from her political chores with *L'Humanité* and merely said, "Bonjour" in a matter-of-fact way.

"Come in," I said, but she shook her head.

"What's the matter? Come in, please."

"Non, merci. You've been with that American woman again. I can smell her on you."

"Look, I'm tired. It's been a bad morning, and I'm in need of rest. I want to lie down, and you're welcome to rest with me."

"Rest with you? Chéri, I know your rest…"

"Keep the door open then, if you're more comfortable that way. But come in and at least sit with me."

From down in the streets, the skirling of Scottish bagpipes began to fill the neighborhood.

"What's that about?" I asked.

"Les Brettones arrivent," she said, explaining that some nationalistic students from Brittany occasionally marched through the quarter on Sundays. It made a riotous explosion of sound when the bells of St. Sulpice clanged the hours. Gaiety flowed.

"Christ, I'm tired," I said.

"Be good to yourself, Tom, and finish with that American woman."

"You obviously don't like her."

"It's not her. She's not very good for you. I've tried to tell you that."

"Jealous?" I said.

"Not at all. You will be attached if you continue."

"And we aren't?"

"Not at all. We are good friends…"

"Sometimes extremely close…"

"But that is something else. We excite each other and there are times…"

With the door opened and Irene draping herself in the entrance, I heard a commotion downstairs. My name was mentioned, and then I heard light footsteps mounting the stairwell behind Irene, who looked at me questioningly. I heard a girl's voice say, "Hi, there!" brightly. It was Goodie Goodstein; and soon the two women were exchanging greetings.

"Not good timing, Goodie. He's tired and feeling sorry for himself."

Goodie said: "If you don't mind, I need to talk to you, Tom…"

"It's nothing," Irene said. "He may give me a few minutes later."

"I'm really sorry, Irene," Goodie said. "I don't mean to interrupt, but something's bothering me…"

"Me, too," Irene said and bid us goodbye to go back up to her room with Tamara. Before she did I spoke to her in French and reminded her of our dinner date, to which she had already agreed. She nodded mechanically and disappeared.

"Now then," Goodie said, "can we shut the door?"

"I'd rather not. It'd be better to keep it open."

"All right," she said reluctantly.

"It's about Fred, isn't it?"

"Unfortunately, yes. And I hate to impose on you, Tom, and I know you're tired, but I don't know where to turn. I'm just about fed up with him, and maybe you can help."

"Chaplain Cortell is always on duty," I said, watching her twist the gold ring on her finger, a custom she began months ago when Stateside people visited and she wanted them to assume she and Fred were married.

"He's making a terrible mistake, Tom. I wonder if you can call him off that English girl, Joyce. She's taking up a lot of his time lately. She's rotten for him and rotten for his work."

"And rotten for you, too," I said.

"Yes, and it's wrong."

"From whose point of view? Maybe he wants to see her…" I soon regretted those words. They led to more than an hour of Goodie's frustrations about her relationship with Fred Furness. I began to make a comparison—Goodie and Fred, Irene and myself. The women were getting edgy about things.

"Do you know how we met, Tom?"

"The museum in New York, wasn't it? You hid inside an Egyptian tomb."

"I wanted to meet him. I felt it was romantic. If he saw me come out of the tomb, some Bathsheba, I knew it would appeal to him."

"And it did."

"Yes, it did. People laugh about it and call me conniving, but it did."

"Look," I said. "I can't help with this thing about Joyce."

"She's not right for him!"

"And you are."

"That limey broad is ditzy, a trollop, in fact. Fred will lose his poet's edge."

I had to smile at that. "His poet's edge?"

"Well, damn it, Tom. I came here to…"

"I'm sorry, Goodie. I know how much you care for Fred, I really do. But it's his life…" I waved a hand and just looked at her.

She left at that. I'd have to find a way to win her friendship back. She had a lot of spunk. But it would have to wait.

Time was getting short, and I had to work in the date for drinks with Ellen planned before the dinner with Irene. After Goodie left, I rushed over to an obscure bistro near the Odéon and a famous bookstore there to find Ellen. Now that I had determined Buck's interest in her, it was time to find how it was the other way around.

"I like this place for our secret rendezvous," she said, lighting up a cigarette. The blue eyes crinkled under the rakishly tilted beret.

"It's about time, I think. After all, we're going to be together in Switzerland soon. Nothing like being familiar with the personnel…"

"Sounds like a spy operation."

"In a way, it is," I said. "Some things have been said, and I'm curious."

"You always have been."

"Is that an accusation?"

"No. Just a fact. Now, Tomasso, what was said that piqued your interest?"

"It has to do with Buck and you."

"We're very good friends. I thought that was clear."

"Do you love him, Ellen? Can you?"

"Why should I tell you, with all those women you've got? Are the farther fields of more interest to you?"

"I only want to know about you and Birnbaum…if it goes deep…because it seems strange to me…Maybe I'm just a guy who likes girls, different girls, but all girls. Of all the women I know in this city, there's only one, you, who baffles me. Despite his deviations, Buck is a stellar person, and I respect something basic in him, as much as the switch-hitting bothers me now and then. It's none of my damned business, Ellen, but I've been puzzled by you and Buck. Is that too blunt?"

She searched in her bag for another cigarette, lit it and inhaled deeply without looking at me.

"I don't know if I should answer you. Tom, you're treading on tender nerve endings…"

We fenced for an hour.

"You'll need to be very careful about this, Tom," Ellen said at last. "Buck's intellect and emotions are involved in what you might do…"

"And what about your intellect and emotions?"

"They don't count right now. We need to know each other better…Then maybe I won't baffle you so much."

"And what after that?"

"We'll have to see," she said with a knowing smile. "We'll just have to see…"

I wanted to get deeper and tried some diversionary tactics. I asked about the conference coming up.

"Oh, he has his big plans to make it successful, but he hasn't told me much."

"I doubt that," I said. "Your relationship has always made it look like you two were in cahoots about everything."

"I can't deny that, but I couldn't possibly compromise him."

"Why not?"

"How nosy you are. Look, Tom, he brought me on this trip. I owe him a lot for that—and for other things."

"I suppose you do."

"Let's talk about something else."

"Sure. Tell me, Ellen, where did Buck's interest in sports come from? He always made a big thing of football, boxing and basketball. They were important to him, but I never figured it out."

"Sports actually brought us together, if you can believe it. That was just how it all happened. You know he played freshman football his first year at Columbia. You were away at war then. But he continued on the varsity. I remember you were there then after the war…and Cornell before that. That was before your transfer from Ithaca…"

"Good memory…And I remember you at the games."

"Especially at the post-war Cornell-Columbia games when you rooted for Cornell in the Baker Field seats. Someone once threatened to evict you from the College cheering section."

"I was drunk and had to be loyal."

"Call it what you will," Ellen said. "Buck was always proud of his football prowess. I remember once he ran right through the whole Princeton team for a touchdown. I met him at that game. It was his greatest achievement, and that day he was quite a hero, even for me who didn't understand anything about the game. He had his reasons for being proud, making a show of it. Remember the dance after the Cornell game? I had come up from Swarthmore for the weekend…"

"I do remember…"

"Columbia rarely won, even in the war years. But Buck changed that."

"I remember dancing with you. That was enough for me…"

"Don't be so moony, Tom. What I was leading up to was a big discussion his sweetie of the time, Bob Kemperman, had with Buck. Until that girl at the next table commented about Buck's good looks. As she put it rather loudly: 'his dark masculinity and his commanding power.' Do you remember when another girl, who knew Buck well enough, almost gagged at that comment. Her peals of laughter were out of control. As a matter of fact, she laughed so raucously that the band had to stop. Then the same laughing one said louder than the first girl: 'If you only knew the whole story—and the boys in his life!' Buck tried to take it well, with poise. My heart went out to him. Anyway, he turned a bright red and walked out of the very dance celebrating his victory at Baker Field."

"I didn't get all the innuendoes at the time."

"Come, come, Tom. Back from war, the Veteran?"

"We didn't dwell on queers . We tried to stay alive."

"Anyway, it was just a part of life. His group at school was all male and somewhat unmasculine. They were rabid intellectuals and emotionally a lot younger than you veterans. He never lived on campus, and you know why. If he and Bob and some of the others ever let on to their relationships on campus, it would have been the end. Same sex love was a no-no. The frat parties could be disgusting with the things that went on. My Barnard friends told me."

"The AC/DC business had to affect you."

"It did, but he went out of his way to be nice to me at a time in my life when not many others did that. So I became his stalking horse show girl…his showcase lady love…what have you."

"Lady love?"

"I said showcase lady love…"

"Am I dense? He's not your love." I recalled Buck's non-committal answer to the same question when we had talked a few days ago.

She stared at her cigarette, her hand shaking. "No, Tom. He's not my love. But there is another side to our relationship. He's a generous, faithful person—with great aspirations."

"I'll say."

"Don't be sarcastic. You have to understand him."

I had heard the fag part before. And I had come to admire him, too, him and his great aspirations. She was avoiding direct eye contact with me now. "It's a problem for me now, Ellen."

"Oh?"

"Look, I just want to know one thing: why did you come to Europe with him?" She was not happy with this, looking away defensively. "Maybe I shouldn't have asked—but I had to."

"No, you should ask. I would if I were you. I just want to be cautious about what I say." She took deep drags on her cigarette. Finally, it came.

"Tom, do you want me to be totally honest? I slept with him once—the victory weekend of the Princeton game.

"How could you?"

"It was a mistake. Never since…"

"Are you serious?"

"I hated it."

"Jesus!"

"I froze up."

"You deserve better than that."

"But the worst thing was something else." She paused, uncertain. "The next morning after he tried to make it with me—oh God, Tom, why am I telling you this?"

"Please go on. There's a reason."

"Well, in the morning I found him in bed with that fag, Bob Kemperman. Seeing is believing, you know. Even so, I forgave him for an insult that wasn't an insult, really. He has no control over this." She held up her hand. "Am I out of my mind?"

"Just out of your depth."

"But I know he needs me."

"It's perverted. It's wrong."

"I can't accept that."

"You just feel you owe him something. Ellen, the fact is we all owe him something. But we can't be blackmailed. And you above all don't owe him your body. And not your heart. A heart has no obligations."

She crushed out her cigarette. "A heart has no obligations. Tom, that's true. I never thought of it that way."

She let me take her hand. "He does care, and he needs to lead. It's part of his nature. The whole conference, you see, is vital to his existence. He's incredibly bored when he isn't leading. At the same time, he's a decent, generous person. Forget his sex life. Just think of his intentions. You've got to respect them at the least."

"No question. But you and him—I don't understand the link. And what about your butterflies?"

Her face went blank. Only her perfect features asserted themselves—the graceful nose, the light eyes against her freckled cheeks, the trim blonde hair. I noticed a single tear, then a quick half smile, like a camera shutter.

"Are you punishing yourself in some way for this trip? If so, I hate to see you do it. Buck doesn't rate that kind of self-torture." Then, without warning, Buck appeared over her shoulder, and I quickly gave him a makeshift greeting.

"Well—well," his high voice came. "And what have we here?"

"We were just talking about you," I said, recovering what composure I could.

"You won't believe this, but I just finished the conference outline—finally—and it's going to be great. You'll both be surprised." We will never know what he was thinking when he walked up on us. Except, of course, his great preoccupation with the coming event in Switzerland.

TEN

"Look at that girl!" Norman Tunison exclaimed, joy on his trowel-shaped Jewish face.

We were seated in the front of the Vagenande Restaurant on the Boulevard St. Germain a few evenings later. Through the street windows and the dusk outside Norman focused his eyes on a brunette girl of medium height crossing the boulevard. When she entered the restaurant he got to his feet and with great ceremony greeted her, much to her surprise. Fred Furness asked who she was, and Norman said he had no idea, but "She fascinates me—just look at her!"

"God help her," Fred said on the side.

In no time at all Norman had the girl in tow and had discovered her name was Betty Lowry—from Denver, and that she was a French literature major at Boulder graduate school.

"I can't believe it," Ellen Cassidy said to the rest of us. "It's not like Norman."

"Only Norman," Buck said in disagreement. Norman introduced the newcomer to everyone with enthusiasm.

"I only arrived this morning," Betty said, "and never expected a welcome like this."

"Welcome aboard," Buck said.

"How nice," she responded.

"He isn't always nice," Buck said, indicating Norman. "Be careful."

She smiled and explained that she would be studying medieval literature at the Sorbonne.

"You'll fit in nicely, too," Buck said, playing host for the group. "We're the unofficial US foreign service. Just be careful with Norman. He's an aesthetic snob."

Norman had already placed his arm around her, saying, "They don't trust me. It's just that I've got better taste."

"Don't count on that, Betty," Fred Furness said. "He even likes Picasso and Braque…"

"I hate Picasso," Norman retorted, "except for the blue period. And I detest Braque. He won't last."

"Guard yourself from these charlatans," Buck said. "They can't even speak French that well."

"Oh," she said and gave forth with a speech in perfect French, some of which penetrated the group.

"Great!" I said to her. "You've put us in new territory."

"How's Pam?" Buck asked me. "I'm concerned about what you told me happened the other night." "She'll be all right," I said, wanting to avoid the subject.

"Who's Pam?" Betty asked.

"She's pamming him," Norman said, pointing at me.

"Very funny," I said and explained to her.

Eventually Norman's excitement calmed down and the two of them seemed happy with themselves. Betty talked a lot about her studies. But all was not peace and quiet, and a certain amount of tension was in the air between Fred and Goodie—and even Ellen and myself. At least, I felt it. With Betty on the scene and her deeper knowledge of French and the very period that Norman was pursuing on his Rabelais kick, it was interesting to speculate how she would fit in. Her value to him might well be immeasurable.

After the hors d'oeuvres were consumed, we awaited the main course. Across the table from Betty and Norman were Fred and Goodie, and the contrast was noticeable. Norman and Betty busily chattering away about themselves and France; Goodie and Fred exchanging few words and a bit morose. From time to time Fred looked over, somewhat enviously, to the other couple and their obvious excitement about each other.

Our waiter was Jacques, who had come to know most of us from frequent visits to the restaurant. When he finally brought the main dishes and carafes of wine, the trouble began. Goodie suddenly exploded when her plate arrived. "That's not what I ordered!" she said petulantly to Fred, who shrugged his shoulders and asked her what was wrong.

"I asked for escalope de veau, and that's not it!" she insisted.

"That's ris de veau—sweetbreads," Fred offered, "and it can be very good. That's what you said you wanted, and I ordered it from Jacques for you especially. And you agreed."

"I did not!" she declared, looking peeved at Jacques. He knew enough English to understand and perused the order slip again with raised eyebrows. "Madame," he began, "pardon, mais…"

Fred was embarrassed and shrugged his shoulders again.

"I definitely ordered escalope de veau," she repeated.

"I thought I ordered what you wanted," Fred said.

"I don't care what you ordered. That's not my dish!" She gestured at the hateful plate in front of her. "I want what I ordered."

The discussion between Goodie, Fred and Jacques continued for awhile and raised enough of a fuss so that others at the table and in the vicinity began to look annoyed. "This is kind of childish," I said. "I've got other things on my mind…"

"Pam, right?" Buck said.

"There's Pam again," Betty said, looking at me.

"What's happening here?" Buck said in surprise, his remarks addressed directly to Fred and Goodie. Jacques' heavy dark eyebrows were still noticeably raised at the ruckus.

"The dumb waiter brought the wrong food," Goodie said.

"Mais, madame," Jacques said.

"Oh, shut up!"

Fred jumped at this.

"Mais, madame," Jacques tried again.

"Goodie, for God's sake…" Fred began, but could not break in.

"Mais yourself and bring me what I want…" she said, as Fred cringed.

"There's more to this than meets the ear," Buck said to me in a whisper. I had never seen Fred Furness so rattled.

So it came as a surprise when Fred, clearly annoyed by the rising tension in his girl's voice, said: "Reorder, then, dammit! We're getting nowhere if you continue this nonsense. It's a veritable tempest in a pisspot."

"Since when have you cared about what I eat?" Goodie said coldly. "You don't care much about anything concerning me any more." Fred rose from his seat at the table and suggested they go. "That's not necessary," she declared. "I simply want what I ordered, and you," she continued, "are no asset in this discussion." Like a puppy, Fred sat down, looking for help that wasn't forthcoming.

Betty said, "Won't anyone tell me about Pamela?"

Buck said, "Come, you two!"

"I'll tell you about her later, Betty" I said. Just then I glanced into the far corner of the restaurant and saw someone I never expected to see: Joyce Frost with her dinner companion, Bill Watson. I sensed trouble ahead. Joyce was listening to the ruckus being created by Goodie. Luckily, she had not made any attempt to attract Fred's attention. Bill turned to wave at our group. I got up and walked over to greet Joyce and Bill.

"Hello, love. What's going on over there?" she asked, tilting her head for my kiss.

"Yes, Tom," Bill said, shaking my hand warmly. "I could hear it."

"Like love, death and taxes," I said, "it will pass. Enjoy yourselves. I want to see more canvas, Bill. Joyce, you're very sexy so far…"

"I'm improving, love – getting hotter all the time."

"Any time you want to come, you're most welcome, Tom. Unless she objects," Bill said.

"I've got nothing to hide from old Tom," she said. No reaction from Bill. Over my shoulder I could hear the food problem still being discussed but quieter now.

"Come, come!" Buck was saying. trying to keep the lid on. "Peace, peace—just re-order, Goodie. It's not that big a deal." His voice was higher in pitch, the way he got when he was upset. He was a born peacemaker, and I realized that now, before his Swiss event, he wanted relations within the group to be as smooth as possible.

"Damn it," Goodie was saying, her face falling apart at Buck's cautionary words. Then she began to sob. She stared red-eyed at Buck, while Fred seemed to wilt, gazing at me helplessly.

Norman was annoyed at the intrusion on his courting of Betty, and he decided to take direct action. He said, louder than necessary, "Does anyone here know how the United States is going to help the French in Indo-China?"

"We've got to stay out of it," Fred said. Goodie was sobbing.

Buck chimed in, "We'll probably support them—and with troops." He went on, realizing what Norman was up to. "As one of us said the other night, we seem to have a penchant for keeping the peasants down, usually by supporting the wrong side, the rich interests…"

"The thing now," Norman said, "is that we'll get in on the wrong side of a purely nationalist movement."

"That's exactly what we'll do," Buck said. "We'll get ourselves involved in something that's none of our business. Ho-chi Minh has even asked for our help, and, of course, we'll side with the anti-communists, just because they're anti-communists…"

"The country be damned," added Norman.

Betty Lowry beamed at Norman, realizing how he had stopped the domestic violence between Fred and Goodie from expanding. "The interesting point back home—in case you don't know—is that everyone thinks we should support the French. Someone even said that on the plane over here yesterday."

"What else would you expect from us?" Buck said. Fred and Goodie sat there silently. Now I noted Fred's fast glance over towards Joyce and Bill Watson.

"I feel sorry for Fred," I said to Buck.

"You always do. You're a peacemaker. We both are."

"Oh, Buck," Goodie said, kissing him as the tears streamed down her face and her eyes rolled. "We need you so much—at least I do." They began to leave the restaurant, and Buck was staring after them, his beady eyes wide with concern.

"What the hell was all that about?" he asked Ellen.

"You don't know?"

"No. Not really. I don't like it. Tom said it was childish, and I agree."

"You're concerned about your conference," Ellen said. "Don't worry; they'll be there."

"I know. But I don't like tension between people I care about." Ellen looked surprised.

"None of us do," I said. I had put off telephoning Pam and now got up to make the call.

"Now where the hell are you going?" Buck asked in a way I didn't like.

"I need to call some people." Ellen was watching me.

"Oh."

I made the first call to Irene, and said: "I need you." She asked why, but I couldn't explain. "I do need you, really." She said I always needed her.

"There's trouble here."

"What can I do with you Americans?"

"You can make peace," I said.

"I thought I was, how you call, a hothead."

"That's your politics."

"Okay. You wait. Your hothead will be there." When Goodie and Fred walked out of the restaurant, she was clutching a sodden handkerchief, and Fred was trying to console her.

"I just lost control, Fred," she was saying.

I thought about Pam's loss of control, the scene on the bridge. I pulled another jeton out of my pocket to call Faith.

"You should be here," Faith said. "She's fine. She slept late, as though nothing had happened. Can you come now?"

"No—how about the morning?"

"Be sure you do, Tom. Be sure. She doesn't remember a thing."

"Maybe that's for the best," I said. "I'll be there in the morning."

"Just don't forget. She needs you."

I hung up and went over to Joyce and Bill just to be nice. She placed her hand on mine and patted it.

"Courage," she said. Bill put his on top of our hands and repeated: "Courage." They seemed to know.

Back at the table Buck was discussing his conference in Switzerland and how he wanted to maintain objectivity along with the "passionate" participation of the group. The dinner storm had subsided, Goodie and Fred had departed, and peace resumed. Buck and Ellen eyed me carefully, both asking if I was all right.

Norman said, "Buck, split the presentations between fact and opinion, and let the discussion leaders take over. It's a challenge for the leaders to separate the two, but if that's agreed on as the way to do it, it will work."

"I saw some books the other day that might be relevant," Buck said, "over in a store near the Boul' Miche. Gibert was the store—on the rue Racine where it runs into the boulevard."

"Which street?" Norman asked, as Irene walked into the restaurant. She was radiant and attracting the attention of all the men in the room.

"The rue Racine," I said as Irene sat down next to me and jabbed me in the ribs.

"I heard you. I heard you." She teased.

"You heard what?"

"Say street again. Say rue."

"Roo," I said, and she broke into peals of laughter.

"Say it again, Mr. Américain. You see, you can't say it properly. It's rue." Her rich voice stressed the soft, slightly guttural "r" of the French word Americans always found difficult to sound correctly. "Rue," she repeated. "Say it!"

"Roo…"

"You're hopeless," she chided. Norman tried and also failed. Irene giggled again. "You see, it's like your foreign policy. It doesn't work." She never passed up an opportunity to satirize things American.

"Good lady, " Buck said. "You are quite correct. None of us are proud of our foreign policy—nor our French, but"—here he paused, knowing Irene's left-wing opinions—"but remember, my dear, we have the right to express those opinions and make those mistakes, which you couldn't if you lived in the Soviet Union you admire so much."

"No. No. No!" she retorted, her eyes shining. "How can you know that? It's not true." Her eyes flashed again. But now I bent over to kiss her on the cheek and said "Rue."

"Aha!" she said, ducking away from me. "It proves you can if you try. Your country ought to try harder, too! You see!"

"We did, you hothead bolshevik. We won the war."

"No, no—we won it."

"Who's we?" Buck asked.

"The Soviet Union and America and England," Irene replied promptly.

"Here we go again," I said, and then, between our seats, patting her arm, adding softly, "Comment va le derrière?"

"Tais-toi!" She grinned, her grey eyes darkening.

'Ellen Cassidy had been watching me ever since I returned from the telephone booth.

Now she observed me with Irene. "Is there something wrong, Tom? You look worried."

"What, me worry?" She must have seen something in my face after the call to Faith about Pam. "I never worry about anything. It's against my rules."

"Nonsense," she said. "Who makes your rules?"

"My rules? Women. Irene, for example. Maybe even you."

"Hardly me," she said.

"Not yet, I'm just testing you. What have you got to say for yourself?"

Ellen found herself under Irene's frank gaze. "You still haven't been terribly specific about the rule-maker."

"Life," I said. "Can we discuss this another time?"

She looked away non-committally, "I wouldn't mind…"

"Nor would I. We'll have to see about it."

Now Irene poked me in the ribs again. "You wanted me here, no?"

"Of course," I said.

"Then, pay attention to me," Irene ordered.

"Oui, mademoiselle," I said and held out my wrist. Irene slapped it hard.

"So when do we go to Switzerland for the grand convocation?" I asked, studying Buck's bitten fingernails. Irene's eyes narrowed on me with this news.

"Two weeks from today," Buck declared. "I'm going down next week to set things up."

"And how do we begin?" Norman asked.

"I'm working out the final agenda right now. You'll see when you arrive. I want you there by next Tuesday week."

"Sounds quite British," Betty said, while they all began chattering away about the conference…

When we broke up awhile later and said goodnight, I had an opportunity to pull away from Irene and ask Ellen privately, "When?"

"Quand tu veux," she responded. Betty turned her head on hearing it. I nodded, pinched Irene, and we headed out.

ELEVEN

In the Paris University Library where I went to deliver a private note to Betty Lowry, I stood off a bit. Norman was grunting with pleasure as he leafed through a volume. He was in his element, and so was Betty at his side while she made some notes. They had become totally immersed in their research on Rabelais. For weeks, everyone in the group had known about Norman's enthusiasm for the Renaissance French writer, but few of us realized how much of a preoccupation it had become or where it would lead. I finally got their attention, and we went outside.

"They're real fussy about silence in here," Norman said.

He paused for a minute to whisper something to Betty and then addressed me: "Do you realize that the wars of Picrochole were no more senseless than the wars of today? I tell you, this man really dug things!"

"Norman, please don't get so carried away," Betty said.

"No, really, when you find something like this and apply it to other times, Rabelais seems like a genius. Tom, I'm going to do a book on this man. I'm really launched on a big project…"

"Like Buck with his conference," I said.

"No. This is something I can control and do myself."

Across the street a cycling policeman—one of the hirondelles—mashed on his squeaky brakes and confronted two Arabs changing some money for tourists. After a few authoritative words with them, he mounted the bicycle again and was on his way. Tourists and Arabs resumed the transaction.

"The law in action," Norman said and grinned in the sunlight. I checked my watch. It was getting late to go to Pam's place. I waved goodbye and wished them well on their research.

Before I left, I gave Betty the note, which Goodie had written and asked me to deliver. I suspected it had something to do with the Swiss conference.

I ran across the street, cut over to the Luxembourg Gardens, and made my way through the park to the Observatoire area. I thought about how Norman had become tied to Betty. It was quite a lucky stroke that she had appeared on the scene, for without her and her knowledge of French, Norman wouldn't have been able to pursue Rabelais efficiently. It was ironic, for of all the Americans I knew in Paris, Norman had the least command of the language; yet he had become the firebrand on his work.

Soon I was through the Gardens and pushing the entry button at Pam's apartment house. It buzzed back, and I went up. Faith Carlson opened the door and immediately touched her lips with a finger. "She's sleeping. Come in."

"What's going on?" I asked.

"You helped a lot when you came the other day. The doctor prescribed some sedation for awhile, but I think she's going to be fine." Faith offered me a drink, and we sat down.

"I don't want to be repetitious," she began, "but Sally and I hope you really love her. She so needs that love." Sally came into the room, nodding.

"I understand that. That's why I came—to be sure she's all right."

"She's not just a patient, Tom. Maybe the worst thing is to treat her like one," Sally said.

"Look, we've already talked about that. I have to be honest, you know."

I glanced at my watch.

"You're in a hurry?" Faith asked.

"Actually, I have to get back to the hotel and make some reservations at the Mediterranée…"

"Oh. Sounds nice."
An awkward silence ticked by.
"Well," I said, standing up...
"Thanks for coming, Tom. Perhaps next time you can stay longer."
The censure was biting.
It turned out to be a gay evening with Irene, Tamara and young Katya, and it was good to hear Irene talk about our visit to the cathedral. The restaurant was festive with inviting southern ambiance, seashell decorations, happy talk. We sat directly across the Place de l'Odéon and had a good view of the theater arcades I had once shown to Pam.
"He opened my eyes to something new," Irene said to Tamara. "I think he's trying to convert me."
"You?" I said, watching her relish her seafood. "Impossible for a hard core Communist. But I never thought I'd see you in a religious building. Remember what Lenin said about religion."
"It's more important that you, monsieur, remember that beauty has nothing to do with politics. Tom, I loved it," she said, reaching her hand to touch me. Tamara observed this with a raised eyebrow. She had never really approved of our relationship, because I was an American and thereby related to the soldier who had abandoned her and Katya in Morocco. "The vitraux—the windows—were fantastic," Irene finished.
"Well, just as long as you remember that many of them were donated by the guilds of the city, the artisan workers in those days."
"Really?" she said, surprised.
"Does that make them any better?" I said, teasing her. "You said they were fantastic. And when Soviet Russians say something is fantastic, they are speaking from the heart."
"You mustn't pay any attention to her, Tom," Tamara said. "She's only speaking that way because of her brother-in-law, the Communist architect. He's fanatical. He does free work for them in eastern Europe. Irene is under his influence, and I don't approve of this selling of *L'Humanité* in the streets..."

"Be quiet, Tamara. You don't know…" Irene said.

I lightened the mood by tickling Katya under the chin. She giggled.

"Tom, how can you go with such a girl!" Tamara said.

"Ten years from now, she won't give it a thought," I said, placing my hand on Irene's. She pulled it away defensively.

"It's not only my brother-in-law!" she said. "It's the way things are!"

"What do you want for dessert?" I asked. For the rest of the evening her grey eyes flashed at her sister and myself as the conversation wandered from Chartres to the Cold War. Sometimes Irene talked about the Swiss conference.

"I don't understand it," she said.

"Neither do I—and I will miss you."

"Horsefeathers!" she said, using an American expression I had taught her. "All those American girls will be with you. I've seen them making eyes."

"It's supposed to be a serious discussion about the world," I said.

"Horsefeathers! When are you coming back?"

"Three weeks is as long as I can stay away—from you."

"Horsefeathers!"

That night when we all returned to the hotel, Irene resisted coming to my room. She mechanically brushed my cheek with her lips after Tamara and Katya had gone, and I grabbed her around the waist.

"You are angry," I said.

"It was a nice dinner, Tom, but you hurt me when you go away like this. We had such a wonderful trip down to Chartres. And now you go away, as if you throw it all away."

"Irene, please. Try to understand…"

"You don't care about anyone but yourself," she pouted.

"I happen to care for you very much." I pulled her toward me in the hallway and kissed her, holding on to her for a long time, even when she started to cry. Then I began to kiss away her tears. She was incredibly sensual when emotion took over.

We were standing in the hallway just outside of my room, and her crying seemed to go on forever. I was tired from the day, but I needed to calm her down.

"I don't want to stay with you tonight," she said all of a sudden, "but I will."

"All right, let's forget it then."

The intensity of her crying annoyed me. "If you don't stay, it won't be the end of the world." At that she shoved my room door open. Then she sat on the bed, leaned forward and cupped her chin in her hands.

"Tom, you are being cruel to me. Not a word about your trip. You are insensitive."

"What do you want?" I asked. It was a stupid question. As a result, her crying resumed. I had never seen her like this and was confused by it. Then she stood up close to me, trembled, and I felt her fingers exploring my chest. Her face was close and the taste of her tears excited me. "Gypsy, what have I done wrong?" She got onto the bed, facing away from me.

"You are so selfish, Thomas," she sighed, but made no objection as I undressed her. I took off my clothes quickly, pulled back the blanket and slipped into the sheets beside her. She was warm.

We lay there mute and still except for her occasional sobs. For the rest of the night, I held her close, until much later she finally kissed me softly, and I felt her probing touches. "Mon Dieu," she whispered in my ear. "I am such a fool." Then she shuddered and began to make love to me. Finally, she fell off to sleep while I lay there cradling her.

TWELVE

"The war?" Fred said one day when a few of us were walking along the banks of the Seine. "That's all over. Forget it if you can, Tom." I had said something about how simple life was when we were in the service.

"Nothing's simple any more."

"Never forget it," Buck said. He hadn't been in it, but talked in a commanding high voice. "Like the Holocaust, it needs reiteration, if only to remind people how rotten it was and that it shouldn't happen again. You see, what America should have learned from the war, it never did." He was warming up his academic style for the Conference in Switzerland. "And that's because of the fact that we've never been invaded. In turn, gentlemen, that accounts for our lousy foreign relations…"

"Maybe that's why," Fred said, going for the bait, "we all had to come over here at this time—to get a detached look at ourselves."

"As Buck once said about Norman's artistic conclusions," I said, "you're both full of shit.' "

"You're too negative, Tom," Buck said. "And you've got to realize that what I'm trying to say is behind my idea for the conference: to come up with a document that will explain the war…to hold up the mirror to our country, show what it was all about and how we can convert the current stupidity into practical solutions."

"We can try, Bucko," Fred said.

Even though we all would be leaving for the conference at Caux in a week, I still had quite a bit of research to do for the article I was planning on the French Maquis, the underground resistance movement that harassed the Germans when they occupied France. This almost prevented me from joining the others going to Caux because the piece was commissioned by a good magazine, and I needed the money. But Irene came to my rescue when she mentioned that her brother-in-law Edouard, who was in the Maquis patrol near Lyon, had been captured and tortured by the Nazis. We had a date to call at his and her older sister's apartment in Belleville. That was to be just before we all were going down to Montreux on a train.

I told Fred and Buck about this and cut off their aimless discussion about the war's lessons and how we might handle the subject at the conference.

"Let's check out the bookstore on the rue Racine you mentioned the other night," I said, and we walked on in silence, admiring the view of Paris around the Île de la Cité.

That morning when I woke up beside Irene I turned toward her. Her face was now in repose as she breathed lightly. Whether or not she had come to terms with my Swiss trip, I didn't know. But she was such a lovely creature in sleep, and I lay there admiring her peaceful face, the high cheekbones and her dark, tousled hair. The telephone buzzer snarled on the night-table. I hoped it wouldn't awaken her, but it did, and when I reached for the receiver, a familiar voice was speaking in clipped British English. It was Joyce Frost asking some questions about the upcoming visit to Switzerland.

I was dazed by the early call and unhappy that Irene was going to hear everything.

"Didn't Fred or Bill tell you about it?"

"No, lovey. Besides, I don't believe either of them."

I gave her a quick run-down of the event. She wanted to see Fred off from the Gare de Lyon.

"That's not very wise," I said, anticipating a catfight between Goodie and Joyce. Meanwhile Irene was now fully awake, her flashing eyes alert to what was happening.

I could hear her muttering: "There he goes again—more girls…je m'en fou, mais…"

Joyce talked about Fred sounding desperate when she last spoke to him. "I know the Goodie problem," she said.

"So why get so impassioned?"

"Because I'm beginning to fall for Fred. He takes me seriously, not like you and me. We just have good fun…" Irene pinched me vindictively and flew out of bed with a scowl.

Anyway, Tom, I'm going to come down to Switzerland after the rest of you arrive."

"Dammit, Joyce…"

"What? The confrontations, Goodie having a fit? I have a right to live and breathe, you know, and Fred is deeply caring…"

"You run the risk of ruining Buck's plans, Joyce, and there could be a lot of ill will there…"

"I'm coming. And who's that woman chattering behind you?"

"Never mind."

"Is she as good as me?"

Let's end this call, Joyce. And I've got to tell you I'm disappointed that you're forcing your way…"

"It's not exactly forcing. Fred wants me, I'm sure."

"I strongly doubt that. In fact, Fred will have a big problem with your visit. Have you thought of it that way?"

"You're crackers, Tom. I'm coming."

"Please talk to Buck first."

"I have. He's unconcerned. He told me water seeks its own level."

"Oh. Christ!"

She hung up.

It turned out to be easy, especially when she called her sister Sylva and made a date for us to come out to Belleville. There was something formal about it, as if Irene were taking me out to be judged like a bull at a state fair. That aspect of it bothered me.

"Now you are pleasing me for a change," she said when we walked down the steps at the Metro Odéon on our way to Edouard and Sylva. "You better prepare all your capitalistic arguments."

She laughed as we boarded the train, "I am so happy you are coming…"

"To subject myself to a political grilling, I guess."

"No, you will like him. You are both blond and blue eyed—and stubborn," she said.

When we climbed up the subway stairs and made our way into the dingy neighborhood of the 20th Arrondissement I saw a new Paris, one without the glamor and glitz of the central districts. It had the dull sameness of any major city working quarter with its unattractive stores and grime on the buildings—an area of Paris free of tourists.

We climbed three flights of stairs to the apartment where Sylva amd Edouard greeted us warmly and immediately sat us down for tea and pastry. Architectural drawings were prominently displayed. Edouard talked about his new drawing for the Warsaw housing project, which I thought well designed and executed.

He explained that he was donating a good deal of this work to the Polish authorities. "They need all the help they can get from the West,"he said. The conversation was in French, and I was a bit hard pressed to keep up with it.

"According to your belle-soeur, you believe in that cause," I said. Irene smiled at him and began a vigorous conversation with Sylva, a plain woman in her thirties who seemed amused to have me there. "Communism, that is," I added unnecessarily.

"You might say that, yes," he said cautiously. "You might say I believe in the future. Don't you?"

"Not really." The words stopped him.

"Why not?"

131

"I'm a pessimist."

"Oh, that's too bad," he said in a consoling way. "I was under the impression that Americans were optimists."

"We have a variety of people in our country—with all points of view. Not like some other countries."

"I think you must be pessimistic because you have no sense of class and the class struggle," he said. "For example, you may have helped win World War II, but you do not comprehend why it all happened." I noticed when he lit a cigarette, his hand trembled a bit and he was missing a finger on his right hand.

"How so?"

"It was the culmination of an historical process. Capitalism had run its course. You in America simply do not understand where we Europeans stand. DeGaulle, Franco, Hitler, Mussolini—they have existed only because of capitalism's failures. But now you will see big changes, historical changes…" There was something messianic about him; he said it all without rancor, actually with a smile in his voice and a professorial tone. I felt like a student being lectured on geo-politics.

"Who will change things?" I asked. Irene and her sister watched us.

"The people…"

"People like Stalin, you mean?"

"Ah! We have come to the point quickly," he said, tossing his head with pleasure and exhaling a cloud of blue smoke. I liked the bitter smell of his Gaulloise cigarette. "Even Stalin is part of the historical process. I know how you feel."

"Stalin never cared about the people, Edouard," I said, declining a cigarette. "That was shown in the struggle with Trotsky, the idealist. And they haven't found all the mass graves yet. Today it's worse. It's always about power, and his concern is power over the people."

"Stalin will pass," he said with a shrug of his narrow shoulders. "Much good will come. It will." He sounded as though he were trying to convince himself, but even his wife nodded in agreement.

He made a fist of his right hand, grinding it into his left palm, the stub of his missing index finger peeking out. Somewhere I had heard this discussion before, I couldn't remember where—maybe Jack Hayden or Buck Birnbaum back at Columbia, or from the radical soldier with whom I had been hospitalized near Salerno—wherever. But the "historical process" of Marx, Lenin, Engels bored the hell out of me. In the long run the people would suffer; they always had. And I knew that America had some destiny to fulfill, just as without us the war would never have been won. And we didn't fight it for Stalin. We fought it with him, not for him.

"I have all the confidence, just as I had for France during the war..." he was saying.

"You were in the Maquis, Irène told me."

"Yes," he said. "My confidence lost me this finger." He held up the stump. "But I still have confidence."

"How did it happen, if you don't mind telling me?" I asked, mindful of my research for the article. The women left the room to carry on their conversation in the kitchen. Irene waved an ironic finger of farewell as they moved out.

"I will tell you a story about our famous underground group in Lyon. We used the 'traboules'—those funny secret passageways in the old town—to make our escapes from the Gestapo. This is about our devotion to a cause. It occurred during the war near Lyon. That was only four years ago, when six of us from our Maquis group were planning to blow up a train carrying a mixed cargo—Jews and special chemicals destined for Germany." He lit a fresh cigarette from the old one. "The chemicals were vital to their war operations. We would detach the back end of the train with the Jewish cargo just before we blew up the track at the front end. Two of us were to divert the Nazis' attention a few kilometers ahead of the train, two would detach the rear cars. The other two would set off the explosives in the middle. I was part of that pair.

"The train came just on time. Another group had tracked it after the train left Valence on the way to Lyon. Everything was fine, except for one little matter. My partner had to piss and showed himself just at the time we were going to press the detonator for the explosion. A German guard on the train spotted us, and before we could carry out the plan we were captured. No traboules to escape to. Naturally, we were interrogated—only we two, since the others got away—and they beat us for information for almost two hours. Later, they took a chisel and cut off my finger. But the information was withheld. They were planning to kill us, but this time pissing saved us. My partner acted his role of having to go to the bathroom and cleverly snapped a wire leading to the room where they had me alone. In the confusion of darkness we got away.

"Such is my little story of devotion to a cause…and of confidence in the future I was mentioning a minute ago."

"That's quite a story, Edouard, but now we're not talking about France and the war. We're discussing principles, political principles and philosophies…"

"You are naïve," he said in a rising voice, its zeal reminding me of Buck's delivery. "Communism and Stalin are not the only issues, though you think so. Consider your own record in America. You massacred the Indians. You were fools in Nicaragua. You exploit the Philippines. You support dictators as bad or worse than Stalin—Battista, Franco, Somoza, Chiang Kai-shek, many others. You persecute the Negroes, the poor whites in your South. The minorities. You dominate with your money to protect it. And you don't understand what you do to the workers and peasants of this world. The worst thing: you fight change." This struck a bright bell; Norman had mentioned it at the Flore just the other night. But I felt defensive and had to reply.

"And the Soviets? And the French in North Africa and Indo-China?"

"Better than you in many ways. Thomas, no one is a hero here. We're talking about the main events, the direction of the world to become an ideal world."

He frowned in an odd, unconvincing way. I leaned back and took a cigarette from him, eyeing him and hearing some things that made me think. It was direct criticism and observation. But there was no point in pursuing it any further.

"We will have to discuss this later."

"Are you angry with me?" he asked.

"Not at all. We need to speak honestly."

"Good," he said and reached to shake my hand, and I felt the nub of his missing finger, a reminder of sacrifice hard to forget.

"Now," I said, watching Irene and Sylva return, "may I see more of your plans for Warsaw?" He smiled but looked questioningly at Irene. She had clearly brought me over to their home to impress us with each other. Before looking at the plans I excused myself to go to their lavabo. There I noticed their new infant sleeping in a tiny crib that had been stuffed into the shower stall. There was obviously no other room in the apartment.

Later I looked over his neat architectural renderings of the apartment complex simply labeled "Varsovie." I admired them and we talked about French architecture, about which I knew little.

"It's for the Polish people and the future life there," he said.

"Yes," I nodded, thinking of the child in the shower stall.

"You see," he said, "architecture, like everything else, is not an end in itself. It must be useful to society. I don't make much money doing this sort of work, but it gives me something back in knowing it will be useful to people."

"But you need to eat, too."

"I have my job in a small architectural firm here in Paris. That's for eating. This other work is what gives me satisfaction."

I interviewed him about his other experiences in the Maquis, and he gave me good references to help fill out the story. At the end of our visit, he asked me about my work, and I mentioned the upcoming interview with Maurice Thorez.

"How did you manage that?" he asked, surprised.

"Well, I just asked the right people the right questions. That's my job: to ask questions. Not to have all the answers."

"I find it more satisfying to have the right answers."

"And how do you know? How can you know?"

Later, after we had talked ourselves out, Irene and I left and went to a café back in our own quarter.

"What did you think?" she asked.

"I liked both of them. Did I pass the test or not?"

"I think you did."

"And will you let me go to Switzerland?"

"That's your affair," she said. "When is your interview with Thorez?"

"Tomorrow afternoon."

"Do you still need me? I have to make arrangements at the office."

"I always need you. Meet me for dinner tonight and we'll discuss strategy." She beamed, grabbed my hand and began making those curious circles in my palm with her fingers.

THIRTEEN

The Thorez interview went well, and Irene was fascinated by the challenge of translating, which I barely needed. However, it gave her a feeling of importance, and her youthful enthusiasm for the workers' cause in the current CGT strike action against the railroads amused the head of the French Communist party.

"C'est une fille devouée," he said to me about her dedication to the party, "and she is Russian, too. Doubly dedicated!" More than anything, the interview fortified my confidence in my own command of French. For me, also, the interview cleanly broke her will to criticize me for leaving on the Swiss venture, and after it there was no pressure of any kind from Irene.

With Buck and Ellen already at Caux, most of us took a train together from the Gare de Lyon east to the alpine country. Between us, we occupied three compartments, more or less, in a second class railcar. It was to be more than mere transportation. It was a journey to paradise, a land so different from Paris that it took us out of ourselves. Bill Watson sat across from me in the six-person compartment where the three Smith girls chattered excitedly, and Goodie Goodstein observed the gaiety without participating very much. Fred Furness was sequestered with Norman Tunison and Betty Lowry in another compartment with some French people. In a third compartment Bob Kemperman and Homer Fangwort, the two fag scientist classmates of Buck, relaxed and talked about what they would say at the conference in their respective fields—astronomy and biology. Others would join us after we arrived in Switzerland. Everybody aboard the train seemed excited about the trip ahead of us and glad to be out of the oppressive heat of Paris.

Near Vallorbe at the French-Swiss border we passed through a long railway tunnel that finally brought us out into the bright sunlight of Switzerland. But before we entered the tunnel I walked down the car to Fred's compartment where Norman was holding sway about his hero, Rabelais. His prominent jaw was moving like a leaf in the autumn wind.

"I do know he studied medicine at Montpellier," Fred said. "That's about it for me."

"Oh, there's much more!" Norman said.

"And I'm sure you'll tell me." Fred smiled

"He acted in a highly anti-clerical play."

"Really?"

"Also, around that time, he had this mission to Rome just when Henry VIII was having his standoff with the Vatican."

"Worthy of a dramatic monologue," Fred said.

Norman looked exasperated. "Come on, Fred."

"I think he's pulling your leg," I said.

"Well, I'm really serious…"

"Let's take a break," I suggested.

Norman gaped at me from his familiar intellectual crouch. "A bit much?"

"On occasion," Fred said. "Let's enjoy the scenery." He glanced at Betty. "You're awfully quiet."

Betty laughed. "I'm not getting into this." "Fred, I need to talk to you," I said.

At the very moment we shut the compartment door behind us, the train entered the long tunnel, and the noise was so great in the dark corridor that we had to yell at each other to be heard. We had to wait to make conversation.

The blackout took more than ten minutes. While I was waiting for the return of light and quiet, I planned how I would broach the subject of Joyce coming to Switzerland. His first words as we emerged from the tunnel into the vineyards around the lake, made it easy for me: "What have you got on your mind—something about Joyce?"

"You bet, just this morning I got a call."

"Yes?" He was on his guard.

"Joyce is worried about you. She plans to come to Switzerland after we arrive."

"She what!" he said.

"Friend, this is none of my business, really, but I had to mention it to you. It's going to be a sticky wicket, as she might say."

"Damn right it'll be a sticky wicket," he said, aroused. The train moved into another world, and as we made the half-moon circle around the north shore of Lac Leman, we were streaking past vineyards bursting with fat clumps of purple and green grapes.

"Right smack in the middle of the conference she'll arrive with bells and whistles," I said.

"Oh, God!"

"I did try to discourage her."

"Shit! Why the hell are you involved?"

"That's my function, I guess. Everyone comes to old Tom—he'll fix things up."

"God, this is awful. Why does she have to come now? I was hoping to end this thing diplomatically with Goodie while we're here…"

"Fred, she's in love with you."

He groaned as the train moved through the vineyards. On the other side of the lake the mountains brooded in silent splendor. They seemed to magnify Fred's problem. He looked me squarely in the eyes and said: "Really, Tom, why did she tell you, of all people?"

"We're friends, that's all. And I guess she thinks I'm neutral. In any event, she sure must think I would alert you to this."

"What kind of friends are you two?" he interrupted.

"Just friends," I said. He muttered something to himself just as I was about to return to the compartment. Then he said to me, "Can we talk further?"

"Yes, if you want. But it's basically your business, and I'd prefer not to get involved."

"It appears that I have to make a decision. Let's go back to the others." We reentered the compartment. Fred sat down moodily, and I left.

In my own compartment, Pam immediately looked at me, and I nodded. I found myself looking for signs of stress. Previously she had shied away from me. I leaned close and whispered to her the news of my Thorez interview.

"Really! What kind of person is he?"

"Moody but confident. Honest answers…and no use for us, America, the enemy. It was the shortest interview I ever had."

"You'd think he would welcome it."

"He barely tolerated it."

"There's something else, Tom…I'll tell you later, if you don't mind."

After the stop at Lausanne, the vineyards climbed high above us; below, the flat purple lake stretching away in an endless dark shadow. To the south, blue-tinted dragonback shapes of the French Savoian Alps plunged down into the lake. They were massive, dwarfing us.

"You know what?" I said to Pam.

"What?"

"All that counts in Switzerland is the scenery."

"Not people."

"Right. And what do we have from this? The cuckoo clock…"

Pam laughed. "The Swiss are people, too, Tom. I'm sure they have their fears, their anxieties. Like me."

I looked at her. "How are you doing?"

"Okay. I've been better."

"No desire to dance on the train?"

An anger smoldered briefly, then she smiled. "No."

"Sorry, Pam, that came out wrong."

"It's all right."

The Street of Four Winds

We passed Vevey and came to a stop at Montreux. There we wrestled the baggage out of the cars and onto the platform of the steep resort town. After the train pulled out, we crossed over to another platform where a blue funicula was waiting to take us up the mountain to Glion and Caux. When Pam sat down beside me, she clutched my arm and said, "Is something going on?"

"Nothing that concerns you and me, but some others are going to have some static."

She raised her dark brows above the thick glasses, and I said now was not the time to discuss it. The steep angle of ascent as we rose let us look down at the massive sheet of lake back to Lausanne where we had come from. Almost before we could admire the view, a small stone church loomed up behind us on the other side of the funicula. And beyond it to the east, the lovely scene of the green Valais ran away under more breathtaking, plunging mountains.

After a stop at Glion, we came to a gentle halt near the station sign marked "Caux." And there, miraculously, were Buck and Ellen waving to greet us as we stepped down on terra firma again.

When she inspected us like troops passing in review, I noticed that Ellen stopped to check me out, gave me an extra warm smile, and then moved on to greet the others. Then her eyes lighted on me again, and I wondered if she remembered our suggestive conversation a few weeks previously in Paris. For an instant I recalled the smile through her tears and how she reacted when I touched her.

Now Buck took over. Everyone had light baggage, and he suggested we carry it through the woods to the chalet. I grabbed Pam's quickly so we could lead the group, just behind Buck and Ellen, but far enough ahead of the others so that we could talk privately. I told her about Fred's problem and Joyce's imminent arrival.

"My, my—Goodie will be pleased, I'm sure," she said.
"Just wait."
"How come you know all about it?"

141

"I'm too well connected. This is an incestuous group—no secrets."

"You mean like you and Joyce?"

"How do you know anything about us?"

"I have friends, too, my dear. And I know you're their chaplain. Reverse confession in action."

This really bothered me; how to handle it? So all I could do was talk about Pam and how she felt. She had to be suspicious of my motives now and merely said, "Fine."

The deep woods around us soon gave way to an open hillside of pastureland overlooking the lake and falling down to Montreux.

"You're angry," I said.

"No, just disappointed. Don't worry about it, Tom. Don't forget, this could be our honeymoon."

Ahead of us the chalet appeared, at which point she asked me what the sleeping arrangements were. I said I had no idea, but asked her if she had something in mind.

"Yes, I do. But I don't know about you with your catholic tastes in women." She grinned spontaneously, and the light glinted off her glasses.

"Thanks a lot, but I did have something in mind, if we can manage it."

The group gathered out on the front lawn of the building and marveled at the view. We were above the light cumulus clouds. It was a view of views, the alpine vastness something few of us had ever seen before. It gave us the prospect of two weeks in heaven, living out of this world, where even the miniature towns we could see—Montreux , Vevey and Lausanne—seemed unreal.

All that time I spent in Switzerland had an element of unreality about it. The matter of the sleeping arrangements became larger than life. Pam sought guarantees in her relationships, and wanted that with me.And I was constantly debating with myself what she precisely wanted to be sure of in her life. All I could suppose was that her pattern of desires was standard American: a stable home, a man she loved, a family she would raise, and security all around, emotional and material. But about myself? I couldn't be that precise. There was too much flux in the picture for a veteran in his mid-twenties who knew he didn't want any standard pattern. There was so much new to do and try.

If there hadn't been the war and the wound, the path to the future might very well correspond to Pam's. But now a lot of that had changed. The women in my life made me dissatisfied with any one woman. Even lusting inwardly for Ellen was a bit of a lie. Nothing could last. In light of this, what the hell difference did the sleeping arrangements make?

I had become a vital part of Pam's life, responsible for something I couldn't name. In Paris we had interminably discussed the Existentialists—Sartre, Camus, Simone de Beauvoir. They had made a key, appealing point: we are individually responsible for our actions in this world. Yet, why didn't I feel responsible for Joyce or Irene? Fred or Buck? Myself? And why was there this feeling about Pamela?

Americans had a problem. In many ways they were all romantics. When it came to men and women, there was the romance of love. The popular music, the lyrics, the films, the family ideals—all of it was Romantic. The very idea of love between a man and a woman was a Romantic notion, more a notion of being in love with love than love itself. It was all illusion never experienced—but sought after. It even spilled over into our politics—being afraid of the Communists, of people like Edouard who had just spoken to me about his fears and illusions. Then the illusion of America that existed during the war. Another Romantic notion. It was a hell of a problem trying to grasp an illusory something or someone. For Pam it was going to be rather simple: "Yes, I want to sleep with you." Well, I said, not permanently, of course. I understood her and what moved her. And it was important to her, this commitment I wouldn't give. So, despite all of the ridiculous self-examination, I then asked her as we stood apart from the others on the edge of the fantastic view, "What do you want?"

And she answered, as I expected: "I want you."

FOURTEEN

It was a large, rustic house just perfect for the location. Its back pushed into the mountain, the front giving way to the "perfect view" we would talk about endlessly. We had already paired off, except for Bill Watson, who was alone, so that when Buck began to formalize the room assignments there were no surprises. Goodie and Fred, Faith and Sally, Norman and Betty, Bob Kemperman and Homer, Pam and myself—there it was. And he told us little cards placed on our doors would confirm the arrangements in both the main house and its satellite cottage. Buck and presumably Ellen had set the "sleeping arrangements."

The windows of my room with Pam were just across from Fred and Goodie's, and even before we had begun to unpack and settle down we heard their bickering.

"When are we going to solve this situation?" Goodie was asking.

"When we terminate it," Fred replied.

"You think that. I'll bet you do."

"One thing I'm going to tell you. We're not going to upset this conference with our own petty differences—not in this magnificent setting. If that is your aim, my dear, you shouldn't have come…"

"Buck especially asked me to join in," she said.

"Well, let's get on with it, Goodie. For God's sake, let's pretend for a week or two that nothing has changed between us while we're here. Please!"

It was only a few minutes later that Pam, almost as a reaction to what we had just heard through the window, said: "How I love you, Tom." And when she repeated it, she threw her arms around my neck and gave me a long kiss. I held her close for a long time.

There then came a hesitant knocking at the door, and we heard Fred's voice asking to see me and apologizing to Pam for the interruption. Pam began to unpack. "Be careful, Tom." There was protectiveness in her voice.

On the way out of the chalet, I passed Ellen and Buck in the kitchen. They were opening some misted bottles of champagne and pouring them out in plastic glasses. He had thought of everything.

Outside, Fred met me at the edge of the dark pine woods. Before I could get my bearings he was talking nonstop.

"Tom," he began, "I don't know what to do. Maybe you can help. I need an arbitrator. You know my problems with Goodie." His head was bent forward, his blinking eyes fixed on the carpet of pine needles as we strolled along.

"She's a strong-willed girl," I said. "What makes you think I want to get involved?" He looked up at me in alarm. "It's your life, not mine," I went on. "There's only one thing, Fred. Try to keep it between yourselves. Pam and I couldn't help but overhear you a few minutes ago."

"Sorry about that, but you know us, and you know Joyce—and, of course, that's the nub of it. You seem to care about people. Actually I've always envied how well you've organized your life and how people respect you."

"Are you kidding, Fred?" I was surprised. "I don't know how you figure things out. Half the time I don't even know what the hell I'm doing. If you don't know what to do, all I can say is, neither do I."

"You don't have Goodie to contend with."

"What happened between you two? I thought you were love birds."

"We were in New York, but something happened…"

"And what the hell was that?"

"Joyce Frost," he said firmly. "I never knew I could love someone so much."

"Aha! The other woman...sex rears its ugly head."

"It's more than that, believe me, Tom. And when Joyce comes down here, that's going to be explosive."

"Joyce is no fool," I said. "She can be determined. She knows what she wants. I guess she's flipped for you, and vice versa. So now there's the classic triangle."

"You sound surprised We've had this thing going on for some time."

"I know. I've seen you together in the quarter. And Goodie must have, too."

"Don't tell me discretion is the better part of valor, Tom."

"Well, it is, when you've got two women."

"Goodie can't stand it. That's why we're on the skids." He stopped walking. " I've made up my mind to leave her."

"Just pack her up and send her back to the States? That's something...and all for Joyce Frost?"

"Yes,"

"And you want my help, right? What the hell am I?" I remembered Pam's word—"some sort of chaplain? What can I do?" We resumed walking.

"Look, I need your help." I was besieged by conflicting emotions.

"Let me tell you. It's not worth it, Fred. Not worth anything. Joyce is just a loose woman—a busy body. And you may be making a mistake to think it's anything more than that—particularly now when you're well along with getting that volume of poetry published. Why get off-target now?"

"Off-target? She's perfect for me, and I don't care for this loose woman talk."

"It's not worth it, believe me," I repeated. "Joyce is just a busy body, I told you, and you may be making a mistake to think it's anything more than that."

146

He stopped again and said with all the blind passion of his verse: "Not the way she makes love. You don't know, Tom."

"Well," I said, trying to look innocent, "before you ditch Goodie, who's loyal to you, you better be sure."

"How the hell can I do that? Joyce is sensational," he said, more than a bit perturbed.

We were getting nowhere.

"Check with others who know her. The list isn't short, my friend."

"Just what in Christ's name do you mean by that?" he asked. "I'm serious about her, you know."

"That's the problem—your problem. None of the others were or are serious."

"Who, for example?" Now he was annoyed.

"The others who've slept with her—and enjoyed it. I told you she's a busy body."

"Tell me, Tom. I've got to know. Who?"

"Some people you know," I said.

"I must know who."

"Why? You're awfully possessive."

"Tom, please!" So I said to myself: the hell with it.

"Bill Watson for one…"

"That nigg—I've suspected Watson, but who else?"

"Me, if you must know."

"You!" he stared in disbelief. "You? By God, Cortell, you're not going to get away with this!" He was angry and out of control, and before I knew it, I took a hard right on the jaw and ended up on the pine needles. Blood trickled. "You bastard!" he shouted and made for me again, trembling in rage. And then he struck again while I was down, this time with his foot, kicking me in the ribs. The pain was terrible. "You bastard, you!" he repeated.

I passed out. I don't know when but later I came to, still in great pain. There was fire around my ribs, and I felt sick. Then Buck Birnbaum appeared in my distorted vision. He had been aroused by Fred's yells, and when he came close and saw my condition he realized that I couldn't move. He called for someone back at the chalet to bring some boards or a door, or anything flat I could lie on for carrying me back to the house. A doctor was called, and before long I was carried to Buck's small car and on my way down the mountain to Montreux. In the doctor's office they took x-rays and found no fractures.

So began the peace conference. Later that night, after my ribs had been immobilized with tape, Buck drove me back up the mountain from Caux to the chalet. They put me down on my bed. Pam sat by me and tried to console me. She understood exactly what had happened and was saying how contrite Fred was. She reported that he said he had "no idea" what he was doing that afternoon and apologized profusely. That did me a hell of a lot of good now.

"Pam, it was like a brawl in a cathouse," I said. Luckily, she had not heard the whole discussion about Joyce and myself. She held my hand and played nurse. Then she brought me some dinner and a few strong drinks. The situation was ridiculous, but it had happened. All on the first day of what had promised to be an idyllic time in Switzerland. I had been taken out of action by an irate poet, a casualty in a conflict that I had no right to be concerned with. The price was a few cracked ribs, a lot of pain and confusion for the others.

Pam tried to comfort me. She kept holding my hand, saying it was "just one of those things."

"How did you get into such a violent argument?" she asked.

"I wish you could tell me. He suddenly got angry about something I said."

She said I should forget about it and get some sleep, but I couldn't. I just lay there, very much awake, bored by my immobility and annoyed with Fred and his passion for Joyce. Why did I get involved with these people? I then realized how much I had become entwined with so many of them—Joyce, Pam, Irene, Buck, the whole lot. The list expanded the more I thought about it: Ellen, Norman, Goodie, Sally and Faith. It was a mess. "Maybe you can help," Fred had said.

Joyce meant nothing serious to me. She was merely a great lay, and I for her. And I admired her free spirit. There was nothing earthshaking about it, merely exquisite, slow friction. And here Fred gets furious about it. When I mentioned Bill Watson and Joyce, that probably was enough to remind him of what he had always really known but refused to face, kindling the fire. A goddam Negro lover of his own lover, her pure white skin mixed up with Bill's evil blackness. The very idea of it: a black painter against his own pure, poetic, lovemaking talents.

That must have been it.

The pain in my ribs came and went during the night. I didn't even think of playing with Pam. Once she touched me in her sleep, and I was wide awake, all sorts of memories flying around in what passed for my mind. One small contact with her was all it took. I tried to pull her closer. Then she curled up beside me and sighed in her deep-throated way. The pain held me on a leash. Then I wondered what Fred and Goodie were doing. Probably arguing, as usual; not making love. I thought about Buck and Ellen and some of the things she had told me in Paris. Were they sleeping together? Probably not.

Finally, I dozed, visions of Irene in the cathedral of Chartres floating before me, the blue light through the windows on her dark cheeks. I saw her wonder at the depth of mystery in the place, the image of the Virgin in her window looking down on us. Above her the high arches and yawning spans of space up to heaven in the nave…and I was off.

FIFTEEN

"Let us begin," Buck Birnbaum said with force and conviction when he opened the conference the next morning out on the front lawn. Moses on Mount Sinai. Chairs had been set up for us in rows, classroom style. Pencils and papers distributed with an agenda.

"We're on the very edge of something great," he carried on. "Considering what this generation has gone through, we're about to investigate our world at mid-century and pursue—let's say, for the hell of it, Stephen Crane's man chasing the horizon." (That was so typical of him, to throw in a literary allusion where he could work it in, if only to reassure his listeners of his academic prowess.)

"The real questions before us today are, one, how do we propose to live now that the world's greatest war is over, and, two, what is that world's capacity to recover and move forward from the brink of destruction. We must keep in mind the global extent of the war—the first in history—which separates it from all prior conflicts…"

Norman's hand was up immediately, and Buck recognized him.

"I beg your pardon. Rome versus Carthage was the big war in the world as it was then known."

"A mere matter of degree, Norman, but not global. And the amount of destruction can't be compared. What I want to move on to is what our country is doing in the way of recovery, the amazing Marshall Plan, for instance…"

Despite the pain around my middle, I understood what Buck was driving at. And it was clear that he was dead serious about the conference. He fully expected us to pay close attention. All faces were fixed on his. A secretary had been engaged to take down every word, and behind Buck's comments came the steady hum of her stenographic machine. Beyond that were the stunning lake below, the giant mountains behind, and above the bluest sky I had ever seen. "God, what a place!" I said to myself.

Again Norman Tunison's hand was waving in the bright sunlight that flooded the front lawn. He seemed very much attuned to what Buck was saying about the Marshall Plan, a smile on his face. It so happened that he had just finished reading the Book of Gargantua by his passion of the moment, Rabelais. Betty had helped him with the original 16th Century French. He cited it and said, "In that marvelous book there's a remarkably similar comparison with the Marshall Plan of today. A fantastic parallel."

Betty perked up: "Obviously the general idea is appropriate, but none of the details. You might call it a just peace—in the interest of long-term human relations…"

Norman went on to compare the generous victory of the Allies over the Axis powers in 1945 with the sympathetic conquest and peace made by Gargantua over Picrochole in ancient times. Despite the ridiculous roots of that conflict in the cakebakers of Lerné not wanting to sell their cakes to Gargantua's shepherds, Gargantua had won the battles. "In victory, Gargantua displayed the same sense of clemency as the U.S. has shown to the Japanese and Germans." He went on, but Buck intervened.

"That's what we want here—parallels, comparisons and contrasts in history, whatever, to show our place in the flow," Buck was saying. "And thank you, Betty." He went on to present a brilliant summation of the post-war world situation. All the participants on the lawn around him joined in with their own remarks. I looked about, somewhat out of phase with them, thinking the discussion a bit strained and pompous; but now the place was buzzing like a wasp's nest. I sat there in my tight bandages, watching Buck trying to accomplish something, perhaps feeding his own ego and playing it off the scenic backdrop. Maybe he could have it both ways. But I wondered if it all made any sense. Possibly, I thought, his friends didn't really know as much as he wanted them to.

"What do you think, Pam?" I said privately.

"It's fun, I think. Better than drinking and telling jokes. How about you?"

"The question is: what's fiction, what fact?"

"It's going to get somewhere. Buck's established good rules. Don't be so skeptical."

"You're generous…"

"I'm from Illinois, I've said more than once."

"Score for you."

I looked at the view and remained quiet. Then I noticed how Buck was observing his brood in action, his fair way of dealing with them, letting each person contribute, exercising his control and playing one off against the other—even Sally and Faith when it came to women's issues. But it was soon to be my turn when he gave me the high sign to get ready. I didn't know what he expected from a skeptic like myself, but I tried.

"Big changes are on the way in communications," I said, "all driven by technology and economics. News media like newspapers, magazines, radio—how are they going to fare in the new world of electronics and still other things to come? How will information technology affect education? Will people read any more or less? Will they even need to read? Will they want to with the new toys? Calculating machines, for example—slide rules made obsolete, manufacturing by automation. All I can do here is mention new items in our lives and ask questions how they'll come into play for us."

I was warming up, like a pitcher on a baseball mound. I wasn't saying anything significant, but working up to the point I really wanted to make. "What we ought to use our time here for in the field of communications is simply this: our generation is the one that's going to have to make the transition from the pre-war world to the post-war world. The World War was so explosive that it's going to separate our generation from all the others. We are products of an older age, an older point of view, older forms of communication. Even an older morality that may have little place in the kind of living that will be done in the future. We are the generation on the spot, the link between two worlds. I hope all of you will explore that subject from other viewpoints before we're finished here."

"Tom, you've brought it right home," Buck said. "That provides a provocative framework for this whole seminar." I looked at them, while I rattled on about the modern world of communications. I was making a living in the field and decided to say something that might raise new possibilities for them, dangers, and realities. Then I thought: you're the imposter in this group. You had been upset by something entirely impractical: beauty in a cathedral that had become a kind of passion, which had flawed your prism of knowledge.

We had a small break, and Pam came over. "I never realized that before you said it," she said, touching my arm. I asked her what she meant. "That idea about our generation being the link…"

"…one that may not link things," I said. "You know, I'm more confused than anyone actually, about that subject."

She smiled and squeezed my arm this time. But I was watching Ellen, who stared at me with interest. I nodded back. Pam hadn't noticed.

Now all of a sudden many of them had questions for me, and I was swamped with providing answers about which I wasn't sure—journalism ethics and the future, how people were going to get their practical training in the field if newspapers were going to die a slow death, many other points. All of this when I wanted to say something to Ellen and get her off alone.

Now she raised her hand and said, "We may have to go back to basics, Tom. We'll have to describe what we mean by news, what news value means, how you distinguish it from feature stories, whether news can be fabricated or genuine, what qualifies a journalist to transmit news, and so forth. Then there's the commercial side of the news, what sells newspapers and how that relates to 'news value.' And then the real question: how a public's reactions can be regulated by the media…"

I stopped taking notes. I was staring at her, wanting to grab her and take her away. I was out of the discussion and only thinking of caressing her when we would be alone. My shutter snapped. I was looking at her well-shaped legs, her sexy body and not caring at all about what she was saying. I said a few stupid things and then sat down, easing into the ambiance of the moment. Pam's hand reached for me as it had that night in Paris. Buck was looking at me in a curious way. He probably thought I had lost it, but then recovered enough to introduce Sally Satterwaite as the next speaker.

Sally spoke about the coming major growth in international business, globalization of corporations and economies of the future. Buck brought up China's emergence, possibly passing Japan as the leader in the Far East, and Faith and Bob Kemperman made a presentation on the U.S lead in communications technology and how women would participate. We were ranging far and wide, sending our ideas over lakes and mountains. Soon it was lunchtime, but people were carrying on the morning discussion in small groups. Time was passing rapidly, and before long we were reassembled for the afternoon session. Kemperman and Fangwort gave a good presentation on new developments in astrophysics first, then bringing in the space exploration race that might well occur between the USSR and the U.S.A. How that would turn out was vague, but the reality of the competition was assumed.

"We covered a lot of ground today," Buck said at dinner, "and I want to compliment you. Tomorrow we'll carry on with some words about the new economics picture that appears to be emerging. Homer is going to try to give us a view on the new information technologies that could well convert the U.S. economy—electronics, data processing and so forth.

"In the afternoon we have to get back to politics—the fate of colonial empires that no longer fulfill a function, since the war has broken up the possibility of colonialism. Then we've got independence movements in Asia, the Pacific—stemming from the defeat of Japan. We're going to give short shrift to Africa since it's out of the mainstream."

Fred Furness stood up at the dinner table and made a point: "Nature, Buck. We've got to cover that in many ways…"

"Right. Very important, but before we get into that, I think we'll need a day of diversion. So the day after tomorrow I plan to take you all down to the Castle of Chillon and let you do your own things down on the lake. I've got a mess of literature on the area…" As he talked, I noticed Ellen catching my eye from time to time. "Then we've got to cover cultural aspects with Bill and myself, possibly some others who may be coming from the States in a couple of days."

Buck had wrapped up our first day, and we all went out to look at the stars. I was tired and still in pain and decided to go to bed. Pam remained up a while, and I heard them singing as I started to climb the stairs to our room.

"In the evening by the moonlight," they sang, "I can hear those darkies singing.

"In the evening by the moonlight I can hear those banjoes ringing…"

I paused to listen to the old college song that went with beer and good times wherever university students assembled to sing themselves hoarse and to share in youthful pleasures. It was a touching note high on this Swiss mountainside. I recalled good times in the Dutch Kitchen at Cornell.

"Nostalgic, eh?" Ellen's voice sounded behind me as I paused at the foot of the stairs. "Wonder what Bill thinks of 'darkies singing!'"

"Oh! You surprised me."

"Were you not expecting me this evening?"

"Only hoping, but I am dog tired. As for Bill, he'll never say anything. He wants to belong."

"How are your ribs?" she asked.

"I'll survive. Maybe they're not really cracked, only badly bruised, thanks."

"So you were hoping," she said.

"I'm always hoping for someone like you. I guess that's pretty direct."

"Buck mentioned the day after tomorrow being free. I want you and me to talk about a few things."

"I think we can work it. Let's look at the literature he talked about—maybe go for a swim if I'm feeling better."

"Why not?" she said and came up behind me. I felt a light kiss on the back of my neck, trembled at her touch, and turned quickly to grab her, when I saw Buck entering the kitchen from the lawn where the singing filled the night. I began to climb the stairs as he noticed Ellen and my disappearing feet.

"Rest easy, Tom. Hope you're feeling better," he said. At least he hadn't seen anything.

"Great opening day," I said, regretting I couldn't return her kiss.

☙❧

I could tell he had been waiting for me the next morning. And when his eyes snapped open in their customary manner, I noticed he was a bit on edge.

"See here, old man, it was my fault," Fred said, while both of us were greeting the sun's rising over the plunging hills in the Valais. Not a breeze stirred on the mountain. The light was intense, and far below us the lake slid away to infinity. "I'm dreadfully sorry I lost control the other day. You'll never forgive me, but I wish you would." At first I said nothing, then relented, particularly when I noticed his popping eyes.

"Women bring out the worst in us," I said.

"How do you feel?"

"A lot better, thanks. You've got your own worries coming up."

"Oh, Joyce. Well, I'll simply have to face the music…"

Just then Goodie came up behind us.

"It's beautiful, isn't it. How can we be so idiotic as to have a serious discussion in such a setting?" She had that surprised look on her face that seemed out of phase with her remarks.

"Yes," was all Fred could manage.

"You've got a point there," I said to her. "How are you two doing? This should knock the tar out of both of you."

"He knocked it out of you," Goodie said. "I don't know why, Tom, but I hope he's apologized."

"I did," Fred said.

But there was going to be interference. Joyce would break in on us, and all hell might break loose. I had discussed it privately with Buck after we all arrived from Paris. As usual, he was positive. How he proposed to take positive action was another thing. In fact, he had no plan, so when in a few hours Pam and I were over at Caux near the funicula station, and Joyce appeared unannounced, it all began.

"Hi-there, you lovely people!" she said in her breezy British way, like a character stepping out of a 1920's novel. When she jumped out of the blue train, neither Fred nor Goodie was there, and Pam gasped. "I've come here to claim my own, in case you didn't know." Joyce knew her role in our universe, and she played it to the hilt. No one took her too seriously, except the men who slept with her. Maybe I was the only one who understood her and the kind of Midlands background against which she was in constant revolt.

When she jumped down from the train like a wood-nymph alighting on the forest floor, she looked fresh and ready. Her pure white skin stood out against the larch trees, and her lively eyes glittered as she greeted Pam, saying, "Hello, darling Pamela, you don't mind if I kiss your lecherous friend." And without any reaction from Pam, she did just that. It was a firm, spontaneous kiss directly on my lips and she purred in her usual catlike way. Pam's eyes snapped wide open.

Looking back, I'd guess this was one of the chain of small, jabbing events that got to Pam. Joyce's kiss held an intimacy that came from earlier explorations. When she let me go I looked at Pam and caught the vulnerability, the betrayal and jealousy in her eyes.

"Steady, Joyce," I said, giving her a theatrical push. "I'm spoken for."

Joyce giggled and said, "A little kiss never hurt anyone, Tom." I wondered about that. "And by the by, you don't look too well. What's up?"

"A minor accident. I hurt my ribs and I'm bound up like an Egyptian mummy,"

"You always need a mommy," she teased.

Joyce patted Pam on the shoulder, and I saw her shrink away imperceptibly.

"Darling Pam, you must be kinder to him. His aggression often gets the best of him. I know only too well." I switched gears and asked her to join us at the nearby restaurant for a drink to celebrate her arrival. While we waited for it to arrive at the patio table, she took up the matter at hand. "I assume Goodie is here and ready to pounce on me."

"I thought it was the other way round," Pam said.

"No, not at all. All I ask you to do, dear people, is help me in one little detail. Can you arrange for Fred to meet me alone this afternoon before the others see me? I'd be awfully indebted to you." Pam looked at me.

"We'll arrange it. How about right now?"

"The sooner the better."

I told them to wait for me and went through the woods to bring Fred over from the chalet. As I left, Joyce was saying to Pam in her brash way, "He's such a dear boy. You are so fortunate. He really knows how to handle women…" I prayed that Joyce would go no further. Then I worried that Pam would get aggressive with Joyce about her patronizing tone. Pam was angry, somewhere deep inside, and it disturbed me.

On the way to the chalet through the dark woods, I was puzzling how to pull off the meeting without creating all sorts of trouble. But when I arrived Goodie was closeted with Buck and

Ellen. Then I spied Fred and took him back to the station café. As we walked, he stared at the ground, and asked me for my advice.

"Look, Fred, don't get me in any deeper." I said. Of course, this did not satisfy him. Joyce's presence was forcing a decision from Fred. Goodie, too, needed a decision. It was still a man's world, and both women knew that.

"Look here," I said after awhile, trying to be objective about the standoff, "don't overstep your bounds. You got pissed off at me for something I said and you hurt me badly. Now you're asking for help. You can't have it both ways."

"Tom, I know all that, but this is a major decision."

"Well, make it, for Christ's sake!" When Fred and I entered the station café, Joyce quickly got to her feet to receive Fred's perfunctory kiss, which she returned.

"So you did come," Fred said. It was a weak opening.

"Of course. Did you expect me to languish in Paris while you all were here living it up? I do have my pride, you know."

"Maybe that's how it had to be," Fred said.

I put out my hand towards Pam, and we waved goodbye, retiring to a table across the patio. When we sat down I looked at Pam. "Are you okay?"

"Why shouldn't I be okay?"

"Oh. The look you gave Joyce when she kissed me. It was just one of those…"

"What does she think of the rest of you? Your scar, for example."

"What?"

"Does she make her silly purring noise in bed?"

"Hey, now…"

She smiled brightly. "Forgotten—okay? I'll not mention it again."

I let it go. "Look, we've got to get Goodie out of here."

"That's not going to solve anything. She's a participant in this. She'll have to be involved," Pam said, lighting a cigarette. "What we really have to do is keep a lid on Joyce…"

We weren't far enough away from them to avoid hearing their conversation…

"You could have waited till the end of this conference," Fred said across the patio. Joyce lit a cigarette and blew a cloud of smoke directly at him. He batted his eyelids.

"Do you really believe I could do that?" she said. " Some things one can't do. You simply have to be a bit more decisive—that is, if we're going to continue on our merry way. You must understand that this is something new in my life."

"What do you mean by that?"

"Just what I said, darling," Joyce said. "What I mean is that with the others, I wouldn't care a jot, Freddie. But you're different. I happen to love you, though God may wonder why. When you love someone you go after him, like I did by coming here." Joyce blew another blast of smoke at him. He promptly coughed, and a smile broke out on her alabaster face, as if she had scored a major debating point. She fairly glowed. She was magnificent at such moments, and I don't know how he could resist her. I had never been able to…

"Why do we have to get involved in this Furness-Goodstein war?" I asked Pam softly.

"Because," she replied deliberately in a strong whisper, "we've gone through something like it ourselves."

"You want us to be civilized."

"After a fashion, at least."

"Son of a bitch!"

"Don't be so crude, Thomas," Pam said. "Look: Goodie feels intensely about Fred. So does Joyce, and she's tougher. She's British."

"What does being British mean? "It means she's more realistic. Joyce has been around."

"And you envy her that."

"What?" she asked.

"Well, you're the recent ex-virgin, right? She must put you on the defensive."

Pam's eyes clouded, and she retreated. It was frightening.

"Jesus, Pam, I didn't mean that. It's just that you keep pushing at her when there's no need…"

"There's need. But you're right, I'm afraid. I'm defensive around her."

It took awhile for her eyes to clear, her mood to return. When her smile revived I was relieved.

Across the way Joyce began to preach. "Fred, I think we need to face facts. That Goodie woman's got her canines into you—right from the time she set her trap for you in the museum when you met her and she pounced."

Fred said nothing. Then he took in Pam and me across the patio. Finally he checked Joyce, grinned and managed: "Joyce, you're absolutely terrific."

"Well," she said. "Blast it. Do something about it, luv." That expression began to sound familiar.

"It's not as easy as you think…"

"Look, she doesn't appreciate the best part of you—your poetry. Think about that. She doesn't have any fundamental understanding of your essence—and without that, it's never going to work. Actually, she doesn't have an opinion worth a leek about anything. All she can do is twirl that bloody ring on her finger to try to prove to herself that you belong to her—and you don't, do you?" "Joyce, when our relationship began I needed her."

"And how about now?"

"Probably not, but I can't just cash her in like a poker chip."

"A dead chippie, you mean."

"Don't be flip…"

"You see," I was saying to Pam, "he's lost his sense of humor This is going to be a disaster. And I don't want to have anything more to do with it."

"I feel sorry for Goodie," Pam said.

"You would. You're a woman."

"And the sad truth is," she said riding over my comment, "she's got nothing to do with it."

"She sure as hell does. She doesn't recognize what she's done to Fred, and she's making it worse as time goes on. I didn't tell you, but just before we left Paris she asked me to intercede. The fact is, she should retire gracefully—admit she made a mistake in believing in Fred."

"Why don't you talk to Fred about it? And I'll talk to Goodie."

"Why the hell should I talk to that son of a bitch, Pam? He hurt me with that attack. Anyway, why should either of us get involved? It's certainly not my affair. You're my affair."

The light of late afternoon was fading, and the woods between the chalet and restaurant began to look forbidding. Joyce and Fred were heavily engaged in talk. Pam and I now had to return to the chalet to help out with the evening meal, so I interrupted them.

"Don't worry about me, Thomas," Joyce said. "I'm staying down in Glion for the night. I made arrangements on the way up."

Pam and I walked to the chalet. I stole a quick look back to see them kissing.

"No matter how sensitive he is as a poet," I said when we entered the dark woods, "Fred's a damned fool. But I guess it'll work out."

SIXTEEN

That night during dinner I sat next to Ellen, who seemed ill at ease. Usually under great control, she was now tense, her eyes darting about from person to person. I had first noted these mood swings during our meeting in Paris at the brasserie, and here they were again, only more exaggerated, not at all like Pam's frightening withdrawal of today. She abruptly asked me for a cigarette. While I held the match for her she stared into my eyes, then exhaled and looked away.

"Can we meet outside this evening, Tom? Just for a minute. Please?"

"With all this noise in here, why not now?" She crushed her cigarette in an ashtray and immediately pushed back her seat, and I followed her, hoping Pam wouldn't notice.

"Thanks very much," she said, holding my hand impulsively when we were alone on the front lawn under the stars.

"You seem out of sorts," I said.

She released my hand.

"What's up?"

"We don't have enough time, but I need to talk to you. Maybe we can go together to Vevey the day after tomorrow—take a swim there, and talk or whatever while they're all at the castle. I've asked Goodie to go with me now that Buck's changed the schedule, and she can cover us." I agreed to work it out with Pam. Our meeting only lasted for a minute more, but as we stood there side by side, looking down on the lakeshore and the lights of

Montreux, she reached for my hand again and with her other hand touched me on the cheek.

"Kiss me," she said, and I did. Then she put a finger on my lips as if to swear my silence. Then we strolled back into the dining room. As we did, Pam's eyes followed me.

My bruised ribs didn't bother me too much that night, and sleep came easier. I wondered about the kiss from Ellen. It had a forced, unnatural quality to it. Then, sometime toward dawn, I had an upsetting dream about Fred and Goodie. They had had a terrible quarrel, so frightful that they came to blows and Fred knocked her down. I must have shuddered or something because Pam muttered, "What!" and after awhile asked weakly, "was that the grenade going off?" Then she pressed her lips to my ear and said, "darling," which is all I remembered when sleep descended again. I slept well until Pam stirred beside me as light was breaking. She caressed me then, becoming more aggressive, taking me over. Her mouth found mine as she rode above me, and I heard her murmurings. Afterwards, she said, "Am I good? That was easy on your ribs, no?"

"Fantastic," I said.

"Are you all right now?"

"Fantastic," I said again.

"I love the way you let me kill you," she breathed, curling herself around me. I thought of Irene, her innocent, uncomplicated love. Now Pam and I slept for a while like spoons in a drawer.

When the sun splashed into the room I felt like I was in a tent. Pam had spread her rich brown hair over the both of us. I quietly crawled out of the tent and began to dress. I could still breathe in her body's scent as I moved about the room. For a moment I thought twice about getting up at all. She had had that sensuous appeal for me ever since we met. Nevertheless, I dressed and shut the door of the bedroom without awakening her.

But once out of the room I froze. I was not alone. Something unexpected stopped me as I moved into the dim light of the hallway. There before me stood Bob Kemperman, stark naked, outside of Buck's room, desperately trying to pull his shorts on. It could have been funny, but it wasn't at all.

"Hi, Tom," he said self-consciously. The door to Buck's room, which I had mistakenly assumed our leader was sharing with Ellen, hung open. The bedclothes were carelessly thrown about the place.

"Hi!" I replied, not really knowing what to say.

"This is some great place, isn't it?" he said and shivered.

I started to move towards the bathroom, then Ellen descended from upstairs and greeted us in a hushed voice on the landing. She trembled in the dim light. I remembered that the room upstairs was a single one in the attic.

"Good morning, all," I said to break the tension, as Kemperman shrunk back into Buck's chaotic room. He kept a watchful eye on both Ellen and myself. I made a point of remaining in the bathroom as long as I could. I heard some sobbing outside for a moment and then it stopped. I changed into a swimsuit and went downstairs to the kitchen. Neither Ellen nor Bob was around.

On the way down, I could hear Buck whistling "Sentimental Journey," a popular song of the time, and when I entered the kitchen he was walking about like a sergeant-major, moving from the mixing of fruit juice to fussing with the coffeepot. Ellen was outside in her bathing suit. Seated on a lawn chair, she was crying into a towel on her lap.

Then Bill Watson walked into the kitchen and greeted us. "Never slept so well in my life!"

"Just like Chicago," I said.

"The silence is like the scenery—overpowering. Man, I love this place."

Ellen remained on the front lawn, and I watched her reach into her shoulder bag to take out a cigarette. She inhaled deeply and leaned back in her chair.

"How did you find this place, Buck?" Bill asked.

"It wasn't easy. I rented it from two French ladies who live regularly in Paris." Almost as an afterthought, Buck said, "I had a rotten night's sleep."

I smiled to myself about that, knowing he had spent the night actively with Bob Kemperman.

"Sorry to hear it. Worried about the conference?"

"Well, for one thing," Buck said, "I'm worried about how to work in your thoughts on the arts."

"Oh, I know the answer to that," Bill said. "The landscape here gives us that."

"How so?"

"It actually sets the pace for us. Ever think how landscape painting's in such a state of decline? It was even before the war. Why? Because people are no longer at peace with their surroundings. Monet was the last great one, you know. So that leads nicely to the focus of painting today: chaos...the destroyer of landscapes. Only the frazzled inner landscapes of deranged artists survive on canvas. Even the human body has gone...degenerated into what passes for nude paintings today. All that's left is Rothko, Bacon, Pollock, and what's left of Picasso. They're not communicating anything except personal nightmares that say nothing to the public."

"Good points," Buck said, "and you know my views on Picasso."

"He's great with line drawings."

"You make a good lecturer, Bill," I said, looking out at Ellen. I felt uncomfortable. The place seemed to be in the grip of a nervous tension and unhappinesss, although Bill didn't feel it. I suspected that something pretentious had emerged during the formal proceedings of the previous day and hoped Buck would turn Bill Watson loose on the cultural aspects of the period we were discussing. I mentioned it to him when he announced he had to go down to Montreux to pick up the stenographer for the morning session. Bill and I had some breakfast.

Out on the lawn was a hollowed-out log filled with cold spring water. Without much ceremony I greeted Ellen who now lay peacefully in a reclining chair near the log. Beyond her was the big view of the lake and mountains. To make a complete break in the morning mood I approached the log and rolled over into the frigid water. The shock was complete, and I had to catch my breath. She giggled like a little girl, and I knew I had broken the evil spell of the day. My teeth were chattering when I climbed out of the log. I grabbed my towel, wrapped my body in it, and sat down in the sun next to her. She continued to giggle and said, "Smarty!"

"Christ, what a sensation!"

"Let the sun warm you and contemplate the joys of the morning session," she said. "And think about tomorrow when we have our talk on the beach at Vevey."

"Oh, yes. I've been wondering about that. What plans do you have for me?"

"You'll find out, if I don't have to go through another last night."

We looked at the view as Fred and Goodie, Faith and Sally and some of the others came out on the lawn with coffee cups and their breakfast toast. Buck returned with the stenographer and he summoned us to begin our conference day.

The morning session, thanks to Bill Watson's comments, was taken up with the cultural scene and how we all felt about music, the arts, design, architecture and public taste. Bill led the discussion for the most part, and Norman and Fred filled in on the music, theater and creative writing areas. It was difficult to predict direction in the arts, but the speculation focused on new conditions for the artists themselves, greater government support for the arts, the inflation in values for paintings, sculpture, the folk arts. On the whole, what actually happened in later years was well predicted by Bill.

In the afternoon Sally and Faith did a workmanlike job of explaining how the war had changed the role of women in society, in family economics—all in light of the growth of suburban life, the exodus of whites from the cities and growing racial tensions. The rest of the day had to do with economics, a field that normally bored the devil out of me, but which Buck and Norman did a creditable job of presenting. The disagreements were unbelievable.

That evening we relaxed over dinner, cooked by Sally and Faith. I obtained the wine at a small grocery in Caux that had a good selection of local Swiss Dole and Fendant red and white bottles. Later at night we listened to some jazz and classical records that Buck had brought along, then wandered out to look at the stars.

Just before we turned in, while Pam and I lay in our lawn chairs, observing the crescent moon, I felt Ellen's hand on my shoulder as she passed by behind us. "Sleep well, you two," she whispered and headed for her attic bedroom.

"I don't like her," Pam said.

"You don't like her or you just feel threatened by her?"

"I want you to myself," was all she said.

I wondered if Pam had been watching us.

SEVENTEEN

The next morning I found Fred alone out on the front lawn again, and the first thing he did was to inquire about my ribs. "I don't think I'll live down those moments of rage. I really had nothing to bitch about."

"You just needed a target for your frustrations," I said. "I always seem to get in the middle."

"Too Many Girls—was the name of a Broadway show years ago."

"You may have something there," I said. "Just watch out when Joyce appears."

"By the way, Tom. We must talk about Bill Watson some time. He did a good job yesterday."

"I'll be happy to discuss Bill's cultural theories, Fred. But that's all."

He pulled a face. "I must take things less seriously than a poet usually does then, is that it? Not ponder Joyce and how she is with her men."

"If you handle this right, Fred, there'll be no other men. It's up to you."

"Well, that's good news. Too bad I can't say the same about you."

I stared. "Meaning what?"

"Oh, just Pam. The way she's skulking about, smiling here and frowning there. Always turning inward—have you noticed that? Not a good sign, me thinks. And Ellen, of course…"

"What about Ellen?"

"Pam watches the way you look at her. It happened just yesterday again. There's Bill delivering his theories, and you and Ellen are exchanging looks. It's all pretty obvious and not good."

I got up to leave. "Stay in your own backyard, Fred. You've got quite enough work to occupy you there."

"Watch the eyes, Tom. They reveal a lot."

That really stopped me, and I felt funny about it. I had been discussing women and had said how eyes make promises they never keep. I thought of Ellen. Well…

※

Some of them had wanted to be by themselves down on the shore of the lake in Montreux, but most of them, including Pam and Fred, went with Buck in his car to the Castle of Chillon. Only Ellen, Goodie and myself opted for the beach at Vevey to swim and relax on the sunny day. As Pam jumped into the car, she turned to me and cautioned me about Goodie and Fred, even though they were now separated. I promised to be a "good boy."

"It's going to be a great day," Goodie said as she appraised the wide view below us and walked through the woods to the Caux funicula station.

"I thought you'd go with Fred." Ellen said to her.

"Just another ruined castle, like our romance," Goodie said. "and I need some room right now." Actually it turned out to be a good idea for Goodie to be with us. Soon we were aboard the next bright blue funicula that descended from the summit of the Rochers de Naye past Caux and Glion and down our magic mountain to Montreux. Once there we walked across the platform and took the next local train to Vevey. There was the grass beach along the lake, where we spread our towels and lay in the mid-morning sun, cupped in the bowl of the mountains. Before long, Goodie made her announcement about going for a long swim out into the lake, and she ran down to the water.

Now we were by ourselves, and Ellen offered me a cigarette. As she lit it, she paused and stared at me, suspending time between us. The grass beach was almost totally devoid of bathers, and Goodie's splashing out in the water kept us occupied. We watched Goodie receding into the lake. She then turned up along the shore, her powerful kick propelling her forward.

"She has an excellent freestyle stroke," I said. "She cuts through the water neatly." I remembered she had swum a bit at Barnard, and I had watched her in the pool when Fred and she were in their early period of courtship. During those days Columbia College's sister school had no intercollegiate varsity swim team, but the girls took lessons and often challenged each other to races in their pool. Goodie had always been unbeatable in freestyle; she was a natural swimmer and would have done well competitively, if the opportunity were there. Right now she was streaking through the waters of Lac Leman in great form, her strokes firm and regular, her kick strong, as she moved parallel to the shore. Every once in a while she stopped to wave at us.

"She's good, that Goodie," Ellen said, "I wonder what's in store for her."

"She'll take care of herself. Fred's foolish about this Joyce thing. I tried to tell him, but he's mad for her." Ellen turned her lean, well formed body to a prone position close to me on the beach blanket. As she did, our feet touched and our eyes met in a significant encounter. She put her head down on the blanket, peeking up at me with her slow, sexy smile. We smoked quietly and time passed. Goodie plowed endlessly back and forth.

"She's really taking a swim," I said.

"And what are you doing while I make eyes at you?"

"Thinking about things," I said non-committally. It was quite a contrast—Goodie's determined activity in the water, our silent fencing on the grass beach. Now I lay back, avoiding her blue eyes, looking up at the darker blue sky flowing behind the white cumulus clouds that seemed to hang like draperies from the mountain peaks. Ellen shifted on the blanket and touched me lightly on the arm. I took a deep breath. Her smile was within inches. Then she held her head high like a proud queen and looked past me. Cortez must have looked that way when he first spied the Pacific.

"You wonder what this is all about," she said finally.

"What do you mean?"

Her reply was to touch me again lightly on the arm. "This rendez-vous, my dear."

"I like being with you. I always have. Are you flirting with me? If so, you're about the most difficult siren to resist."

"I am flirting with you," she said, touching my cheek with her lips. "You are not to resist me, either."

"You mean, get in more trouble than I already am?"

"Yes." She rubbed her nose against my face. "You saw that scene on the stairs yesterday?"

"Yes."

"Well, Tom, it bothered me—bothered me awfully. Since you saw it, I needed you. It confirmed our date here on the beach. Pam has nothing to do with this, either. Forget her, please. I have no intention of hurting her. But I need you to share this with."

"That stair scene—was it unexpected?" I asked.

"No. But, as I say, it confirmed something I didn't want to recognize. It made me want to be with you, more than anyone else and to talk. Tom, I care for Buck very deeply. I owe him a lot, but I don't like being taken for granted. I don't want to be window-dressing for his deviations with other people." She was being frank with me when she didn't have to be, and I noticed her eyes tearing the way they had in Paris and on the lawn before breakfast yesterday. Her hand reached out for me again.

"Ellen," I said, "how do I come in?"

She looked at me without any pretense. "I think you know how." Then, without any warning, the revelation she had once mentioned fleetingly came at me again:

"Tom, when I was fourteen I was raped by my uncle. My reaction at the time was both disgust and excitement. He was very nice about it, and I sympathized with him, because his wife had left him, and he needed a woman. But he took my virginity—so casually. It scared me when I thought about it later. But then, I was pleased to be the vessel. In a way, that's how I've often felt about Buck—there's nothing particularly unusual about queer conduct."

"What!" I said, amazed. "Are you serious? That sort of thing isn't commonplace—not where I come from."

"And neither is it rare," she said. "So I accepted him, vowing never to let it happen again."

"And did it?"

"No. In fact, it was a long time before I slept with anyone." She smiled a sad smile. "Then I met Buck. I guess I had high hopes for him, a sexuality to match his intellectual gifts, his protective ways with me."

"And it was no good," I said.

"It was dreadful. I was frigid. I remembered how it was with my uncle. I think Buck's invitation for me to come to Europe with him was to try and make amends. It's the sort of thing he'd do, isn't it?"

"Yes. Very much so."

"And there was Bob Kemperman. God, it was all so sordid, yet I do care for his wellbeing, Tom. It's just…"

"Just what?"

"That I'm angry. That I don't know how to be a woman. That all my circuits have been crisscrossed and messed up by uncles and queer friends."

I reached out and touched her shoulder, trailing a fingernail across her skin. "Is that why we're here—old trusty Tom, counselor Tom, preacher Tom, solver of problems?"

She didn't fight me on it. "Yes, it's more than that. I care deeply for you, Tom. And it's not easy watching you with other women. Haven't you noticed?"

"Pam has, apparently."

"And she's watching us. But I want you here, anyway."

173

She began to rub her wet cheeks on my chest, then gently pushed me away. She motioned to Goodie down the beach from us, who sat at the water's edge gazing at the alps. She acknowledged Ellen's wave. "What do you think of her and Fred?"

"Just now I don't know, what with Joyce arriving the other day."

"Do you suppose Goodie knows Joyce is here?"

"She doesn't know yet, but she will. If I know Joyce, she's going to want a clear decision from Fred. Really clear."

She slumped on to the beach grass and looked at me probingly. "How well do you know any of them?" At this point, lying on her back, her breast close to me, she again reached toward me with demanding fingers, playing with the hair on my chest, twisting it until it hurt. "I mean," she went on, "are they important to you?"

"Ellen, everyone's important. To me? Variously. It depends."

She said in a whisper, "I want to know more about you."

"You're out of order, Ellen."

"I agree," she said, still playing with my hair. I grabbed her fidgeting hand to stop it. "I've been living with it too long." I watched Goodie walking up from the shoreline.

Ellen grinned at me. "Let's go for a swim. It'll cool us off and dampen our passions." She jumped lightly to her feet and pulled me up after her. We ran to the water.

If Goodie was a strong swimmer, Ellen was stronger. She struck out into the lake with a freestyle that made her fly over the water. Then she stopped and waved, beckoning me to join her farther out in the lake. I did, and as soon as I approached her, a bit winded for the effort, she grabbed my right arm and kissed me aggressively.

"You've been wanting to do this for a long time," she said. "I know you." At that she placed my arm around her and nuzzled me. Then I felt her hand inside my swimsuit. I looked at her a long time, as she caressed me, then pulled her to me. Our bodies were trembling against each other. She kept hold of me tenderly while I held her buttocks. She shuddered.

"Let's go into warmer water," I said.

"There's more to you, is there?" She giggled.

"When it's warm—I want you."

She kissed me. We swam side by side to the shore, stopping now and then to embrace and fondle each other. "Over there," she said, pointing. When we arrived, she forced herself deeper into the water beside me, and I felt my bathing trunks being removed.

I stripped her. "Bundle everything in my suit," she said, eyes sparkling in the sun.

We were close enough to shore so that our feet touched bottom, which made the lovemaking easier in the warmer water. "Tom, have you ever done it this way before?" Our hands were all over each other. I pinned her like a butterfly.

"You'll be the death of me," I said. "Slow it down." We held on to each other for a long time in a slow rhythm. Her legs encircled me while she writhed. We held on and moved until she cried out, arching her back, both of us gasping. We fell in the shallow water and I set her gently on my lap. Her hands wandered all over my back, and we kissed with a new trust. We were locked together like that for a long time. Then we uncoupled and struggled to the shore where we collapsed. Later we pulled on our swimsuits.

"What is that scar on your thigh? It's like a cross you've been branded with."

"It marks the time I got religion in the war," I said. "You might call it a forced conversion."

"Dear Thomas," she said. Then we were snoozing on the grass, holding hands all the time, as though someone might separate us. Her body pressed down on mine. If Goodie had seen us, she was circumspect when she came to awaken us. She was smiling. "Bless you two," she said softly. Then she said, "Pardon me, you lovers, but I'm going back up to Caux if you have enough Swiss francs to get me to Montreux on the train. I'm broke." She awaited our revival for a final swim. We then took a walk to where our beach things were lying, and we all went together.

In the funicula, Goodie sat in front of us during the ascent up the mountainside. At first Ellen and I held hands and smiled, confident in our new intimacy. That was the beginning of a great, secret dialogue with myself for the duration of the climb. The four women in my life were good to me—Irene, Pam, Joyce and Ellen. How had I become involved with them and why? Strangely enough, pride in conquests wasn't important, and I didn't feel especially proud of myself at the moment, having added Ellen to the string. Maybe I was easily persuaded. In many ways I was their victim, their tool and toy, their need for possession and domination. But also their touchstone, each seeing in me solace for their own needs. Whatever it was, it wasn't merely their active pursuit of pleasure, for I was their foil.

Ellen had planned it all. "I need to talk…we need to talk." Perhaps we did. As we held hands in the seat behind Goodie on the way up the mountain, it was clear that she needed more than talk. Playing stud once in a while wasn't normally a problem for me, but that afternoon in the funicula a sense of guilt overtook me. Ahead of us Goodie was immersed in herself. We of the Paris "bande" obviously needed more than we were getting. A deficiency in peace of mind could not to be solved by physical satisfactions of the moment. What greater peace of mind could I have than with these promiscuous women? None, really. Pamela was the real problem at hand. Now full of Ellen's affection, I was blinded to Pam by her cloying need for fulfillment that no one else could satisfy. Her breakdown in Paris frightened me. The last thing I wanted to do was hurt this sensitive woman who had opened herself to me in utter innocence.

I thought of poor Goodie—the opposite end of the axis. Fred was her problem. She wasn't accepting the prospect of losing him. Her investment of so much time and faith in their relationship was far more specific than mine with any of the four women with whom I was involved. Fred had invested much as well, but now he heard the inevitable siren song of Joyce.

The Street of Four Winds

Riding in that funicula, I felt magnanimously sympathetic to everyone, a true man of the cloth. I, Thomas Cortell, had claims on these women, these friends, these comrades—at a time when all of us were trying to sort things out, to evaluate ourselves and determine how we wanted to be. It was Hamlet's problem. As Betty Lowry once said in Paris, all of the members of "la bande" found themselves connected by common questions. In ten years or less we might never again see each other. We just happened to converge on postwar Paris, where so many had before us. Paris, the magnet of centuries. Like the war, the stage setting could never be shared with others who hadn't been there then.

Like Chartres. I found myself staring at Ellen's lovely face, the blonde hair cut across her blue eyes. "How important was this day?" She regarded me with passionate concern.

"Very."

"Any butterflies?"

"Only when you pinned me so deliciously." She looked out of the window like a princess observing her domain, freckled nose held high, eyebrows arched. "You gave me something I needed badly, Tom. Before, I felt worthless. Remember that. I needed to feel like a woman again,"

That morning scene on the staircase returned to me. Yes, Buck had deserted her in a basic way.

"You have more of me than you think," I said, squeezing her hand.

"Tom, you are such a romantic and you've always been generous. You make us feel like women."

"All things to all women. I thought I was selfish."

"No, not at all. And never change, please." She tugged at my hand. "Promise?"

"I'd promise almost anything to you."

"Don't flatter me, please. I'm like the poor little rich girl in Noel Coward's song. Just don't say anything to spoil this day for me—such as, for example, that you love me."

"I don't make it a habit to share orgasms with women I don't love."

She touched my cheek. "But, darling, it wasn't love. You've got Pam and Irene. Remember."

"Ellen, where does love fit into your priorities?"

She looked away to check her domain outside the car window. "I often wonder," she said at last. "I've been deceived the few times it ever happened. That's why, Tom, I'd rather you say nothing now. Just accept what we had as a sublime act of nature."

We looked at each other. But I wasn't sure I heard her words correctly. Ahead of us I noted Goodie again.

"I'll go sit with Goodie a while." Ellen smiled as I moved forward.

Goodie looked up in surprise. "To what do I owe this honor?" Pleasure spanned her oval face.

"I wanted you to know something," I said.

"And what is that?"

"In the first place, Fred is a fool. Secondly, do you know that Joyce is here?"

"What!" she exclaimed.

"I'm not proud to be the bearer of ill tidings."

"You're not serious, Tom. Not really serious."

"Serious as I can be. I'm concerned for both of you, too."

"Oh, my God," she said, as I patted her hands that lay clasped tightly in her lap.

"Can I help?" I asked. She was silent for a long time. The funicula climbed, and as it moved upward through the mountain forests I watched tears form in her eyes. She tried to wipe them away. "I want to help," I said.

"Tom, the priest, but it's not really your problem. It's mine. Fred's already attacked you physically—about what I don't know—but it's better for you to stay out of it. I think I'm leaving anyway. It's becoming impossible to live this way."

"He's a damned good poet, you know. You've been such an asset, a vital support for him."

"No longer. He's losing his touch, you know. His most recent work is weak. He's relied on all the World War I poets. If you look at his work fairly, you'll see how derivative it's become—Sassoon, Owen, Blunden, even Graves—not Fred Furness." Her comments were surprisingly astute and entirely unexpected. I hadn't given her any credit for being able to appreciate Fred's literary qualities. I had thought of her as a mere hanger-on—sitting around, twisting that false wedding ring. And Joyce had badly underestimated her. If anything, Goodie knew more about Fred's poetry than Joyce did.

"The early work was something else. It had a freshness that was exciting. It actually reflected a poet's bitter edge in direct reaction to war. But now it's not Fred any more, Tom. Unless he changes. If that freshness doesn't return, he'll never even end up in a decent anthology of mid-century poetry.

"Please stay out of it, Tom," she pleaded with me, bending toward me on the facing seat of the car until her lips gently touched my forehead. "I know you want peace, almost at any price, but…" Behind her I saw Ellen listening. Her expression didn't change as Goodie kissed me.

"We'll soon be there," I said as we passed Glion. Now what would happen? I wondered.

EIGHTEEN

She rediscovered her courage. Sadness did it. By the time we arrived at the chalet that afternoon, Goodie recovered enough to greet both Fred and Joyce, who had come up from Glion, with confidence. I watched her assess Joyce's figure, voluptuous and pale. It was amazing to see how well she had reestablished herself after the shock of learning about the British woman. Joyce was decisive as usual, but she understood the situation enough to avoid it.

"You all seem so serious about this conference," she said, "but I wonder about something. What makes you think you're so well qualified to be pronouncing judgment on this world?"

Buck rose to defend his turf: "My dear Joyce, we're not playing God here, but we are thoughtful people. Do you have anything to contradict that?" He was smiling all the way, and she smiled back, taking in the whole group with her dark, flashing eyes.

"Fred tells me you intend to come up with a document of sorts regarding the post-war world. But only a few of you went through the war at close range. And here you are, about to make enormous conclusions about a Europe you may not really understand. I say it's a bit presumptuous."

Betty Lowry perked up. "Joyce, darling, don't confuse discussions by thinking people with conclusions by idiots." Joyce was striding around the room with the obvious authority of what she thought was going to be a winning role. Lost in her own performance, the force of Betty's comment passed her by. Goodie merely sat there, somehow above it all.

"I second what Betty said," Buck said.

"Really? Well, I think you are all a gang of intellectuals who know no end of self-stimulation. And God love you for it, but I do suggest you might be overstepping yourselves. We've had jolly times together, but I don't want to see you run away with yourselves on this."

"It's comforting," Norman volunteered, "to know that we have a lady policeman with us."

Buck looked chagrined. His head was lowered like an injured bull taking an inventory of his options in the ring now that he had been assaulted by the picadors. He shook his dark head, his eyes staring here and there.

"Anyway, I hope you really don't take me too seriously," Joyce said lightly, the damage done. Pam's cheek was close to mine, and I took a peck at it. Ellen observed this with a Mona Lisa smile. In the meantime Buck motioned Ellen to join him outside.

They moved out into the darkness on the front lawn, while effusive conversation broke out in the chalet, a needed change from the tension that Joyce had created. Buck soon returned with a frown on his face. A few minutes later Ellen drifted in while Buck tapped his foot. He was definitely preoccupied with something, and I only hoped it had nothing to do with me. I put my arm around Pam's waist, nuzzled her and led her out on the lawn to see the stars. It was a dark night, the stars clustered heavily around the Milky Way that split the sky in half. Vega was high overhead, and when I pointed out the bright star to Pam, she hugged me close. I needed it just then and kissed her eyes.

"Not really relaxing in there tonight," she said.

"It's Buck."

"Buck's disturbed about something—probably Joyce."

"Maybe we ought to get back in there."

When we did Buck had restored his command of the gathering and suggested out of hand that we resume discussions in the morning.

"What's the subject?" someone called out.

"The Cold War between the US and USSR."

"Who'll lead?"

"I'll lead," Buck declared.

In the morning he took over as if nothing had happened the previous night. Bill Watson began it all when, after we had assembled out on the lawn in our outdoor classroom, he asked Norman Tunison how Rabelais would have reacted to the beautiful scene below us.

He beamed. "Bill, he once contemplated the future we all face and said he didn't know about the others, but that he personally was going 'to the great perhaps.' That should satisfy you skeptics."

"Be that as it may," Buck said, "the question before the house is: are we, the USA, pursuing the right policy by 'containing' the Soviet Union?"

"Fat chance," Fred said.

"But we've got to be cautious how we do it," Norman warned. "Our problem is the former colonial possessions of European countries—even our own in the Philippines. If our policy is based on a confusion of coping with truly national movements—like the Indo-Chinese breaking loose from France—confusing that with fear of the communist agitations in these new countries, we're going to have serious problems."

"We'll surely confuse things," Bob Kemperman said. "We've always confused that issue."

"Independence is the point," Sally Satterwaite said, "Not Communism."

"You're a slogan-maker," I said to her. "You should be in public relations."

"Is that a compliment or insult?" she asked.

"Sally, you know I never antagonize women," I smiled.

"That's his foreign policy," Pam said.

"Just as long as he can get away with it!" Faith Carlson threw in.

I put up a hand in protest. "How long is my notoriety going to delay proceeding with the discussion at hand?"

"Just as long as you mask your real motives," Buck said, keeping me on the griddle.

"Can we eliminate this nonsense in the official minutes?"

Betty Lowry sympathized with me. "Can't we keep the focus on one issue?" Buck took her obvious hint and started in on the east bloc countries bordering the Soviet Union.

Just then someone shouted my name and said there was a telephone call for me. I went to the kitchen.

"C'est moi," Irene's distinctive voice leaped out from the receiver. "This is a warning, chéri."

"About what, my love?"

"Stop that," she objected. "One of your women called a few days ago and was desperate to speak to you…someone called Belinda from Espagne. It sounds serious—she's in trouble, and like all your women, needs your many attentions…"

"Very funny. I love you."

"Je suis sérieux. I gave her your address…"

"Why not this number?"

"I was upset," Irene said.

"That's the trouble with Slavic women. Did she leave a number?"

"I am not your secretary. Besides, you have not called me once since you went away. And I have met a new man."

"That's why you called—to tell me that!"

"She is writing you a letter in Switzerland. That's what I tell you, Monsieur Méchant!"

"I miss you,"

"Horsefeathers!"

"I do. I miss your pommettes."

She hung up. A bit stunned, I returned to the conference, which occupied us for the rest of the day. That afternoon the letter Irene had referred to was delivered at the Caux post office. I left the conference to go pick it up and saw that it was marked "Urgent." I tore it open.

"I am about to get into a lot of trouble," Belinda began and went on to tell a long story of love and danger for her personally in Madrid. She had met a young Spaniard, a kindred anti-Franco youth who had squired her and her girlfriend around the city. After awhile, she had fallen in love with him and participated in smuggling activities for the cause. The young man, she said, had been apprehended by the police at one point and was still in jail…where, she did not know. All she did know was that the police had been following her for several days, and she was worried.

The letter ended by pleading with me to come to Pamplona where she had a mission to perform for the anti-Franco group. Since it was the end of the bull-fighting season, she was certain it would be safe for her in that city. The police would be preoccupied with the famous San Fermin Festival where they ran the bulls in the streets. The time was "ripe," she said, for me to help her. She assumed that my presence as an American journalist would be useful. She also assured me that the Pamplona police were more pliable than other authorities in the country. She seemed to have it all figured out. "Please come, Tom, I desperately need your help!"

I recalled her parents' original request in Paris for me to chaperone her and her friend for this very reason—and my refusal. I remembered her mother's matronly bosom at the cocktail table, the brooch she fingered like a talisman. Now, once more, old trusty Tom was being pressed into service for the cause. I didn't see that I had much choice in the matter now. But I would have to figure out how I could withdraw from the conference gracefully.

Meanwhile, Buck had called off the next day's proceedings. He had substituted a touristy event which seemed out of keeping with the seminar, but it was clear he was upset about something and figured the group needed a bit of diversion. He himself appeared to have some matter in mind that involved Ellen, and my hope was that it had nothing to do with me. As things had turned out, I was highly focused on Ellen and even considered that Spain could possibly be a kind of "out" in terms of my relationship with Pam. She had stared at me when I left for the post office, and she would grill me on the letter. As for Irene, she was already unhappy with me for having "abandoned" her, as she put it. I wondered about the new man she mentioned. Bluff or not?

What Buck had in mind was a trip that would put us all on the funicula up-mountain from Caux and deliver us to the high point on our side of Lac Leman, the Rochers de Naye. This was supposedly the great view above Montreux. So after lunch I made sure I had on warm clothes when we all walked through the dark forest between the chalet and Caux. Then we all were aboard the train and rising to heaven.

As much as I was preoccupied with the sudden trip to Spain, I couldn't escape the new Swiss scenery Buck had put before us. No one could avoid it, not even the Swiss themselves. The view was sensational. As we climbed in the funicula, the blue car gave us a new, wider world, the very thing we had come to Switzerland to see and appreciate. Off to the southwest was the famous mountain we could not quite make out—Mount Blanc over the French border—and directly across the lake to the south were the massive Savoian Alps. To the west and now below us was the Dent de Jaman, a gothic tooth jutting up out of our mountain's lower jaw, and there in the distance far down on the lake were Ouchy and Lausanne.

Sally Satterwaite sat across from me on the aisle next to Faith Carlson. She leaned toward me and asked, "Is Buck's conference dead in the water now?"

"Who knows? Seems like Joyce threw in the monkey wrench…"

"That's a crime, in a way, because I wanted to make a point today. Now there's no audience to react to my big thought."

"What's that?" She was an enthusiastic, good-looking, optimistic girl; she had shown her spirit in Paris when Pam had been so out of it. Like so many Mid-westerners I had known, she was direct and friendly.

"Well, it's simply this," she said. "The world we're entering may never again have to go through what we just did—another world war. I believe that business interests will become so international in this new world, so global for most industrial companies, that they won't tolerate the dislocations caused by world war. Madmen like Hitler will never again have the opportunity to upset the flow of goods and services the way he did from the 1930s on. That seems so logical. I know it sounds like pure economics and doesn't take into account many other factors, but what business wants it usually gets. World markets are the key to the future."

I looked at her profile against the afternoon sun. There was some elusive element in her open face that reminded me of Ellen. Only her gaze lacked the excitement conveyed by Ellen's desperately blue and expectant eyes. And there was also her flat chest. Sally's words were special, however, and I found her idea startling, intelligent and worthy of attention. I had never heard anything as interesting about the subject before.

"Sally, that's a great idea. Joyce did us a disservice by questioning our credentials." She smiled back at me, and as she did, I had a wild thought. Here was a graduate of one of America's better schools—cream of the crop—a woman exposed to a superior education, coming up with an idea worth more than most, an honest reaction to her world. What lay ahead of her? What was going to become of her when she returned to Minneapolis? The answer was obvious. She'd get a job as a secretary. Maybe she'd be lucky and marry someone interesting. And maybe not. Here was a whole generation of bright women who'd have to claw their way to as close to the top as they could get, being women—or, worse, screw their way up because no man would be willing to accept their intelligence on its own merits.

That was the way it had always been, and it wasn't going to change. An odd thought for a woman-chaser like myself.

But I was wrong there, too, because Faith, overhearing Sally's words, came up with another pregnant thought:

"We postwar women will get beyond our traditional roles of helpmates. As a result, marriage as an institution is going to change. It might even become unnecessary. Rosie-the-riveter gets a decent paycheck now, and the man might well lose his financial authority in marriage, which will change things a lot. Two incomes will be the rule. And so will smaller families. Maybe marriage itself will lose its allure as a way to security for women. None of this is hard to imagine, and it comes directly out of the war. End of speech."

"And a good one," I said, "maybe two of the better thoughts to be aired at our conference." That was where Buck was right. He had faith in the idea of bright people expressing themselves.

In front of Faith sat Goodie. Far ahead in the car Fred and Joyce chatted animatedly, and that had to bother her, sitting there sad and alone. When love ends it ends more than your emotional security. The illusion of caring for someone else leaves you with jagged shards of glass in your hands. I knew it well when I left New York, and the girl in my life went on to other conquests. Now Goodie was going through the same misery.

I noticed Pam beside me, staring straight ahead, silent.

As the funicula swept up the steep mountain, I recalled how, with me, it began before the war at Cornell. She was tall, lively and exciting to be with. She attended architectural school and when we planned our times in bed together it was with the same meticulous attention to all of the architectural specifications of pleasure that went into her school drawings. We began just as I entered the Army enlisted reserve corps, and when Pearl Harbor happened, and my unit was called up, we were devastated. But after the war we resumed the passionate relationship with even greater intensity while I was at Columbia working on my graduate degree. It was only after she broke it off, after weeks of recriminations, that I knew I had to get away. It was like pulp fiction, the first time in my life that had been notably full of such emotion.

I thought that by putting space between us—the Atlantic Ocean in this case—I would be able to forget her. But I was wrong. Even Europe's women couldn't erase the personal loss. It wasn't until I met Irene and her saucy, fresh dark face in my hotel on the rue des Quatre Vents, that I began to feel free of the damage. The street of the four winds brought refreshing breezes into my life…four, three, two, even one breeze was enough to soothe the hurt. And that was only the beginning. Then Pamela

187

and Joyce came along. Still, I hadn't learned really to care about people, not deeply. Which is why "tough Tom" was merely an illusion, softened a bit by the other illusion, "chaplain Tom." And it all stemmed from the damage in New York. The pleasure of women solved nothing. Pam had come along, and now I was on another threshhold with Ellen.

High in Switzerland, in paradise, and watching Norman and Betty sitting side by side in the funicula, I realized how fortunate they were. They shared so much that's essential to any strong relationship. It was a matter of proximity and comfort in all things. Like lovers still in the surprise of each other's affections— and the joint pursuit of academic truth buried deep in the Rabelais project. When they were in the Paris University library no one from our group failed to note the happiness they shared. The more they became immersed in their work, the closer they became. It was great to see. Now before me were Joyce and Fred, infatuated —and Goodie, suffering. And Pam, wondering—and fearless Tom Cortell, wondering about Ellen.

※

Life was unpredictable, and probably because of that I had developed a great habit and capability for getting out of tight situations. This time I didn't have to engineer my escape—it came right on schedule and entirely of itself: Belinda's letter. That had a certain benefit to me, for, in contrast to the other women in my life, where a commitment was involved, here was a girl to whom I had no real attachment. Diplomacy was called for, and I found the ride up to the Rochers de Naye a fine opportunity to do a bit of planning.

The only real worry I had was how to avoid letting Pamela down too quickly. She had nursed me back to health after Fred had knocked the tar out of me, and she was making plans for us. Not in jest she had told me already that she considered the trip to Switzerland together a kind of honeymoon for us. Therefore, to help her along with that illusion without risking a recurrence of her mental breakdown in Paris, I would pull her aside when the funicula arrived at the top and break the news that I had decided to depart for Spain as soon as possible to do what I could to protect Belinda. It was my obligation, and she would have to understand.

Almost at the same moment I hatched this devious plot, the funicula came to a gentle halt at the highest point on our side of the lake. We filed out with other visitors and walked to a spot where the view was best. It had been marked off by the tourist people. Since we arrived first, there was ample time for me to make my case and solicit Pam's opinion, which was an important part of my strategy to get away scot-free.

"You must go?" she asked when I broke the news.

"Do I really have any choice? You remember my reaction to her parents' proposition. If I had taken them up on the offer, you and I wouldn't have had this trip at all." She could see the logic of it. "Look what we've been able to learn about each other here. And the place itself has been marvelous…"

"I don't feel any closer to you here than I did in Paris, darling. I'm fine wherever we are. It has been wonderful. Besides, if you have this obligation, you know that I can't and don't want to make a big issue of it." She smiled. "I know we'll carry on in Paris when you return. But promise you'll come back as soon as possible."

"I do promise," I said. That was the least I could do. And that seemed to do it, until she suddenly looked away. "Sure, I've lost the only playboy of the western world," she said, echoing the sad lament of Pegeen in Synge's play. We drew near to the magnificent overlook, each of us amazed at the mountains rolling off in splendor to the distant horizon. We held hands, and I watched her soft eyes behind the large glasses. They were tearing.

Just beyond her Ellen stood stiffly by Buck, a wall of indifference between them. Buck was chewing at his nails. Ellen's intensely blue eyes probed the marvelous view. She seemed to be seeking something in the yawning distance, some response from the ends of the earth. I remembered her next to me on the beach at Vevey, and I swallowed hard at the memory. Why did love create these problems?

Then it happened. Buck was gone. He had been next to Ellen, while my imagination had run hot, and now he had vanished. We lurched forward to a point of land where the mountain fell away. There was no guard railing. And he had disappeared. Then we heard his high-pitched scream, a desperate cry for help, coming from below. I inched to the very edge as far as I dared. There, some thirty feet below on a ledge jutting out over the mountain's sheer plunge of hundreds of feet, I saw him flat on his back. He wasn't moving except for a flailing arm. Next to me Fred and Joyce sucked in their breath. Pam, Sally and Faith looked blank, and I heard Norman Tunison's frantic "Jee-sus Christ! How are we going to get him up?"

I spied a worn, narrow path that seemed a safe way to approach him. It snaked down the side of the dropoff. I started down. Trying not to look beyond Buck in fear of the acrophobia that plagued me, I moved towards him. While everyone in the group shouted warnings to me and I worried about my footing step by step, I groped my way out on the ledge. He had passed out, probably from the shock and pain from his fall. Now he was within reach. I tried to revive him, without much immediate success.

I felt something strike my back, and then heard Norman's voice yelling, "Here's some water!" He had lowered a plastic bottle by rope. I splashed the water on Buck's pale face. In a few moments he blinked and mumbled about losing his footing—"I think."

"Are you okay?" I asked.

"No!" he grunted. "My sides hurt like hell!"

"I know how that goes. Where else?"

"Something with my leg." When I touched his left leg near the knee, he groaned. A swelling was visible on the calf of his leg. While I did what I could, there was some commotion above—and shouted questions. Luckily, Fred Furness and Bill Watson had already gone to the funicula station for help. In no time a stretcher was brought by three Swiss bearers. After some sweating and cursing on the descent down to us, they put Buck aboard the litter. Then all of us were climbing back up. Buck Birnbaum was carried along the heights toward the funicula station. The entire group scrambled to keep up with the litter, talking all the time. Buck was unconscious again.

"I simply can't believe it," Betty was saying to Norman.

"Couldn't be more untimely," Bill Watson said.

"I had the feeling," Sally Satterwaite began, "we were really beginning to warm up…"

"That's true," Fred said, "and for the first time I was thinking that the whole project was worth while."

"Still, how did it happen?"

"It was bad luck," Norman said."One of those things."

"I'm not so sure," Bill Watson said. "It was too coincidental…"

I was watching the group from inside the cablecar at the station when I noticed Ellen off by herself at the far end of the platform. Her shoulders drooped as she watched. When the blue car moved away, a smirk formed on her lovely face. Then Buck, the Swiss attendants and I began the downhill run to Montreux.

Buck had suffered a complex leg fracture and badly bruised ribs. The medical people in Montreux assured me that a relatively short healing period was all that would be required. He'd need a cane for support after the cast was removed. They were very solicitous at the hospital and competent, for in no time at all they had set the leg and put him in a lightweight cast. Mountains and broken bones seem to go together in Switzerland, and the Swiss know how to cope with both.

I stayed with him in his private room as the day came to an end. He dozed on and off, and I was bored to death. I kept thinking about Ellen's smirk. He lay there, looking awful. He was in pain and was sweating as he lay on the bed. Every once in a while he rolled his eyes toward me with a look of distrust and anger. Once, almost casually, he said, "Somebody pushed me, you know. I remember distinctly. Oh damn, it hurts!"

"Who the devil would have done that?" I asked. "And why?"

"Maybe I know who and why," he growled in his odd voice. "Tom, what the hell's going on between you and Ellen? We've been good friends in the past. Today, I'm not so sure."

"Sure of what?"

"Come on, Tom, for Christ's sake. This afternoon she said that you were a 'generous' man. That's a weird statement. So I asked her what she meant, and she was kind of angry at the question… Hell, this leg hurts now, really hurts! Cortell, it was more than obvious what she meant." His eyes found mine. "I think it's damned ungrateful of you, Tom. Damned ungrateful."

I sat staring out of the hospital window. Far out in the lake, the day was beginning to fade. The haze was lifting and being replaced with growing shadows. A boat was on its way to a port—probably Evian in France—and gloom was gathering it in. The world of darkness was on the way. So was mine.

"Look here," I said, "I don't know what you're talking about."

"You know damned well what I'm talking about. Something's happened between you two." "Yes, it has. I've learned to understand her…"

"What the hell does that mean?"

"She's missing something and feels mistreated."

"What kind of mistreatment?" he demanded. "Not by me!"

"You have no idea?" I stared at him and hoped he would change the subject. He asked me for a cigarette, and when I lit it for him the flickering light of the match highlighted a defensive, helpless look on his face.

"No, I don't know, damn it! I don't know anything any more."

"Look here, Buck," I said. "You're still in shock, you're confused, and you're angry. It's not the time for stuff like this. And it's not for me to criticize you when you're flat on your back."

But he wouldn't be pacified. He kept after me. "Shit, Tom! Did you screw her or not? Just tell me." I really resented him now but refused to respond in kind.

"I'm getting sick of his, old man. If you want to know the truth, I'm actually more concerned that your great plan is going down the drain. It was a good idea, really—impractical but noble, and an injury like this is a rotten way to end things…"

"You're not telling me what I want to know." he insisted.

"I realize that, Buck. I'm leaving now."

"Why?" he demanded angrily. "To screw her?"

"Because I've got some rotten problems of my own and some obligations. I have to leave tomorrow for Spain. You know that. Do you think it's easy explaining all of this to Pam?"

"That's of your own making," he said. "What I'm talking about is more to the point. All right, be close-mouthed Just drop your bomb and go on to another target in Spain or somewhere else. The trouble with you, Cortell, is you don't want to face the music. Go ahead. Make your escape! Screw my girl and take off!"

"The only trouble with that remark, Birnbaum, is she isn't your girl. She never was. And in case you want to know, she sure as hell isn't mine. She simply wants to be treated like a woman. That may be a tall order for you—and that's all I'm going to say. Goodnight!" With great guilt and pointed anger I walked out of his room.

As it turned out, that was the end of Buck Birnbaum's grand conference on the fate of our post-war world. In a bar near the funicula station, I thought about how Buck would react when he recovered and got his bearings. There was little time for me to worry about it, for in the bar I was accosted by an attractive young woman who began to proposition me.

"My name is Anna," she said.

"Are we interested in similar things?"

"That might very well be possible," I said, looking her over, her slim legs and perfect breasts.

"That didn't take very long, monsieur." Her smile almost seemed sincere.

"They call me Hugo. I'm a great one for good rapid understandings." I offered her a cigarette, which she readily accepted.

"So am I."

"But we have to establish certain things, don't we?"

"That is most important. The Swiss franc is a solid currency."

"Yes, indeed," I said. "But I do have my limits. This was an impromptu trip."

She raised one brow and asked me to name a price. I did, and the reaction was somewhat negative. "You have nice blue eyes," was all she said.

"Yours are green, I believe"

"Very green."

Her English was good, her tone and accent devastating. She had a deep, somewhat hoarse Germanic voice that reminded me of Dietrich in the films

"You mentioned the Swiss franc and its value," I said.

"But of course. Then there is the matter of location, which I am quite happy to provide."

We arrived at a price at the same time I realized I could not keep my hands off her. In an hour we completed the transaction and I was on my way up the mountain, sated. As I arose in the car, I lolled in the pleasure of her and thought, self-accusingly, what a bastard I was. Another score for Tom. But I was purged of the displeasure encountered in the hospital with Tom—and could think of Pam and Ellen without remorse.

When I arrived at Caux and walked through the woods to the chalet I stopped once when I glimpsed through a gap in the trees the grand view of blinking lights of Montreux below and the lake beyond. "Cochon!" I muttered accusingly to myself. But she had met my need, a business transaction to underwrite my fears. Then I walked on to the chalet, whose lights beckoned me forward.

When I pushed the front door open, they were drinking and talking. I gave my report, informing them that in the morning we could probably pick Buck up at the hospital. We would call to see. Pam came up to me after this, but kissed me tentatively. She was cool.

Later when we were alone in a corner of the room she asked, "Do you really have to go?"

"What choice do I have? Belinda is in trouble, and it's the least I can do, if only for her parents."

"But why? I need you, too."

"Look, I know that. But you remember what I told you about her mother in Paris?"

"Tom, you could have agreed to be the chaperone in Paris. You didn't. You came here with me. We wouldn't have had this"—her hand swept wide—"if you had. And now you're going back on it."

"You came first then. You knew that. Besides, this conference was a hell of a great idea, even though Buck kind of defeated it in his own way. For us it was a treat," I was reaching for reasons. I tried to pull her close, but she resisted. "Oh, come on, Pammy, do you think it's easy for me? It's a duty…"

"Life is duty," she said testily.

Norman Tunison and Betty were sitting nearby and overheard Pam's remark. "This sounds so serious," Norman said with a smile. Betty had an inquiring look.

"It is," Pam said. Norman said he was sorry for interrupting.

"Nothing to regret," she responded, returning Betty's frown, her glasses flashing in the light.

"Thomas is just reacting to his obligations—real or perceived."

"With friends like you, who needs…" I began.

"Enemas," Norman said. "You know, you and Buck are so much alike in your stubbornness. In a way, the only concrete result of this conference is pain."

"You think it a total waste, then," I said.

"Nothing's ever total, but this is ironical. Modern man unable to avoid combat. Men versus men and women," Norman continued. "Look here, chum, I'm just as guilty as you. The two of you, however, are symbols of our time, both intellectual disasters!"

Pam laughed.

Pam was far too passionate for me that night. My interlude in Montreux had taken its toll, but she was persistent. I did my best to keep up with her, but she was so intense in her movements that I gave up. There was something desperate about her lovemaking, as if she had no control of her desires.

As if, indeed, there were no tomorrow.

"I do love you, you know," she said as we finally fell asleep.

The next morning it was evident that many things had changed. When Pam and I picked up Buck at the hospital and purchased my rail tickets to Spain, he readily admitted that the conference was in trouble. As he hobbled along on his crutches, he made it clear how disappointed he was. Once we left him in the car for awhile, picked up some groceries and grabbed a quick drink at the Kursaal.

"You know it wasn't entirely an accident on the mountain yesterday," Pam said.

"You're kidding."

"No, not at all. Ellen did it. I saw her prod him during an argument. He lost his balance and slipped. Whether she alone caused it or not, I can't say. I noticed the angry look on her face, as if she didn't care. Something was bothering her. Whatever, she did absolutely nothing to stop his fall."

"Unfortunate," was all I could say.

◉◉

That night brought me no sleep, tired as I was. Life was becoming too complicated. Sometime after midnight when Pam was finished with me I left her in bed and went downstairs to get a drink. I poured it in the kitchen. While imbibing, I heard a noise in the parlor, and there I found Faith Carlson, also sleepless.

"Hi," she said. "You, too?"

"Hard to avoid. Can I get you a drink?"

"Fine," she said, "and then let's go outside. I want to talk to you. You don't mind, do you?"

For a moment she sounded like Ellen, and I wasn't so sure. We settled down with the drinks on the front lawn chairs.

"Christ, what a relief," I said, watching the twinkling lights down on the lakeside. Above, the quarter moon dragged through the black sky.

"Wouldn't it be great to find out what went wrong here," she said.

"What do you mean? Everything's fine, Faith. During the war we said: 'situation normal—all fucked up.'"

"It is a snafu, all right," she said.

"In this case, it's the people, not the situation." Moments passed by until I went on. "Why did you three ever come back here after graduation?"

"Suckers for punishment, I guess. But Pam found you. That was something. At least she got you anyway."

"A bad discovery—really bad."

"She's completely devoted to you."

"I'm not comfortable with that. She's too fragile." We both lit up and stared straight ahead.

"What about you? Find anything—anyone?"

"Not much, but at least I'm consistent." She laughed self-consciously. "Some things you have no right to know,"

"God, Pam's fragile," I said.

"And you're not." I turned to her.

"I'm a tough sonofabitch," I laughed, equally self-conscious. "I'm not devoted to anyone. I was once, and it hurt me." I thought of the girl from Cornell who dumped me—and the Swiss hooker I had just met and enjoyed in Montreux. The first hurt, not the second. "I'm not devoted to anyone."

"You must be insecure. Do you trust others?"

That was a hard question. "I could trust you," I said, because it was a way of avoiding her.

"That's because you're not passionate about me. But, with your record, you might be. As things are, I can't damage you or your ego. You have been hurt, Tom. I can sense it about you."

"How can you tell?"

"You're transparent, Tom. Your language covers you too neatly."

I looked at her in the same way she was appraising me. The dim light from the chalet hallway was on her plain face. It was honest and cool. I wondered why she had known all along that I had been hurt. "You are correct. I have been hurt. Never again."

"Perhaps you're now hurting others—people like Pamela, which you are. You'd be kinder, if you hadn't been hurt. Kinder to Pam in her dilemma."

Again, there was a long stretch of silence as I tried to pin down when I had been damaged the most. The hell with it; I would tell her. I trusted her in this conversation. "Maybe once when my parents left me alone in our big house—but our maid, Dorothy, took good care of me. Or later, at college, a girl at Cornell before the war and afterwards at Columbia and how she tossed me after she took my heart and soul. That did hurt. I had assumed a perfect world with people being very considerate of one another…"

"Like you aren't considerate of Pam."

"She's too fragile, as I said."

"And you can't be a man about it. You got her to bed, and you chucked her like an old ear of corn. One of your problems is you've got too many women."

At that moment I tried to grasp her hand, and she said, "What's this?"

"You're trying to help me. I hear it, Faith. Can't I hold your hand?"

"Yes, if you want. But I'm as tough as you say you are—which you aren't."

She dropped her head on her breast and took a deep breath. To test that toughness I put an arm around her. She responded, looking up at me. "God, I'm glad I've got some self-control at this moment. Darn it, Tom, I've never been in love. And I shouldn't tell you…"

"Never been mad about a boy? Even in Geneva?"

"Just once for a short time, but he was weak. I wanted to fly away with him. But he wasn't up to it, like Pam's friend. That killed it for me. The same for her." She seemed close to me at that moment, but distant in a way.

"Well, why not make up for it now that Geneva's in the past?"

"I suppose I could, but I think of Pam and you…how she's so keen on you…and not happy, like I would be."

"That doesn't make me feel great, as I said."

"That's unfortunate. You know, I still suspect you've been hurt," she said. There was a pause, and I wondered. Then she pushed me away gently and inspected me.

"You're thinking about it," she said. "I can see it."

"You're trying to reform me."

"Not really. But she's so delicate, Tom. Whatever you do, don't hurt her."

I said I'd try and put my arm around her again. She stiffened and looked directly at me, her face open and trusting. She held both her hands together, as if to contain them. She was nervous.

"Don't worry about me, Faith," I said. "I'm merely expressing friendship by this." I gripped her hard. "I'm really listening to you. I am. I understand how you feel." Trying to be just as cool as she looked, I held on to her and turned her face up to mine and kissed her lightly on the cheek. "I wish I had as good a friend as you are to Pam. I have no friends like that, Faith." She dropped her head on my chest and took a deep breath.

"You have your women," she said coyly.

"I miss having friends, though," I said. We both got up and stood gazing at the dark lake.

Then she looked at me while I held her arms, facing her. "Are you going to be nice to Pam? Are you going to avoid hurting her? I've watched you with Ellen. There's something there. A secret."

"Oh, Christ, Faith! Are we so transparent?"

"Yes, when you're infatuated—and you are with each other. Pam has to see it."

"Oh. How could you see it?"

"I'm as messed up as you, Tom, but I can tell," she said. "You two look at each other with love."

"So, to summarize," I said in Buck's manner. "Your analysis is that I've been hurt, that I need to be kind to Pam, and that I'm a softie."

"More or less—mostly less…"

"Less women, you mean, for me."

"Right—also more understanding."

It was a strange conversation, and we could both see the sky lightening in the east. The day was coming. And I didn't like it one bit. She stood there before me, her hands on my arms, holding hard. I said thanks, and we returned to our respective rooms. Again, I couldn't sleep.

∽∾

Pam was half awake. "Tom, where have you been?"

"Out on the lawn. I couldn't sleep." She focused on me with her wonderful eyes.

"Oh," she said. She reached up and put her arms around my neck. Then she dropped off. While she slept peacefully, I thought of Buck, how he must be fretting down at the hospital, and thinking about me with anger. He probably still refused to admit that he had let Ellen down. It was a mess. I couldn't wait to get on my way to Spain and escape.

Still unable to sleep, kissing Pam's shoulder from time to time, I tried to think about everything that had happened in the last twenty-four hours: Ellen, Buck, the fall, the damage, the argument with Buck in the hospital and his unwillingness to see things my way. Finally, the weird conversation with Faith and how she had probed some of my deeper problems. I needed space to digest all of it. Listening to the silence of the early morning there on the mountainside, I drifted away, imagining Spain and what might happen during my mission to rescue Belinda Vorst. Then the rest all seemed so sad—Buck's conference coming to an end, his intellectual pretensions stripped away and his own twisted personal life and pursuits laid bare—Buck and Ellen, Buck and Kemperman. It was bewildering. With the exception of Norman and Betty, Sally and Faith, they were all screwed up. And I was as unstable as any of them. Faith had said that in one way or another. Impossible questions wafted. Was it only the war that affected Fred and myself? We were always escaping, and from what we never knew. Perhaps Faith had touched on it when she talked about my "hurt." At least Fred had his poetry and his unique ability to capture in a phrase or line the fear and redemption and the awareness and joy of being alive. And what did I have?—a stable of women sapping me of energy Fred had, and leaving not much else.

It would be a relief to be free of them in Spain. I would solve all of my problems just by running away. Or so I thought.

NINTEEN

In the morning we picked up Buck Birnbaum at the hospital. He wore a cast on one leg, using crutches to move about. In sharp contrast to the previous afternoon, he seemed cheerful and joked with us.

"Some expedition," he said. "Some group leader, too." At least he had the good grace to poke fun at himself.

"We never knew you could do such a beautiful swan dive," Goodie said.

"Well, I've been too close to the edge of late."

"And that time you went off."

"Shows to go you," Norman said.

"Look, I'm going to be out of action for a while. We'll really have to reexamine the conference now. With Tom going away like a white knight to the land of Navarre, it'll give me time to rethink the whole thing. Maybe we can even carry on back in Paris."

"It's a damned shame," Joyce piped up. "And I was just getting to appreciate your collective pretentious mentalities."

I noticed Goodie watching her with an ugly look. I pinched her buttocks.

"Oh, Tom, I didn't think you cared!" she said with a smile.

"He always cares if a woman's involved," Pam said.

"Well," Buck said, "I'm glad to see your spirits are up, if it's only to buck up old Bucko. I appreciate it. You are a loyal band."

Ellen kept silent. The sky began to darken, and after I drove Pam, Buck and Ellen up the mountain to Caux, Buck made his generous gesture. He told me that he was giving the car to Pam to drive me around the lake to Geneva to catch the train to Spain.

When I shook hands with him, his hospital anger had diminished.

"Take care in Spain, Tom," he said. "Watch yourself." He hesitated. "I've thought things over, and we'll have to talk about everything when you get back to Paris. I'm going to close up shop here as soon as I can get around. It'll be a welcome time to think about all of us and the future."

"Okay."

"And, Tom," he said, checking out Ellen on the front lawn, "I'm not satisfied with everything at all. Just wanted you to know."

"Mind what I said last night," I said. "I hope you don't harbor any mindless grudges. But I meant what I said."

"So we'll talk."

"If you want." He began to bite his nails.

"I'm not a gentleman when it comes to some things. Remember that, Tom."

"I'll say this…"

"What's that, old man?"

"Regardless of our problems with each other, Buck, I did want to say how much I appreciate what you've done here at Caux. It was only a beginning, but it was worthwhile. And it was a privilege to be asked. Just wanted to let you know that." He waved me off with a half-smile. I wondered what would happen when just the two of them, Ellen and Buck, were alone in Caux. As I got into the car, Ellen gave me a searching look. When I returned it, she ran up impulsively and kissed me. Then Pam and I drove down the mountain, around the lake, and to the Cornavin railway station in Geneva. She joined me in the underpass, and as I scooted up the stairs to the platform, I waved to her. She was in tears. I felt rotten.

Once aboard the train and rolling, I felt great relief. Life would renew itself for me with a clean slate. It was always that way at the beginning of a long journey. The clean slate was vital;

it purged me of my cares, at least for a while, and then the ghosts would return. I called them my Furies, the Furies that haunted everyone once in a while. They lurked, always threatening…

The train rolled on smoothly into the Savoian uplands at the French border. Then we swept into Roman France, where the legions of the Empire had moved into Cis-Alpine territory and set up colonies two thousand years ago. I was sensitive to that history, especially now when I wanted to take my mind off my current malaise. It was another form of escape. Then we stopped at Lyon, where the Saône and mighty Rhône River met under the Roman ruins along the shore. Before long we would be at Avignon, spinning along under the Papal Palace, there, and then over the river towards Nîmes, Montpellier and Béziers. They were all places I had visited, places that, like Chartres, put me in another world— the past that had always fascinated me and taken me away from the confusions of the present.

It began to rain at Lyon, and it depressed me. In fair weather, this was one of the great train rides in Europe, and I had taken it to get to the roots of my stories. Across the compartment from me was a young French-Swiss woman chatting with her father. She eyed me from time to time. I knew they were Swiss when I heard her talk about "septante hectares," using the counting system of French spoken in Switzerland. It was a key to the difference between it and the language of France. It was one of those unimportant variations that made Europe so different from America. The thought took me away from Pamela and Ellen, Buck and the rest of them.

I spoke with them in French. It helped me escape from the Furies. We talked about the U.S. presidential election—Dewey versus Truman—and the possible consequences for Europe. They seemed well informed, but were sure that Dewey would win. We agreed up to a point, but there was something about Truman's tenacity that made me think he might appeal to something deep in America. I mentioned it to them, and it attracted their interest.

"What do you do?" the old man asked in French, and I told them.

"Ah, journalist. C'est important, un métier très important," she said.

"Merci," I said, and we talked about that for awhile. But I was tired and every once in a while tried to shut my eyes. They noticed my fatigue, commented on it, and politely looked away from me to carry on their family discussion. The energy expended the previous night with the cocotte in Montreux, Faith on the lawn and back in bed with Pam, who always took a lot out of me, had to be replenished. But fragmentary dreams intruded, the wings of the Furies beating. And memories of childhood, triggered by what Faith had artfully extracted from me, rushed in…

In many ways we were an "old" American family. My sister Martha and I were brought up to believe that the land was ours by inheritance. We were the ones, with a background and sense of the continent's past back as far as the Louisiana Purchase—not terribly old but old enough. We had the substance, the endurance, the comforting sense of continuity—all of which gave us a proprietary feeling about America and our place in it. However, behind our WASPy prejudices, we really weren't so damned hot, after all.

Faith had said last night: "I know you've been hurt sometime." Yes, there were two things, and now one of them welled up from the days of my adolescence in our home along the Hudson River…

I was scared to death and blaming my parents for it. Very tense and frightened and alone, I remember sitting in our large colonial house one particular night, a loaded rifle across my knees. Father gave it to me before he and mother left the house, separately. I was twelve years old and scared beyond belief, every muscle and tendon in my body tight as a guitar string and poised, like a cat, for action from any unexpected quarter. The house was empty, and I had switched on every light on all three floors; when I walked around it once—just once—the familiar rooms were somehow hostile and full of ghosts. It was a weird feeling in a terrible brightness as brilliant as Times Square down in New York City.

Not only were my parents out. Even our pert and sexy maid, Dorothy, was away on her weekly night off. She was my confidante and I was constantly amazed at the way her lively breasts bounced around under her blouse. Once she caught me staring at them and shook a warning finger at me.

That night my sister Martha had been billeted to sleep at a friend's house in the neighborhood. We had talked frequently about mother and father, who apparently had a "mistress," a word that I had little understanding of at that age. Martha seemed clued in on those things; however, it was clear mother and father were having serious problems, usually surfacing around the dining room table at the evening meal when there were verbal potshots. I remember coming home early from school one day and finding mother in the arms of some man I had never seen before, an "old friend," she said.

Now I was alone, twelve years old, fearful, and guarding the big house in Cold Spring, warding off all sorts of thieves and avenging Furies that threatened. The enemy lurked just outside. I gripped the rifle tighter.

Then I heard a noise at the front door, and instantly I felt my skin crawling over my body. There followed an eerie silence as someone outside fumbled with the lock and finally turned it. I pushed off the rifle's trigger lock, waiting for the intruder's next move. Shivering, I heard the door pulled to—and then footsteps creeping into the front hallway.

"Who turned all these lights on?" came Dorothy's lilting voice. Suspense was broken. I was relaxed and took a deep breath. My body went limp, and the rifle was loose in my lap. She walked in, removing her jacket and unburdening herself of pocketbook and hat. As she turned toward me and asked what I was doing, her breasts bounced lightly, and I didn't even react, merely telling her what she could see for herself, that I was alone and had been keeping a vigil.

"That's too bad, you poor thing," she said and came over to stand directly in front of me. "You're not frightened now, I hope." I admitted my fears, and she patted me on the head. "No need to be. I'll take care of that. Have you had dinner?" I said yes, but she soon brought from the kitchen a dish of ice cream for each of us. As she put down the dish in front of me, I looked up and noticed a tear on her cheek…and asked about it.

"Oh, it's nothing," she whispered. "I was just stood up, that's all. We all have our disappointments, Thomas. No need to dwell on them." She turned on the radio to some dance music of the day and asked me to dance.

"I'm not very good. Martha just began to teach me." Her eyes and body beckoned me. She was so cheerful and wanted to bring me out of my fears. She saw me staring at her, and I remembered being admonished before, but there was something stirring that aroused my curiosity. She reached for my hand, and I felt embarrassed.

"I think you might at least try to dance with me," she said. "Come on. Try it. You're getting to be a big boy." I felt warm and shy, as I moved toward her. In a halting, awkward way I put my arm around her narrow waist and we began to move to Tommy Dorsey's theme song: "I'm Getting Sentimental Over You." It was slow and easy, and I began to enjoy it, especially when she brushed my face with her lips. "You're good," she said. "You dance well. I can see the results of Martha's work." When she said this into my ear, I smelled her perfume mixed with perspiration, which was inviting. It had the smell of the sea early in the morning when the air hardly moved. I breathed it in deeply.

Soon the song ended. She was smiling at me, pausing to turn off the radio. "I'm getting tired. Maybe it would be good for you to get some sleep, too."

I saw her pick up her things to go to her upstairs room, watching her move with rapt attention, and thanked her for the dance—and for rescuing me from the evening ghosts. At that she laughed brightly, saying goodnight. Then I was alone, walking about, trying to figure out what had happened. Something had. First, I clicked the lever on the rifle and put it away in father's gun rack. Then I ran up to my room.

I undressed in a rush and jumped into bed, but I couldn't sleep, merely lying there and reliving the dance and the smell of Dorothy. Finally, I must have dropped off…until I heard a soft tapping at the door. Then, almost before I could understand what was happening, I felt Dorothy's fingers on my chest, and then, further down her other hand held me delicately. She had crawled into bed with me, taken my hands carefully and laid them on her soft, firm breasts, one at a time.

In the warmth I began exploring her body, she mine. Dampness came, and she began making a noise in her throat like a purring cat. "You like it, yes?" she whispered and kissed me with her open mouth. Then she was on top of me, straddling my hips, leaning over me and brushing me with her breasts. I felt myself smothered, and she purred more, saying we both "needed it." The dampness came more as I expired under her body, pulsing into her soft arms, kissing the very breasts I had watched for so long in wonder. We both said, "Oh!" together when I felt a great warm rush and throbbing. Before I knew it she was out of bed, leaning over to kiss me as if it were a reward of some kind.

"Not a word," she cautioned, her fingers at her lips as she stood in the doorway. "Not one word to anyone; it's our secret." I slept in perfect peace, exhausted and was satisfied in a way I had never been before. I had entirely forgotten my fears…

I remembered my first seduction on that rainy day between Geneva and the Spanish border. Looking back I recognized that a morality play had taken place. I realized that when I had a personal problem to solve, I rarely resolved it myself. Women like Dorothy always came to my rescue. I prayed that was not true with Ellen.

TWENTY

The rain continued as I dozed now and then. I noticed that the Swiss father and daughter had left. I was now alone approaching Narbonne where I had to transfer to another train that would take me to Oloron. Night had overtaken the train, and the rumbling rain on the car was comforting. I wondered if Pam, Sally and Faith had arrived in Paris yet, knowing that they planned to take the next possible train from Montreux to Lausanne and from there move on to Paris. Pam must have had a bad time driving back to Montreux and up to Caux before the three of them left for France. I could still see the tears in her eyes at the Geneva station when we parted. I tried to think instead of my assignment in Spain.

The old night train carrying me on to Oloron clunked along. From Oloron I took another train in the early morning, then a bus to Pamplona, one of the worst rides I had ever taken. That morning toward noon I arrived, proceeded as rapidly as possible to Belinda's hotel and learned, much to my surprise, that she was being held at the local police station. It didn't sound good.

Too late to accomplish anything that day. I checked into the same hotel, and as evening came, walked about the town and finally into the Plaza del Castillo.

It was a large square with many outdoor chairs and people enjoying themselves in pre-dinner festivities. At the table, I ordered a manzanilla when the waiter brought a bowl of those small, natural olives that are so perfect with a dry apéritif. I settled into the entirely pleasant and relaxing Spanish routine, but thoughts of Belinda in prison reminded me of Spain's suffering during its painful civil war and the many cruel incidents described by Orwell and Hemingway in their books. It was a romantic night with many stars strung in a black sky over the square, but I was there to rescue a crazy American girl. Nothing fit, least of all me. But I was determined to see it through. After a paella dinner, I walked back to the hotel and slept soundly.

In the morning at the police station there she was, looking at me hopelessly through the bars of her prison room. One of her eyes was blackened and her expression showed complete bewilderment.

"Jesus, what happened? Are you all right?" I said.

"Tom, these fucking police are driving me mad," she responded in language that surprised me. A policeman stood outside the room watching.

"Tell me what you can," I said, knowing we had to be careful.

"Better come back later. They're suspicious." So I left her to investigate on my own at the gobierno civil, hoping to learn why she was incarcerated. But the guardia civil wouldn't say anything worth believing. I got angry at that, angry at the plight of a fellow American. That had always worked in the past when I had gotten into tight scrapes with the European police. After threatening American consular action, I went back to her cell.

"Tom," she wailed through the bars. "Thank God, you're here. Before wasn't the time to talk. Remember the group I wrote you about, those I met in Madrid with my friend Shirley? Well, they're the problem. They're opposed to the Franco government and bent on its overthrow. To be against that son-of-a-bitch Franco is all you need to be detained. That's why I am here."

"But you're an American. They just can't put you in the clink like that."

"Yes, they can. They did find something against me. Not much, but enough."

"And what about your eye? That's quite a shiner."

"Nobody hit me, Tom. It wasn't the police. It's that I tried to run away—and fell on a curb downtown, not far from here. I was trying to get rid of some papers the Madrid group gave me—to take out of the country. I had to do it through some people here first, but I never could. I almost broke open my head on the curb. When they caught me they took the papers away, so now they know what it's all about…"

"Was it intelligent of you to get involved in the first place?"

"Tom," she said stridently, "Yes, for love." Then her voice became plaintive. "That's worth anything." Youth and idealism had brought her down.

"Is it worth going to jail for?" I asked, but she didn't hear me.

"Tom, these people are good. They're for a good cause. They're against fascism. I was only trying to help. You read my letter. I'm in love with the leader, Vittorio."

Looking at Belinda Vorst, still very much the kid she was in the States, I felt the whole thing was nonsense. Maybe it was my lack of political commitment, but it sounded to me like nothing more than a crazy, romantic notion, and reminiscent of those songs of the Spanish Civil War.

"Tom, I need you to get me out of here and back to France. Just talk to them. You're a charmer. They'll get someone who understands English. Besides, you're a journalist and could cause trouble for them."

I finally did "just talk to them," but I had to sound very angry, ready to call the American Embassy in Madrid. That appeared to settle things. I got enough of the Spanish to understand that they were going to release Belinda. But they would keep the confiscated papers.

When she walked out of the building with me, guards spat on the floor. We were bad Americans.

Out on the street she thanked me. "I really needed you here."

"I did it for your mother, and where's the girl Shirley who was with you?"

"Oh, she's probably back in Paris by now. She got over the border ahead of me."

"You didn't coordinate it?"

"No, she wasn't involved with the cadre."

"Oh, the cadre, was it?"

"Yes."

"But she was involved with you?"

"That doesn't make any difference."

"I see."

She eyed me suspiciously. "Vittorio was all that mattered to me. But"—her voice lowering noticeably—"he's dead now."

"How come?"

"In an automobile crash near Madrid." She was making the most of her revelation, sounding like a Jewish princess, wounded by the Gentiles. I wondered, as we walked along, if adolescent infatuation with political action had led her to "the cadre," Vittorio and all the rest of it.

We walked along the Avenida de Carlos III, the main drag in Pamplona, on our way to the Plaza del Castillo, where I had had that pleasant drink and bowl of olives the night before. Posters announced two Venezuelan matadors were going to fight Spanish bulls. The drama of the posters was difficult to resist. I had only seen one bullfight before. The key performer had received a big horn in the crotch, not a pretty sight. Only a day away, this fight might be better, so I suggested we go together. She was amenable but wanted a few hours to try to re-establish contact with her anti-Franco friends. I didn't want to have anything to do with it, so I went back to the hotel to order the tickets and get something to eat. I had done my job, and it was good to look forward to an afternoon on my own in the city.

When I strolled up the Curia to inspect the cathedral, I thought about why I was there in the first place. The mission had actually been accomplished that very morning with Belinda's release from jail. There was no need to stay, but I had this thing with cathedrals. They gave me peace, even if they were hideous. This one wasn't much—a typical Spanish church: dark, garish in decoration, somehow full of space without much meaning. Nothing like the French gothic creations. But it did have an elegant cloister.

I walked around that still, peaceful space, then stopped. I wasn't alone. Close by was a young girl, perhaps fifteen, sitting on the low wall. She was reading a book, holding it before her in a studied way, her coal black eyes shining in the shadows. There was something regal about her and the way she concentrated on the text and leaned forward gracefully. She was a stunning and rare sight. Her curved neck was contoured against jet black hair. There was something familiar about her olive face, soft against the cloister and its deep shadows. And I remembered Chartres, the face that followed me in dreams—full, superior, looking out over the pilgrims coming to the church through the centuries.

Now before me was a sister face. Her lovely eyes focused on the book before her. The olive skin of her neck plunged under the white chemise that pressed against her breasts. I couldn't take my eyes off her.

She didn't seem aware of my rude stare. Then she lowered the slim volume to her lap and met my gaze. Such a fast visual touch remains forever.

I strolled past her. She was entirely lovely, like the 12th Century princess at Chartres. She was my Lady of Spain, and I adored her.

☙❧

Then it was Sunday, the last day of the St. Fermin festival of bullfights that summer. I was sitting there in the sol y sombre seats around the bullring and beginning to wonder about Belinda.

"Isn't it exciting!" she said.

"Prelude to blood and sand."

"To what?"

"Hot blood."

"It's more than that, Tom."

"No matter," I said. "It's still cruel and one-sided for the bull. They call it fate, but he's doomed from the beginning."

"But he's trained to be a killer."

"Trained by those who'll enjoy seeing him killed. But there is the excitement you talk about."

"You admit it, then."

"Why not? Tell me, did you see those contacts of yours yesterday afternoon?"

"No. They're gone. So the whole mess was pointless, I suppose.

"Mine, too—to rescue you from Franco's clutches."

She put her finger to her lips. "Don't talk like that—they may hear you."

Below us toreros milled about, checking their uniforms that fit like their skin, little things tinkling on the jacket as they moved. They were colorful as they gestured and paced under our seats behind the barrera. The procession that opened every bullfight had just finished and the trumpets cooled down.

"Isn't it exciting?" Belinda said again, as the first young bull tore out into the ring, snorting and looking about in a surprised way. His furious, theatrical charge completed, the bull simply stood there. He had found his querencia, his place of accommodation, and was feeling at home in the ring. The seats surrounding the ring burst into yelling as the beast just stood there waiting. One of the toreros brandished a cape and shook it vigorously. The animal moved his big head, lay down and dozed. The audience groaned in disappointment. I smiled, watching as one of the other bullfighters tried to tempt the sleeping beast. He gestured grandly. The bull lay there.

It continued for a few minutes until one of the officials signaled and the assistants brought a couple of cows into the ring. Immediately the bull got up, following the cows out of the ring, favoring them over death. They brought in a new bull who charged menacingly about the ring, just below us, where he farted with spirit. Belinda cheered. What would her mother think?

I wondered why Americans like Sidney Franklin and Hemingway were fascinated by this Spanish entertainment. Perhaps they read a lot into it, the rigid ritual and mystique and bloody spectacle. Witnessing the torture of the animal, leading up to its death, had never fully taken me in, nor had the hunting of deer back home in that American autumn ritual.

Our generation had experienced enough death, torture and destruction. Even before the war in the final bloody rounds of boxing matches I could appreciate the artistry of Joe Louis, Tony Canzoneri or Lou Ambers when my father had taken me to Madison Square Garden or Yankee Stadium. But I didn't need the coup de grâce in the bullring that follows the placing of the banderillas, the clever faenas and passes with the cape, the veronicas and other arty dances of inevitable death. One Monte Cassino was enough in my life.

So, that afternoon about halfway through the second fight, I suggested we leave. For Belinda it was unthinkable. I was being a traitor to one of the great traditions of Spain. So we stayed for the carnage. By the time the third bullfight began I noticed that one of the buttons on her jacket was missing, ripped out by its roots of white thread. During the excitement, she had pulled it off with the passion of the moment. And she refused to go. I leaned back and stopped observing the action taking place in the ring. Rather, I looked at the row upon row of riotous response to the gore, the sea of faces and bodies rising and falling in the rhythm of the fight. I was reminded of autumn afternoons at Schoelkopf football stadium in Ithaca before the war when each play of promise moved me and my half drunken fellow students to wave and cheer in the same way the Spaniards of Pamplona reacted to the violent turns of action within the barrera. Finally, it was over.

"What's the matter, Tom?"

"The first bull was great, not the others."

"Oh, that was a disappointment. He didn't do what he was supposed to."

"I thought he was damned smart. He's alive, coupling with the cows."

"But he was supposed to die." she said defensively.

I couldn't resist the opening. "Even so, he copped out like you copped out on your friend Shirley."

"You don't understand, Tom," she said. "She wasn't really involved in the movement. She didn't care about Franco and the other fascists. She didn't even like Spain that much. So I didn't care about her. Besides, Vittorio was my focus." We entered a tavern through a beaded curtain and ordered a drink with the tapas. Then she finally said, "He's dead now anyway."

I changed the subject and asked her what she was going to do.

"I'm going to get the hell out of this fucking country."

"And what about your movement?"

She shrugged. "Vittorio's dead."

"But what about the cause?"

"It'll go on without me."

"Then was it the man or the movement?"

"That should be obvious."

"But is it right—for you? They obviously needed you from what you said in your letter, and even now."

She shrugged again

That bothered me. Her fervor was grounded in whim, not passion…

The food and drink were good, and I looked around furtively on the chance that someone might have overheard us. Basques and Spaniards ate and drank around us. Their smiles wrapped us up. Then beyond the beaded doorway I saw the girl I had seen in the cloister. I turned to Belinda and her blackened eye. The contrast was striking: a princess out on the street and a spoiled American beside me.

Then the princess was gone as the beads swung behind a fat Basque. I had lost my otherworldly vision. Reality closed in again.

"What a great corrida!" Belinda was saying.

Later in my room I found a message from the concierge and checked with him about it. Irene had called me, although how she traced me remains a mystery. I telephoned her in Paris at the Hôtel des Quatre Vents. She had just returned from one of Maurice Thorez's Communist Party rallies and was all fired up. That gave her a tie to something big and vital in her world. Edouard was there and talking about me, she said. "He wants to speak to you again…to teach you more about the Left."

I laughed. "Je t'aime, " I said.

"Go tell it to the Marin-es!" she said in the American slang I had taught her but with the wrong accent.

"Sincèrement…"

"Chéri, you are such a clown—si faux. Mais, my call—le but, les choses importantes."

"Tu es importante pour moi,"

"Merde! Maintenant: I couldn't reach you en Suisse but had to open a letter for you here at the hotel. It was marked urgent—from your home in America. Mauvaises nouvelles. I am sorry…

"From your sister…about your father…a heart attack. 'The circumstances are not good,' she writes, 'so call me as soon as possible. He's paralyzed on one side. I wrote a letter but I need to speak to you.' Assez, chéri, call her right away. I'm sorry, bébé.

"Tell me, how is that American woman, Pamela"

"She's fine…in Paris now. Somewhat nervous." I said cautiously.

"Nervous? That is not what it is, chéri."

"What is it then?"

"She wants to draw you totally into her world and possess you. And she is realizing that it cannot be done. As I said before: prenez garde!"

Her insight was upsetting.

"One more thing," she said.

"And what is that?"

"She suffers. Be aware that suffering can turn inward, chéri. This is not good, Thomas."

Silence spun down the phone wire.

"Remember Chartres."

"Of course."

"Remember how you were there. Spiritual, you said."

I got uneasy. "So what are you saying?"

"Be careful with Pam. That is all I can say…except that I have a new friend."

"Ah, so that's what this is all about—a new man."

"Don't be silly."

"The young man I saw at the hotel."

"Oui."

"Odd, isn't it? You always said I would leave you—not the other way around."

Irene sighed. "C'est la vie, mon chéri. Now come home."

"Merde."

"Go tell it to the Marin-es! Now call your sister, chéri. Viens vite! Au revoir!" And she hung up.

I called Martha in Cold Spring. My sister was a straight shooter, and, without hesitation, told me about the "circumstances."

It had all happened on the previous Sunday. Mother had received a message from father's mistress, Florence McTeague, a divorced woman who lived in Ardsley. Everyone knew about Florence. Martha went on, "She notified us as quickly as she could after he took ill in her apartment. His heart just gave out. She only had one option—let mother know about it right away. Quite tacky, what?

"We then took over and made all the medical arrangements with his doctor. Telling his business and social friends was pure hell, especially in light of the circumstances. A blot on the family 'scutcheon, dear brother. But things worked out. We simply didn't discuss how it happened. It was damned embarrassing, Tom."

"What now?" I asked.

"He's in the hospital for a short stay. Mother's all aflutter…"

"I suppose it'll save the marriage…"

"You're more cynical than ever, Thomas."

"No. Just realistic. Should I come home?"

"That's your call," she said. "I don't think it's necessary. I've got things under control." Then she paused a bit. "Still, it's an idea…By the way, how are you?"

"Thanks a lot for asking."

"Where the hell are you, Tom?"

"Spain…Pamplona"

"What! What in God's name are you doing there, running the bulls?"

"At least we read the same books."

"But I get more out of them."

"Honestly, Martha, should I come?"

"Probably not. Besides, it's expensive by air, and you've got to work, I assume."

"Put mother on, will you?"

"Martha's told you everything. I'd love to see you, darling, but don't worry," mother said. "He'll be all right with a little rest, and your presence might well annoy him, Tommy, as it always has." She was absolutely correct, and I let it go at that.

That night in the Plaza del Castillo I tried to make sense of things, mainly what was to come next. Under a black sky, now with just the sliver of a waxing moon, I thought of Irene, who had shown her presence of mind to call me. She could get what passed for my brains back on track. The fino sherry was good, the food pleasant, but I really missed her. I thought of the blue light on her wide cheeks in Chartres that day we made our visit. We used to walk on Sundays in the Tuileries Gardens above the Seine, and I remembered her dark skin, the grey eyes and her sexy, gypsy smile. Outside, the traditional paseo began. People came from everywhere, joining in the night parade. My romanticism took over.

Here I was in a forgotten town far from home, where my father was ill. Home, I thought, the place where I had grown up, had my first piece of ass, familiar, comfortable, and, after the war, not so satisfying. As if anything would be so again. Did I belong there any more, now that the links had been broken by the war? Beyond the Plaza, the chip of moon sought an unknown horizon.

I was out in the wide world now in strange cities, wonderful cities, but cities meant nothing without the people. Especially women who could take me out of myself along some inviting trail. Without people, cities and places didn't mean much—even my wonderful Paris. Or my old, abandoned battlefield in Italy where I almost had it. And Caux where our group had literally been in paradise high above Lake Geneva, and I was with a girl I thought I really cared for. Sadly now, I realized there was no going back. Pam was not the girl. Who was? Maybe Ellen, probably not. Two days ago I had visually feasted on that lovely, eternal Spanish princess in the Pamplona cloister. She had barely seen me. But she reminded me of the lady at Chartres—she offered a continuous beauty. One could settle for that. There was so little of it in the world.

ÎLE DE LA CITÉ

TWENTY-ONE

The ride back to Paris had been long and tiring. And there was too much time to indulge in idle thinking rather than organizing the research and reporting that had to be done for my various work assignments. All the time in Switzerland and Spain I had neglected the working notes I carried with me.

After the flat Landes country flew by we were in Bordeaux, then went on by the farms of Charentes and on up into the lush Loire country, whose picturesque castles seemed to elude the train tracks. More time passed, and I was back in the city I called "home"—for the time being. Between Hendaye at the Spanish border and Paris a lot of planning was done but no real work. When the train came to a quiet halt in Gare Austerlitz I lugged my gear into the Metro and soon arrived at the hotel. There was an encouraging note from Martha about father's improved condition, and one from Pam that I purposely didn't open. I decided it would be better to go out and walk around the quartier after the long, inactive day confined in the train. It felt comfortable to be back and to check out the familiar territory.

Before I ventured out, I wrote a short note to Irene and shoved it under her sister's door upstairs in the hotel. On the street I was attracted first to a bookstore window holding several sets of the French classics. Then for some reason I remembered Jacques Pelletier, my old waiter friend at the Vagenande restaurant, and I crossed the boulevard to say hello.

"Do you remember that night many weeks ago when you got the ris de veau mixed up with the escalope?" He burst into fast laughter. "You see, you will have to get the customers' orders correct the first time, my friend."

"Ah, les femmes américaines," he said with a deep sigh. "They have very strong opinions, don't they?"

"She just got jilted by her boyfriend, if you're interested."

"Ah! I now feel better!" he said and we both laughed. Then I moved on leisurely to the west on the Boulevard St. Germain. It was good to be back again among the noise and bustle of the city. Off to one side was one of my favorite places: the Marché de Buci and its open food market. People were still picking up their vegetables and gelled cold cuts, engaging the merchants with their persistent and often serious observations about everything from the quality of the merchandise to the latest government changeover.

I passed the small church and looked ahead to see who was causing a stir across the street. My stomach tightened. There in the Café des Deux Magots was Buck Birnbaum, very drunk and waving his arms and cane at passersby on the Boulevard. He flapped about in one of the outdoor seats like an injured bird trying to take off, waving wildly. As evening settled in, people filtered into the café, most of them giving his clowning motions a wide berth. From the pile of saucers on the table in front of him it was clear that he had been drinking heavily. Not only was he out of character but out of control. Almost like Norman used to act when he had too much pastis. What he was saying was entirely unintelligible as he talked aimlessly to himself in a weird soliloquy. How removed he was from his role as conference leader. Once the focus, the font of energy, now he was shunned.

I had come all the way from Hendaye at the Spanish border after a harrowing bus ride from Pamplona to witness this scene with an old friend. I stood watching him.

He finally recognized me and tapped his cane. He eyed me contemptuously, slurring his words: "Well, I'll be damned, if it isn't Iscariot himself. Dumm de dum, Is-cawr-iote!"

223

"Not a nice greeting for an old friend."

"Dum-de-dum, Judas himself."

"At Montreux you said we would talk in Paris. This isn't the kind of talk you suggested, Bucko."

"That's the way the cookie crumbles, Judas." He kept tapping the cane. His dark hair tumbled over his face. He brushed it back. His voice was hoarse now with the influence of drink. "So where is she now?"

"For God's sake, who do you mean? I thought you'd ask me about Spain. I've been away, you know."

He held the cane tightly and brandished it. "You know damned well whom I mean: Ellen."

"How the hell would I know about Ellen? I just told you I got back from Spain two hours ago."

"Oh yes," he said gruffly, "You went there, I remember." Then he looked a bit sheepish, tapping the cane.

"I'm glad you remember, Buck—and I'm damned tired." In a move of conciliation, I added, "I told you in Montreux how sorry I was the Conference broke up the way it did."

His eyes opened wide in reply. "In view of what you did, Iscariot, your sympathy is much appreciated!"

He had a sarcastic way of putting things when he was out of sorts. It made me angry, but there was no point in showing it. I wondered if he knew that Ellen was the one who knocked him off balance up on the Rochers de Naye.

Suddenly Lizette, the one who liked dancing, appeared. She spotted Buck and rushed up to him and caressed his cheek. He grinned in his drunken stupor.

"Mon très cher, Book—ça va?" she mumbled at him. He patted her head, mumbling in his fractured French. It was an appropriate time for me to leave. I gladly withdrew, while she squealed with mock affection into his ear. "Mon petit chou!"

Walking back to the hotel, I passed the Relais Odéon and noted some familiar faces. There was a heated discussion going on over a plastic table. Fred Furness and Joyce were there with

Bill Watson, Betty Lowry and Norman. Joyce saw me first, and brightened markedly. She hailed me with a spry, "Hi there, mate! Do join us! You're looking glum and tired." I waved a hand, and she beamed. After the jolt of seeing Buck, I needed a drink and willingly joined them.

"We're discussing our mutual friend…" Bill said.

"Charles Dickens," Fred interposed.

Bill ignored him. "Our mutual, brutal friend Buck Birnbaum, and what a mess he's made of himself."

"You should see him, Tom," Joyce said.

"I just ran into him at the Deux Magots—drunk as a coot," I said.

"That's just it," Bill added. "He's been that way ever since he came back from Caux…"

"…and he never used to drink," Norman said. "I think it's got to do with his family's business and maybe something else. Maybe—don't know. Maybe Ellen. She's been noticeably absent. You remember how they were always together."

"It seems I'm involved, too," I said. "He just called me Judas." Betty held me in a fixed stare, as if she knew something, but said nothing.

"He's called all of us something or other in his dizzy state, Tom, ever since we all came back to Paris," Fred said. "Mostly ingrates, peasants or something like that…"

"Even called me a black bastard," Bill said—"not a nigger, but a black bastard."

"When lofty ideals go, they really go," I said drily.

"Quite a change," Fred went on. "But in his sober, sane moments, he's talking about publishing."

"No kidding," I said. "You know, he first asked me about Ellen and where she was, as if I knew."

Betty said: "I know where she is," and everyone snapped their heads around in surprise. "Don't ask me too much," she continued, "but I just happen to know." We waited. "She's in Paris, and I'm worried about her. We've had several meetings…"

"There's a new Picasso exhibit of line drawings of satyrs in the woods down on the Right Bank," Norman was saying to divert us. "It's terrific—far better than the maddening things elsewhere—and I recommend you take a look when you can."

Fred leaned over to me. "Buck approached me about publishing some of my poetry. It's a new venture of his, a press devoted to young authors—Americans living in Paris." Others overheard him and showed great interest. With everyone's curiosity piqued and the new direction set for the conversation, I figured it was a good time to get some sleep. "I'm bushed," I said.

"How's Pam?" Betty asked as I began to walk away.

"All right, I suppose." That didn't seem to please her.

"Let's talk outside, Tom." She led me to a bench on the Boulevard St. Germain where we both sat down while the traffic sped by.

"Tom, I don't know about Pam, and you can tell me if you want, but Ellen needs you again."

"Again?"

"Yes, again. She told me what happened between you two, and she's incredibly grateful."

"Look—"

"For years she's had this odd relationship with Buck—really odd—and she's terribly upset about what occurred between you two. She had this 'duty,' as she calls it, to Buck, and now there's you."

"Buck's a switch-hitter," I said. "She's known that for a long time."

"Tom, do you know what love is when you see it? You have enough women; you should know."

"That may be the problem…"

"Well, be that as it may, you've given Ellen something that goes deep. I won't say anything else about it. But I'll give you this." She reached into her purse and handed me a sheet of paper— "I've been keeping it for you and I want you to use it. Only you." Her eyes got wet. I looked at the paper and saw it contained Ellen's address in the 6th Arrondissement and a phone number.

"Thanks. Really—thank you, Betty."

Over my shoulder I could hear the others talking in the café we had just left.

"Where are the three Smithies since we've gotten back?" Fred said. That reminded me of Pam's unopened letter in my room—another reason for me to go. I would get back to the Hotel des Quatre Vents, greet the concierge and move up the stairs to my room…

I turned to Betty on the bench beside me. "How's the Rabelais project?"

"Norman's so enthusiastic. I think he's really going to do an elaborate book about it all. I'm so pleased."

"He's been looking for this opportunity for awhile; he was drifting before he met you."

She blushed. "Everything's fine," she said, accepting my kiss on her cheek.

"Now I can see why women love you, Tom."

"I'd better go," I said. "Thanks for the key to Ellen."

"Use it wisely."

I crossed the street to the carrefour and ran to the hotel to read Pam's letter. My heart fell a notch or two.

"Dearest Tom," she wrote in a few lines. "Whenever you get back, I wanted to reassure you that I'm more sure than ever our affair is over. I saw the signs in Caux. You tried to be so brave about it, but I knew. You are such a gentleman about your changing moods. It's been wonderful, and I still love you very much. But I'm no fool. You are off to other flowers. All my deepest affection… Pamela."

It was like a strong kick in the stomach, but it did relieve me of a duty. Again: escape. But I was too tired to think. Just before I drifted off, I heard the door of my room, which I had accidentally left unlatched. I heard it open and shut with light footsteps in between. I felt a warm body snuggling up to me under the covers. I caught the tang of garlic. Irene's hands were all over me.

227

"Oh, my God," I muttered, pulling her close.

"C'est moi." She laughed her unmistakable laugh, deep and sexy, and kissed me on the ear, then on the neck and shoulder. I responded sluggishly and she purred.

"How are things back home in America? Your father?" she asked.

I told her about calling Martha after her own call to me in Pamplona. I thanked her with kisses.

"It was my duty to my lover," she said. "The trouble is your lack of consistency."

"That's been my trouble all my life."

"You are like a bee—going from flower to flower."

"That sounds familiar."

"What?" she asked.

"Nothing worth mentioning," I said. I stroked her back and buttocks, and she purred some more.

"Bees are buzzing around your family. Like son, like father. How is he?"

"Resting. No women now."

"His son is compensating for him," she said. "I missed you, and you were very bad not to write or call."

"I know."

"Then why didn't you?"

"Because I'm bad."

She kissed me. "I want you to meet with Edouard again."

"Why? We disagreed on the USSR, remember. But I liked him and Sylva."

"He liked you—why, I don't understand. I'll arrange it. By the way, you had a letter." In the reflected street light, I could see her wide, knowing eyes flashing at me as she rolled over on top.

"Yes, many letters."

"One in particular," she said.

"Oh, you inspected my mail."

"When you are away. Like the urgent one from your sister."

"All right."

"You are bad, entirely bad." As we talked, we made love, and it was disconcerting.

"I did miss you, believe it or not." I said, fatigue leaving me.

"Horsefeathers!" she said softly. We slept in each other's arms, the garlic permeating our breath. And not a word about her new man.

※

In the morning we had breakfast together before she went to work.

"You were tired last night, but it was good," she said, biting into a croissant.

"You are an evil woman—and wonderful. But you worry me."

"How so?" She arched her dark eyebrows, a show of dominance. "You are not to make love to cette femme américaine!" She was emphatic, and I was a bit taken back by her. This was new. She had checked out my mail, and now this.

"Who said I will?"

"I know you—like your father, as I said last night. You told me about his wanderings."

Someone at the next table on the sidewalk café left the morning issue of *Figaro* on a chair within reach. I noticed a headline story about one of those fast, periodic strikes against the transit systems and railroads. Irene saw it, too, and said:

"You see, it arrives—union action—another moment of truth for the workers' low wages. Edouard may be involved in this one for the Party."

"I thought he was an architect."

"De temps en temps. He always has one foot in politics. You remember."

"Yes, I do. I hope you can arrange something soon, even though we disagree."

"He said the same thing about you."

"But you must join me."

"We can talk about that interview with Thorez. It was a good article, Thomas. He will be impressed."

"I don't care about impressing anyone, but I respect a person who does things, who gives of himself, like Edouard did during the war with the Maquis. Losing a finger for principle is no ordinary thing, mademoiselle."

She looked at me with those large, wide-set grey eyes and I thought how young she was but, like her brother-in-law, honest and forthcoming. I really liked her and would hate to lose her to her new lover.

"When are you free?" she asked. "We can do it any time."

"That's your decision and Edouard's."

"I'll call today from work," she said. "I have to go now." We kissed on both cheeks, and I pinched her flank as she went to the Metro entrance. "Méchant!" she said, waving goodbye, her fingers to her lips.

<hr />

She worked quickly. That night we were invited to Sylva's and Edouard's for dinner. In the afternoon I called Pamela, and we met at a café over on the Boulevard St. Michel near her apartment with Sally and Faith. It was such a pleasant day, however, that we elected to go to the Luxembourg Gardens.

We sat down in chairs near the steps where I had found her in disarray that unpleasant night before we all took off for Switzerland.

"So you want to break it off," I said.

"You do, too," she said. "Besides, I can't go on this way. You have so much of me, Tom."

"And you want more of me. I feel rotten about it, because you made me feel so special. I have never felt so much for any woman before…"

"Well, I'm now part of your resumé." Children ran by us on the path near the stairs.

"You are not nice when you say that," I said.

"I do not feel nice saying it. It's simply a matter of fact. I want more of you than you want to give. You are the most important person in my life, but I am not the most important person in yours. Now I realize how pointless things are. There was a marvelous beginning, an intriguing middle, and an unhappy end. That's a good definition of Greek tragedy, right?"

She stared ahead, as if frightened to look me in the eye. Tears came. Another group of children whizzed by. I put my arm around her, which she resisted. When she collapsed I pulled her in. I watched more children around the big pool behind the Palais Luxembourg. Their toy boats, their eagerness, their shrill cries of delight when the vessels collided—she saw and heard nothing of it.

"Pam, I still love you. Why can't we go on?"

"Because it's hollow, darling Thomas. And I feel terrible. I'm an American girl from Illinois. You keep forgetting."

"Maybe you've forgotten who I am…"

"Ah, that's the question, who are you?"

"That's my question," I said suddenly, angrily. "Who am I? Pam, I came to Europe to try to answer that question."

"We all did. We thought it would be easier to answer in Paris. Something of a conceit, I suppose."

Across the way an outraged parent admonished an innocent young boy about allowing his large toy boat to crash into her own child's sacred motor boat. Pam was sobbing as she peeped at me. Then a young girl in a pinafore came up to us, staring at Pam with an inquiring expression on her wide-eyed face.

"In some ways, I'm more confused than ever," I confessed.

"That's because the more you know, the less you know," she said, trembling as the girl continued to stare. "I found something here—you—and I'm loath to part from you. And I opened the can of worms by writing that letter to you. I blew the whistle on a man who's meant more to me than anybody in the world."

I tried to kiss away her tears. "Pam, I do love you."

"Sorrow brings it all out," she said, her throat tight with emotion, as mine was. The little girl in the pinafore skipped by in front of us. Suddenly, she stopped, turned and stared at us both. She slowly asked in French why we were crying. Pam broke down completely. I got up quickly to kneel in front of the girl. She was not an attractive child, but with her question she was irresistible.

"Because we are foolish," I said to her. "When we are grown up like you, we will not cry." She scratched her head full of black curls and said: "I do not understand."

Pam stopped crying, got up and joined me. "We think we understand, but do not," she said in flawless French. "We wish the world was the way we want it."

The girl inspected us with smiling eyes. "I do not understand," she said, "but you are nice to me." She ran off up the very same stairs where Pam had done her desperate dance weeks ago. Pam did not remember, but I did. I always would.

⚇

That night Irene told me we were invited to her sister's for dinner. Irene met me at the hotel to be sure I didn't get lost finding the apartment in Belleville. Her confidence in me was unbounded. When we met at the Hôtel des Quatre Vents, I had a paper bag full of sweets and wine, including two bottles of Morgon Beaujolais for our dinner. Sylva was impressed.

I began the dinner with a statement that surprised Irene. When I did, her head snapped around and she stared at me.

"The last time, Edouard, we disagreed, but you taught me something."

"About causes?" he said inspecting the bottle. "Excellent wine."

"If you believe in something enough, you will die for it."

"Well," he said, "that's nice to think, but in Lyon when the Nazis controlled it, there wasn't much choice."

"What choice—political choice?"

"Personal choice."

"But you made it. You didn't just let it happen to you."

"But politics is another matter," he said. "That has to do with your conviction about things to come—how you want to live and in what kind of society. In Lyon, the choice was more basic—to live or die."

"You could have told the Germans about the Maquis to save your skin," I said.

"Betrayal is the worst of sins, mon ami."

"You have a sense of honor. That's very French," I said.

"Honor is a personal not a national matter. What is your honor, Thomas?" He held me in a direct stare.

The question stopped me cold. "I suppose it has something to do with fairness…"

"Ah, Christian morality. A bourgeois concept." This was a hell of a way to begin a meal, but he seemed to want it that way. And I had started it.

"Why bourgeois?" I asked.

"Because it's about money, fair dealing in business."

"Not necessarily." But I realized he was partially right. "It really has to do with loyalty—loyalty to one's fellow humans." I felt Pam's cool tears again, recalled the sad look she gave me, which had to do with my lack of loyalty to her.

"Not to faith in Communism, Socialism, Democracy?" he asked pointedly. "I was asking about your personal sense of honor. Loyalty may be more important."

"Being fair with others," I said. "Loyal, too."

He smiled. "What's fair in your mind?"

"Christian ethics, I suppose. I prefer the Chinese version: not doing to others what you don't want them to do to you."

"And the positive view?"

"Living your life in a decent, considerate way."

He leaned back in his chair. "And you do that?"

I sat there, questioning myself.

"Sometimes you have to kill as I did during the war, or at least I thought so at the time." He lit a cigarette, leaned back and shut his eyes for almost a minute. Irene frowned, Sylva talked about the food getting cold, and Irene hated the silence. Edouard's eyes were clenched shut, the lids trembling. We hadn't eaten a thing, and Irene proposed that we begin.

"Bonne idée," Edouard said, opening his eyes and looking around

"However, now you wonder if it was all worthwhile," I said. "The war was, but…"

"That's the problem," he said. "You never know. Not for certain. You carry on. You try…"

"C'est une lutte éternelle—a constant struggle," I said, and he brightened.

"Exactly."

Sylva interrupted now. "If you please, let us eat," she insisted.

"My dear," Edouard said, "we should, but it seems for us conversation is food." We all laughed, and Irene said sullenly, "You are all crazy."

"Pas du tout," I said. "Not at all; it's stimulating."

Edouard took a forkful of ragout in his mouth. I poured the wine. Sylva inspected the label.

"Morgon," Edouard said. "You can never go wrong with Morgon from Beaujolais—or Fleurie or Moulin à Vent."

To this day, I remember words like loyalty, betrayal and one's personal sense of honor in a different way, trying to employ them properly. But for me it was like trying to touch a woman's skin or exquisite porcelain through rubber gloves.

TWENTY-TWO

After calling Ellen, I tried to organize myself for the encounter. We had agreed to meet for lunch. Now separate from Buck, she was living in a room rented on the rue du Vieux Colombier, not very far from the church whose bells struck brightly during my sleepless nights, St. Sulpice. She had broken her relationship with Buck since the Swiss events. Needing the time to recuperate and switch gears, she placed a barrier between herself and the group. That included me.

And now we were meeting again for the first time after several weeks of separation. All of this occurred during Pam's decline and growing malaise. Naturally, what passion Ellen and I shared in the lake at Vevey never left me. It had been something special—full of exciting sensations, animal pleasure and something on a much higher level I often tried to define. We were former lovers, and probably both wondering what to do now, what our mutual assumptions were, and how we would react to each other after the break.

She had selected a brasserie in Montparnasse as our luncheon site, and when I sighted her beret sitting rakishly on the blonde hair and the usual white dress across the street, I waved. She immediately arose, and gazed at me with a questioning look on her stunning face, now that it was bronzed from the high altitude exposure in Switzerland. Her freckles, somewhat darker, stood out in an exciting way across the receding bridge of her royal nose. Even though her blue eyes softened when our glances met, it was like meeting her all over again, and all of the past in America had disappeared. Instead of embracing in the customary French way, we reached for available hands and merely held them together in silence. She began by asking me about Spain, which I didn't want to talk about, but it was a good way to begin again with each other. I told her about the bullfight and how the first bull had not been very interested in struggle with the matadors and how they led him off with the cows. She laughed spontaneously.

"Has Buck forgiven us about the conference breaking up?" I asked.

"No, I don't believe so," she said dispassionately. "But that's all over. He's crazy, you know…"

"I saw that the other night." Across the street a young couple walked briskly, then stopped suddenly and embraced. The kiss was long—very long.

"Now he's going to waste more money publishing Fred's poetry. The Presse de Seine, he calls it."

"He could do worse," I said. "Fred's entirely competent—a disciplined poet."

"But Buck's drinking now. That's a new wrinkle—a lot of drinking."

"Does he see you?" She swept my face with her penetrating blue eyes.

"He says he wants to but doesn't. I'll do it, of course. He calls now and then but seems frightened."

"So, the show is over." The couple across the street came unstuck from the kiss and resumed their swaggering walk, disappearing behind a kiosk and kissing again. "Just about, I suppose. He's still angry with you…in a fit of outrage, even asked me if you were good in bed."

"Someone named Cassidy once passed around a gratuitous comment about my aquatic techniques," I said.

"Yes, you were quite accomplished. It was a matter of tempo, if I recall correctly." She was smiling. She was all right.

"Slow and easy." Her eyes danced.

"Precisely," she said

"You are lovely, you know."

"I didn't hear that, because we have to establish some rules at this time."

"What are they?"

"For the time being, Thomas—rule number one is: keep your objectivity; rule number two: now and then keep your distance; rule number three: keep your sense of humor. Four: don't jump to passionate conclusions. Did you ever see the letters Scott Fitzgerald wrote to his daughter at Vassar? They're kind of pretentious but they have some wisdom about living a decent life. Of course, he never did obey his own advice." "He was Irish that way," I said and watched her carefully, marveling at her own form of Irish wisdom, finally saying straight out:

"You are the cat's whiskers, lady. You really are. Now tell me something: where are your butterflies?"

She sat there with our lunch before us. Then she looked up at me with a message I didn't understand. But there was something special about the expression on her face. Her voice was suddenly soft. "I've found something more important."

"Oh?"

"You must know, Tom. You must."

I frowned in confusion.

"Remember the four rules, please. Please."

I raised my glass of wine to her. "Here's to us. None better." She laughed.

"Now tell me about Pamela?"

"We've split."

"Why?"

"Run out of gas, I guess."

"Sorry to hear that. It seemed so ideal."

"Not really. I've been rotten to her."

"I thought she was so right for you."

"So did I, but who is right for anybody?"

"For you I can think of a few—Joyce, Irene… and someone else." I let that fly past me without comment. because I wanted to get off the subject. Later I would wonder about the "someone else."

At this point, Fred and Joyce, hand in hand, appeared across the street and waved hello. We waved back. Then, just behind them, Bill Watson walked up on our side of the street with Pam and Faith Carlson in tow. I remember Faith glancing at me questioningly. She knew all of my weak points, having spotted them that night in Switzerland. She must have been confused about me being with Ellen. Pam, meanwhile, wore a set smile, almost a mask.

"Hi," Bill said, "I just saw Buck at the Flore. Drunk as a coot again. Called me nigger—and not even a nice nigger—said I was hurting Fred." Across the street Fred and Joyce were waiting to cross over.

Ellen said, "He doesn't mean it, you know."

"I'm not so sure about that," Bill said. "He's mad at everyone these days and out of control."

Joyce came up now. "Hi there!" She gave me a fast kiss on the forehead as Ellen took notice and sat up straight. "Let me add a comment," Joyce said. "Behind all of Buck's disenchantment, he's trying to accomplish something important. We should feel sorry for him and help him. Couldn't you all see how out of it he was at Caux—how depressed he was after the fall? It was so bloody sad."

Ellen looked away. "That was because of me."

"No, it was the end of things…his tether had run out," Joyce said.

Joyce surprised me with this defense of Buck, but she probably was right. I greeted Pam warmly, and her artificial grin carried through the scene. Her sudden reappearance after our earlier session in the Luxembourg Gardens surprised me and put me on the defensive. Others wondered, too, looking for clues from each of us.

"Goddam it," Bill was saying, siding with Joyce, "couldn't you all make an attempt to be nice to Buck? He needs help, even from niggers like me."

Fred, who hadn't been part of the conversation, perked up with "Who? Who said 'niggers'?"

"This nigger," Bill said. "Just a figure of speech…colored speech. Buck needs help these days, what with the booze."

"What good would that do?" I said. Pam looked at Ellen, her brows knit.

The mood broke as Ellen froze. "Oh, God!" she said

I turned to see. Buck staggered along the street, oblivious to everything around him.

"Oh-oh," Joyce said.

I got up and hailed Buck, not knowing if he could make me out amid the whirling traffic. Pam wasn't amused, looking sad and preoccupied. Buck saw me at that moment and began babbling:

"Aha! Judas again! The stud of our world!" He raised his cane uncertainly. "My dear Judas, shall we talk?—or shall we battle?"

Ellen began to walk away. Bill looked surprised, and Pam said quietly to me, "Let's get the hell out of here. Please! Take me out of this. You don't have to talk to him. Please, let's go!" There was fear in her eyes, and I found it upsetting to see her this way. Everything seemed to be falling apart—Buck was out of control, Ellen retreated, Pam frightened. The street scene was like a battlefield. There was no point in keeping the group together. Even Fred and Joyce stood stymied on the bustling sidewalk. I lost sight of Ellen.

"Let's go," I said to Pam, who was trembling, and we began to move away. Buck was yelling above the crowd: "Come back, Iscariot! Come back, you bastard! Come back!" It was embarrassing with everyone in the brasserie staring at us crazy Americans in a state of disarray. As Pam shook by my side, I tried to steady her, gripping her arm tightly. We continued walking away when behind us I heard Joyce's crisp voice rising above the traffic's din: "What a lot of bloody fools!"

∞∞

Fred Furness wrote good, not great, verse, and every once in awhile I was reminded that Goodie had actually recognized it for what it was: derivative. Now and then his work glittered with great insight, a heavy brilliance that caught you off guard. Once in the Odéon Relais he gave us a reading, and it impressed all of us who were listening that night with a sense of the battle of the Ardennes in which he had participated:

> They were rolling on, like famished crocodiles,
> Tanks that crept along, bellies dragging,
> Jaws wide for prey of any kind, ready to deal out
> Decisive death day or night,
> Their glistered, reptile eyes so fixed and blank—
> Guns spewing mythic fire dead on line—
> Cain killing, prowling, then rolling on again.

Although Goodie knew the score about Fred's artistic deficiencies, none of us wanted to accept her verdict. Mainly because we didn't want to own up to our own poor assessments of people. But I couldn't deny the validity of Goodie's insight. As angry as she was with the cards fate had dealt her, she held nothing against Joyce. All of her ire was concentrated on Fred, who had betrayed her.

She was the first of our group to go. Her pride couldn't take the rejection, and her only option was to return to America. She would sail from Le Havre. I was with Pam the day she left Paris, and we saw her standing alone on the Boulevard Raspail with her baggage in tow. When she saw us, we joined her for a moment, but she looked so lonely on the street that I suggested she have a farewell drink with us. In a way, I felt sorry for her, even when she turned bitchy after Joyce had come into Fred's life. Despite all this, she was part of the picture in those Paris years. I had first hoped she would stay, get another lover, and carry on, but it was obvious that she had to go back to the States. Her pride was too strong.

Pam made all of the expected comments about missing her, but Goodie deflected them.

"This is a happy occasion," she said with a smile at the table, holding her drink high. "Thank you, people. But I need to get home." For the rest of us, Paris was our home. "We all learn," she went on. "Like Buck, I always expect too much. I just don't drink away my sorrows. I'm over that, anyway."

"We all expect too much," I said. "If our friends lived up to our expectations, we wouldn't know how to cope with it."

"I'm kind of a special nut," Goodie said, "and Fred was a mistake." She drank her kir rapidly.

"Not so," I said. "It all works out…"

"…comes out in the wash, you mean, Dr. Pangloss," she said. "You'll all go back to the States one of these days, you know. None of you is the true expatriate type. However, Buck will publish Fred's efforts. It's a matter of his stubbornness. Such is life. He deserves it, publication, I mean."

"Will anyone else recognize it as derivative of Sassoon or Graves or Blunden, like you did?"

"Of course—when they realize what a horrible war it was…" Raucous horns of taxis drowned us out. Red-faced drivers cursed through lowered windows.

"It's still running," Pam said. "It's like a constantly re-cycling movie. It's not over, Goodie."

"Pam, you're right. Wars never end," I said.

"Fred will never get over it," Goodie said. "It was too much for him, those tanks in the Ardennes. He was scared shitless." For some reasons I winced at the word, but said:

"We all were," I said, " but we were young. Fred was an old man when he was born. That's why he couldn't cope with battle— also why he could write the kind of poetry he does. Frankly, I don't know—still—how I coped."

"You?" Goodie said. "Tom, come off it! This may sound strange coming from a Jewish girl, but you're so wonderfully Christian." The horns persisted, while we shouted above the racket.

"An hour ago Buck, another Jew, called me Judas Iscariot."

"Why did he do that?"

"He must have his reasons," I said. The taxis moved ahead as relative peace returned.

"Well, they're not good enough for him to say that to you. Pam, just look at that man, Tom Cortell. His main trouble is that he cares too much for others, even bitchy me when I was vexed with Fred. He helped me a lot in Switzerland. Tom's no Iscariot."

"Goodie, you're talking to someone—Pamela Batterford—who has a right to call me that." Pam looked at me quizically, then to Goodie, and finally back to me. Then she said, with great effect: "My dear Goodie, when this so-called saint finds himself, he might just possibly merit your praise. But not quite yet."

I grabbed Pam's arm and squeezed it. "Will you write me?" I asked Goodie.

"What's my reward?" she asked with a laugh.

"A Christian blessing," I said, laughing back at her. She came over to kiss both of us, and hailed a taxi to take her to Gare St. Lazare for a train to Le Havre. As she pulled away from the curb, Pam asked why I said that. She watched the cab disappear into the traffic, looked at me for a second, then began to sob.

"Because she's one of us."

◉◉

When I returned to the hotel, I met Irene downstairs. She had a strange look on her face indicating she was not happy about seeing me. I glanced out of the doorway and noticed a young man pacing up and down with an expectant look on his face. He was the one, I knew. I was still very much concerned about Pam and her being upset with Goodie's departure. We had walked through the Luxembourg Gardens together, and I had tried to console her, but every time she looked up at me with a pleading expression on her round face, she let some tears fall.

The Street of Four Winds

"What's bothering you?" I asked.

"You wouldn't understand," Pam responded with more tears. "Tom, would you please leave me now? I've got a problem that only I can solve. Don't take me home, please. Just go your own way—please!"

Then, without saying anything further, she walked away from that same spot again—the place where she had broken down on the stairs. I walked north out of the gardens, confused and unhappy, so that when I ran into Irene in the lobby of the Hôtel des Quatre Vents, I wasn't prepared to engage in our usual banter. I checked my key and mail, and went upstairs with a small white envelope in my hand. When I settled down in my room I recognized Joyce's handwriting on the envelope, got up to pour myself a drink, sat down again and read the note.

> "Darling,
> I hope you get back soon. I called you earlier and you were out. I need you today. Desperately need you close. Bill's got to go home in an emergency, and I too.
> Can't speak to Fred. Call me as soon as possible.
> Joyce."

I reached for the phone and dialed her number. When our talk was over—rather quickly—I ran downstairs and over to the Odéon Metro station. In thirty minutes I was at her apartment, breathless.

She opened the door to me in her usual spirited way. "So glad you came so quickly. I do need you, Tom. I'm frightened and worried. And I'm imposing again on your good nature."

"There's not much I wouldn't do for you. You're a big light in my life…"

"Only one of many bulbs," she managed, looking strained.

"Not so many, really. And the lights are dimming. What's going on?"

"Tom, it's a terrible time for all of this to happen. I left a note for Fred, and he's already reacting badly."

"How?"

"Well, I've told him I have to go back to England, and he's angry about it. Trying to get me to postpone it. But I have to go soon. From his point of view, you see, he's burned all his bridges by taking up with me. Now he says he's lost."

"Another lost poet. I'm going to miss you a great deal myself. You know, I once thought how much we have in common."

"You're sweet, darling—and we do have fun," she said with feeling, pulling me towards her. "You're the only one here who takes me for what I am—and the best lover of them all."

"What about your agreement with the Duhamels and their children?"

"From the beginning it was understood I'd be leaving in the autumn. The problem is Fred and his anger. You've seen that in action in Switzerland when he lost his temper. Every once in awhile, he loses control. And I'm sure now he's furious with me. I broke the news to him yesterday on the phone after I asked for someone to deliver that note to you."

"Why are you going?"

"I've had a fantastic offer of a job in London. It's something more important than Fred."

"Getting away from the Black Country. I know…"

"And away from him. That may sound odd and somewhat cruel. And just after I forced myself on him in Switzerland. Now I'm bored with him, even though he's mad about me."

"I understand that. The job…?"

"I'm going to be a copywriter at one of the large advertising agencies, and the money's fabulous. Tom, it's my ticket, my real ticket. I had the interview for it just before leaving in the spring. And now it's come through!" She went on to tell me about Bill's quick departure to see his ailing mother.

"Bad news?"

"She was taken to the hospital—and, believe this, he's giving me three of the paintings before he goes."

"What about us?" I asked to bring her down. She looked away and sighed. Then she shook her head from side to side, mischeviously.

"Darling Tom, we've got this afternoon; the Duhamels are out at Fontainebleau until tomorrow with the children. So—you spend the night with me. You're my protector, my lover, my savior, all in one. I'm frightened what Fred might do. And I want you very much, darling. Inside I crave you and feel for you. Please stay with me; I even bought some special food for us—so we won't die of overexertion. Quiche and great religieuse pastries." She giggled, then bit her lip.

"Has Fred really threatened you?"

"Yes—and refuses to let me go. He's also on edge about Buck's proposition...that book of poems. Now, can you imagine me with a poet! Honestly!"

"Yes, I can. It might really gratify you."

"But he really expects the book to work out."

"You don't think that's going to happen?"

"It'll happen, yes. And it will mean so much to him."

"Buck's not in any condition to follow through on anything, Joyce. Faith Carlson does some work for him, and she told me a lot the other day about what's going on there at the publishing house, so-called. With his frustration and the heavy drinking, my bet is that within a month or two he'll be back in his father's New York office, working in the family's textile business. He's stuck with it. His brother's launched a good career in journalism and teaching as well. So there's no one left to carry on the business. That's what all the drinking's about, Joyce. Faith told me a lot."

"There's something about Ellen, too—something working on him about her. I noticed it on the street during that crazy scene the other day."

"Maybe," I said, wanting to avoid that. Joyce sat ensconced on the apartment's best couch. Its Gobelin-like tapestry fabric suited her as she stroked it delicately.

"I'll bet Faith told you about Pam, too. Some romance, that is, Thomas. You ought to be ashamed of yourself. With me, it's sport; with her, it's totality. Obviously, she's unhappy with you."

"That's because I've broken it off, Joycie. She's not for me, not now. She wants to get married."

Joyce was busy undressing both of us, and in a moment of enthusiasm kissed me long and tenderly on the chest. Her loose hair tickled me.

"She wants to get married…and you want me right now, don't you?" We were facing each other on the bed. She took my hand and buried it between her thighs. "Right there." Her head was high and her eyes slitted with passion.

"And you," I said. "What do you really want for yourself?" I pulled her close so that we were eye to eye.

"I want you—right now." Her voice was inviting, commanding as I sank into her. "That's nice." She never denied being pleased. We lay there, sated, and finally I said:

"How do you get that way?"

"What way?"

"You're like a child: honest."

"Isn't that the way we all should be—and aren't?"

I have always remembered those words, said in her special, innocent way. I was curious about Bill.

"How's the modeling going, the picture? Are you still seeing red?"

"No, silly you. I really like it. He was doing a series of me. He's made me proud of my body. I never was before, you know. Do you remember how you looked at me when you pulled back the blinds that sexy afternoon and the sunlight bathed me? You looked at me with such appreciation, you began it all. Bill liked my body, too. He's leaving in such a rush I'm lucky to be getting those paintings."

"I've always thought your body was just right. So does Bill, obviously. Joyce, it's not only your body and how I react to it. What interests me—and satisfies me in an ideal way—is something else."

She propped her head up on my shoulder and appeared terribly grave, as if she were preparing herself for the worst. "What's that?"

"Your spirit. You're the closest thing I know to a free spirit."

"That's all show, you know...but kiss me now...here."

"It's some show. Did Bill ever mention it? Does his work capture it?"

"He's such a love, poor Bill. He's trying to find his way in this white world," she said. "He has so much to overcome, Thomas. America must be awful for him. If it weren't for his mother and family, I think he'd never go back. No one seems to understand him there."

I cupped her cheek with a hand, brought her face as close as I could and said, "Does anyone understand you in Wolverhampton?"

"Yes. Oh, yes. Even David does. He's the one I was going to marry. He does understand me. He accepted my leaving in the spring without any remorse or reservations. He knew what I needed…"

"But you're not returning to him."

"I may. I don't know. Let's not talk about David now." She clung to me, and I wondered if I had opened a wound in her. She was incredible, her shifts in emotion enormously wide. And for the rest of the afternoon and evening I was her toy. I sensed behind her extremes of temperament there were many questions she needed to resolve. But Paris had given her free play with her emotions, something she needed…and dispensed generously to me that memorable evening. I felt exhausted under her spell.

After, we dozed in each others' arms. We were floating on the clouds of our feelings of the moment. Until hunger asserted itself, we were oblivious to everything but ourselves. That night she cooked a fine meal, which restored us. She made a special sauce for the veal she had bought for me, and I spared nothing in the way of gratitude for the great meal. And we talked incessantly of the Paris group. She really liked all of the Americans but said she didn't understand them, except for one thing.

"Why is it you are all escaping something?" she asked.

"For some of us it was the war, others their background, others something else. Weren't you?"

"No. I can't escape myself. I realize that. All I needed was a change of scene for awhile. Tom, you and I, what we do so well together is not an old habit with me. At home, there were enormous inhibitions. This freedom of the mind and body were what I knew I'd find here. For you all, Paris is an escape. For me it's freedom."

"Aren't they the same—escape, freedom?"

"No. I have no ghosts," she said brightly, and then I understood how right she was. All of us, except Joyce, had ghosts from which we needed to escape. The Furies.

At night she consumed me in her usual fashion. I never knew a woman like her, she made such intense and considerate love. The luxurious setting of the Duhamel's apartment with its Victorian furniture and rooms decorated in such elegant style became our perfect playground for lovemaking. It seemed to energize her, and she enjoyed herself so much it was absolutely necessary to please her this last passionate time. We slept afterwards in the night sounds of the city. She had said some significant things to me, and I couldn't help hearing them again.

Shifting restlessly as the traffic carried on and the occasional voices down on the street drifted upwards, I wondered about her concepts of escape and freedom—all the emotions involved in escaping from oneself. Was I escaping the war or a woman or myself? That brought up other questions. I held her closer. The outside noises of the early morning intruded, and we both held fast. Preserving our proximity was our protection.

We were still close and quiet and warm, our thighs pressed together, generating our own heat, while the great heart of Paris beat into the morning. The city carried us along while it went through the first stages of the day. But as it did there was an odd atmosphere developing, a sense that important changes were imminent. All around us, people were moving away from one another, attachments pulling apart like thin fabric, old sailing vessels breaking formation in the frivolous breezes of the sea. Some were going home, others changing direction like the winds. People were coming and going, moving aimlessly. Even the street where the four winds blew. Joyce and I clasped each other, our lips glued together, totally merged, trying to withstand the forces of the city that had brought us this bliss and now drove us onward and away.

◎◎

That previous afternoon at the hotel Faith Carlson had called me. She seemed upset. We agreed to meet near Buck's temporary office where she was assisting him with his plans for the publishing company. Nothing was going well, she exclaimed when we met for a drink directly in the heart of Paris on one of the few side streets of the Île de la Cité.

"Two things bother me, Tom, and I don't know if my reactions have any significance for you."

"Of course. We are close after that talk in Switzerland. That was important to me, Faith. Tell me." A waiter brought us some kir royal.

"I had to sneak out early to make this," she said, glancing furtively as we took our drinks. "I hope he doesn't spot us. By the way, he has nothing good to say about you. He calls you a traitor and thinks you're out to get him."

"The old persecution complex."

"I'm concerned about what's to become of him. His good heart and generous nature are going fast, Tom. He's consuming enormous amounts of liquor, and he's rarely stable, frequently drunk by noon. When you think of all the careful planning that went into the Caux conference and how high his hopes were, it's hard to understand what's happened. It's more than the broken leg…or maybe something that's happened between him and Ellen. Something very basic is bothering him, and I think I've found out what it is." I was listening to every word. "Even Bob Kemperman's disappeared—both Bob and Homer.

"I couldn't help but see his reactions to several letters he's received from New York. And then, one day last week, I wasn't able to resist the temptation to read parts of them lying around the office. All of them were sent from his home, either the father or mother. One had been carefully slit open, then resealed. The day it arrived I saw him read it, and, when he did, he made a fist and slammed the table. That high voice of his was a screech, and frightening. Then he jabbered something about: 'I will not return to that God-damned business! I won't!' I got that letter and read it. His father had ordered him to return to New York and take on his " familial duties" at the company office. Nice kettle of fish."

"It's the one thing he had resisted," I said. "He talked to several of us about this, even back in America. He not only hated the business, but he desperately wanted to make his own career."

Faith leaned back in her chair and looked at me. "The other thing I've simply got to mention, Tom, is Pamela."

"I see."

"Do you? That's the question. I've never known how vital to her you are. She's utterly devastated now that you've split. Sally and I are taking turns keeping an eye on her. Her words sometimes don't make any sense, and we often wonder if it's safe to leave her alone."

"That bad, eh? You know she wrote me to break it off herself. Once I got the letter, I was sure she was over it, but now, after hearing you, I don't know."

"I'm seriously worried about her, and I know how you feel. That's why I had to mention it."

"Life is full of surprises, and no one's immune to the problems they bring," I said. It sounded trite. "Look, I already feel guilty about this situation, Faith, but there's little I can do. Pam and I have simply run the course. That she's taken it so hard bothers the hell out of me. But look at it this way. Who made the first pass in the game? You don't know, but I do. It was that early night here when we all went to the Chat Jaune, the night Buck sort of took over and treated us to the dancing at the boîte, the onion soup place on the rue Dauphine and the first drinks we had. It was a hell of a night. I'm not going to go over it. In any event, that's where she started the whole thing—and I, the great man of experience, let it get to me. But I'll have you know, I didn't start it."

"You merely took it to the next step," she said. "And you became the man who took her virginity. She was utterly innocent and naïve. Didn't that convey any sense of responsibility, even a little?"

"Yes, it did—and furthermore, I fell in love with her for quite a while. See that couple over there? Kissing and making open love to each other. I felt like that with her. Look here, Faith, I'm not a rake. I understood what happened, but I don't appreciate just now your taking me to task for it…"

"I'm not taking you to task, Tom,—and I'm just trying to defend a good friend who's been hurt badly. Please understand that." She sipped her aperitif and stared hard at me. Tourists around us made too much noise. "Do you understand me?"

"I do, but as my father used to say, 'It takes two to tango.' I didn't plan the seduction. She asked for it, and I was as careful about it as I could be. You know I'm no angel. And if you don't behave yourself, I might make a significant pass at you." I said this as quietly and unaggressively as possible.

"You wouldn't."

"Why not? You're good looking, intelligent and more than a little sexy…"

"That's not enough to turn your head from the European ladies. I'm American…"

"So is Pam…"

"What are we proving now, Tom? I do like you very much. I wouldn't have asked to see you, if I didn't think we had some real basis of understanding …"

"You do know that you taught me something that night in Caux. I even held you close, but it wasn't predatory."

"Oh?" She looked startled, then laughed.

"You analyzed me correctly…which makes a lot of your talk now seem ridiculous. Maybe you didn't know what you said when we talked about people being hurt."

"Oh, yes. I do know…"

"And I've thought about it a lot since you mentioned it. Because you were right."

"Tom, I don't bring up Pam now to try to corner you. You'll do what you have to. She's my good friend, and …"

"…and you're worried about her. I appreciate that, more than you know. If you think I should speak to her—and I can do it without hurting her more—I'll do it. But I'm nervous about it. It's not anything I can do much about. Almost the same thing applies to Buck Birnbaum. I like him, I have a loving feeling for him, because he's so damned ambitious and well motivated. Look at him now."

"So we're back where I began," Faith said. She sat there, staring at the small park across the street. "I wonder if our meeting was necessary." Her forehead bunched up in a frown, and I felt rotten.

"Faith," I said, "your feelings for people you care about are fantastic. But you're talking to a person you already know a lot about, and I'm as sorry for Pam as you are—almost—but what can I do? Realistically?"

"I could say, you might be less selfish, but I'm not sure that's fair."

"Thanks for that."

We parted without recriminations, but I had the feeling the whole world was slowly disintegrating.

TWENTY-THREE

Irene came downstairs past my open room door on her way out of the hotel, when I said: "Hey!" Her steps came to a halt, and I heard the silence. "Aren't you going to say goodbye?" The stair creaked as she turned and retraced her steps, and soon she appeared in the doorframe. Then her eyes opened wide when she noticed the blonde hair of the woman sitting in a chair next to me on the bed.

"Irène, you know Ellen Cassidy" I said, purposely using her French name. "You ought to get to know each other better."

"Enchanté," said the Russian girl, her eyes still wide. "We've met." Ellen stood to shake her hand.

"She's an old friend. Come join us."

"Non, merci. I have to go out now. But I hope we may meet again," Irene said when she began to withdraw. Ellen sat down again as I went to the door with Irene. When we were outside I said the encounter was no accident, that I was serious about saying goodbye. "It is not proper at this moment," she whispered.

"But I thought it proper to ask if you were going to say adieu."

"I will say what I will say when you next invite me to dinner," she said firmly, still in a whisper.

"I thought you had forgotten."

"I forget nothing," she said. "When you will."

"This evening?"

"Maybe. I have to inquire of someone. I'll return soon to tell you—unless you are seeing her."

"I'm seeing her now about something important, but we will be finished in an hour."

"I will return then," she said coolly, still looking confused by the situation I had created. "Au revoir."

"À bientôt," I said, trying to touch her, but she pulled away. I re-entered the room.

"Excuse me, Ellen, it was an inspiration of the moment."

"She did not look happy," Ellen said. "You caught her off-guard." She held her head high appraising me as I sat down. Her look conveyed curiosity but discretion, so I had to explain.

"A fellow resident in this establishment."

"That sounds convenient."

"It is. We are like a family sometimes. She's not French. A Moroccan. You know her. Lives with her sister and her child upstairs."

"Aha. She's very pretty. Exotic. Your tastes have always been good, Tom. Yes, I've seen you together—several times. When you called her that night to make the peace. Now let's get back to Buck. I've seen him once in all this time since Caux…"

"Since us," I said.

"Since Caux, please. Remember the rules. And he wasn't very sober."

""Does he know your role in the so-called accident?"

"It was an accident," she bridled. "I had no intention to cause what happened. But he doesn't seem to realize what really occurred. Tom, I was angry and out of sorts that day, but I'm not vindictive. Anyway, I'd rather you drop it. What concerns me is his condition, his throwing away money in that publishing adventure, its effect on Fred, who's banking on it, and some other things. What I don't want to happen is that I turn into a nurse for him. I'm not good at nursing, especially now that you're here…"

"You did begin something, you know."

"Let's not discuss that now, please. We'll resolve it, because it's not over…"

"That's reassuring," I said. "So what do you propose to do about Buck Birnbaum?"

"That's why I'm here. Can we do anything? We certainly can't let him go to pot here. He's got no friends in Paris. His relations with his poufy friends are poor now that the drinking's taken over."

"He's an idealist, Ellen, and what we've got to be sure of is why he's dropped down so far. I think it was the failure of the conference that did it—that and what Faith Carlson told me the other day…"

"What's that?"

"The prospect of being forced into the family business back in New York."

"Oh, God, that's too much! When did that come up? That's one of his oldest nightmares."

"Some recent letters."

"Dear Christ!" she said uncharacteristically, "what terrible timing. The youngest son in the family…you can't imagine how he's worried about that for so many years. He talked and worried about it back at Columbia. I'm intimately familiar with that old fear."

"So what we have is: that plus his broken leg plus the termination of his dream conference plus his suspicion about you and me. A nice kettle of fish! And—oh, yes: the interruption of his affair with Bob."

"Exactly. Can any of them be resolved?" she said. "By us, any of us?"

"We'll have to try. He's an important person."

"The reason I'm here, Tom, is that this has to come first. Ahead of us." That stopped me; it confirmed something that had been on my mind for weeks.

"You're right, and I have no idea how. Faith Carlson's extremely disturbed by him. We need more minds on this than ourselves. Tonight we all ought to get together. Sometime after dinner…"

"After your dinner with Irene," she said. "I couldn't help hear you two."

"Oh, Jesus," I said, "If you must know, we're parting, and we have to talk."

"Oh, Tom. What a life you live!" She regarded me with full affection in her eyes. "I'll see if I can arrange something with the others, sometime before midnight."

I said fine, and as she arose, I held her around the waist and looked deep into her blue eyes—and, reluctantly, released her. The gaze she gave me was indescribable. She frowned, looking away, as though she wasn't sure.

※

There was sadness in Irene's face that night at dinner. She indeed had found someone new and didn't quite know how to break the news to me. So I took the initiative after the waiter came with new serviettes, glistening cutlery, plus, of course, the fresh bread and the Dijon mustard I had come to love.

"I hope you didn't mind this afternoon. Everything has to come to an end, but I wanted to see if a Moroccan girl and an American could be civilized about saying goodbye." One tear popped out of her eye. "It's important to me because of what happened to your sister. This time the shoe's on the other foot. But you know damned well it was just a matter of time. I don't mind it, except how I still feel about you."

A long menu was delivered to us when she sat up straight and looked into my eyes—grey into blue.

"Thomas," she cried, "you don't know how…"

"…much you mean to me," I said. She broke down, and I squeezed her hand hard. "I didn't think your social conscience would take to this sort of thing."

"You are the last person I would want to hurt. You have done so much for me."

I ordered a carafe of Côte de Rhône, which I knew she liked. The waiter then took our order of gigot and biftek…both saignant or bloody.

"Look, you gypsy-face"—at that she brightened—"no one owes anything to anyone else in this world. Whatever I have done for you I wanted to do. Yes, I have been crazy for you—but when I saw your face become so beautifully calm in the cathedral that day—that was enough for me—just to see it. Until now I've taken pleasure by putting myself inside of others. Not sex—I mean helping others see the same things that make me happy…"

"You were meant to be a teacher, I think," she said. "You've been wonderful for me, even in your room when we've had such a grand time making love. But I don't mean that only. I mean the little things you've shown me in Paris, things I should know but haven't until you showed me. But now I believe you have changed. Something's happened to you. It's affected me, and things have changed. I almost feel you are somewhere else, even now. It's almost as if you were in a deep love affair with someone—maybe that woman in your room this afternoon. Someone."

I stopped thinking at that moment. She went on. "I have met someone new. You are right. But it's happened at the time something's happened to you. Maybe we are trading lovers, because…I don't know…in a way we have traded places. It's so difficult to talk about. And I am confused…not sure."

For dessert we ordered our usual fromage and fruit.

I said: "You live for the moment. I once told you that when we first met. That was the thing I admired so much about you… and still do."

"Perhaps that's true," she said. "Tom, I will never forget you." She held out her hand for me to take, and I kissed it.

"Enough of this nonsense," I said to break the sentimentality. "We've had fun, and this should be a celebration." I raised my glass of wine to her. "To us," I said.

"I still feel awful about it."

"Because you are a woman of strong principles, and at heart you are sentimental under that political skin of yours."

"You've always liked my skin," she said with an element of pride, "my derrière," she laughed.

"I hope your new man does, too."

"Yes, he does, but not like you," she leaned toward me across the table and kissed my nose. "Pas comme toi. He's very shy. We may marry."

"That sounds good," I said and kissed her hand again. "If you are sure."

"That is why I am waiting."

It was a strange, mature way of ending things between us, but I had the feeling that she was immensely happy about how it had worked out. Inside, we both were crying; outside, it wasn't so bad. Pas mal, as the French say.

"There is irony," I said.

"How?"

"As I told you before, twice you said I would leave you. Instead…"

"A good omen for me perhaps, chéri," she said.

I smiled at her and raised my glass again.

⊚⊚

I felt like I had passed a tough examination in school. But I also knew that many things were getting beyond my control. Both Pam and Irene were ladies of the past, and Joyce would soon return to Britain. My harem was dwindling.

I walked briskly down the rue de Seine to the quai Malaquais, where the group had been told to meet by Ellen for the Birnbaum pow-wow. She was serious about the gathering and had lost no time in naming the café. The only one not coming, she announced when we had all gathered and ordered drinks, was Pam, who was ill. And Bill was putting in his final appearance.

"We saw Buck for a brief moment on the way here," Bill Watson said. "At the Lipp," he continued, "we caught a quick view of him staggering along the boulevard. I guess the leg is still weak. He's still using the cane to keep his balance with all the booze in him. Lizette was with him. She had to steady him."

Norm Tunison raised a brow at that, looking sheepishly for a second at Betty. I wonder if she knew that Lizette and Norman had lived together at one time. Joyce sat between her two lovers, Bill and embittered Fred, mildly amused at the conversation and every once in a while flashing her smile at me. Homer Fangwort had come, but not Bob Kemperman, and was sitting with me and Ellen.

"What's this all about?" he asked Ellen. "That was pretty short notice."

Ellen explained her concern for Buck and his present condition. Almost as if we were resuming the conference at Caux, she presented all the facts about him and what had happened since the Swiss conference had broken up. She was very thorough about all the details, even covering her own involvement in his fall down the mountain, dismissing it as an "accident," as she had with me that afternoon.

"The problem is," she said, "if we all respect and care for him, we can't see him go to pieces here in Paris, where he has no friends and no one to guard him. And the vital thing we need tonight is some intelligent suggestion about what he needs and how we can help provide assistance. He's one of us, after all."

"I assumed," said Norman, "that you were his guardian, as you put it. You've been with him all the time."

"Not any more," she said, surprising several of us. She went on to explain in her own way that their relationship had changed—without going into any details—and that she couldn't assume that responsibility any longer. "I do, however, have an obligation to help him get through this terrible period."

"Can't we be straight with him?" Bill said. "Just get together in a friendly way and…"

Everyone expressed their concerns and gave their solutions to the problem Buck presented, and it went on for more than an hour. I sat back and looked out of the café to the opposite shore where the Tuileries Gardens ran west of the Louvre. The Seine was blinking with the lights of Paris, spreading necklaces magically. I had little to contribute, having several of my own reservations. Buck was indeed a problem.

Norman once asked me about Irene, and I avoided answering him directly. Not satisfied with my answer, Betty carried on in her solicitous way with a few words of encouragement.

My eye followed the small lights on the Pont des Arts, the narrow bridge spanning the Seine just west of the Vert Galant at the tip of the Île de la Cité, the bridge on which Pamela had done her wild dance. And where we had shared dreams—our bridge. Then I looked up-river to the great illuminated squat towers of Notre Dame Cathedral at the other end of the Île. It was such a pleasant sight, this heart of the brightly lit city where all lines north and south spanned the river, a crossroads that had fascinated so many people over the centuries. Jewels gleaming on a woman's breast. Nearby was the Pont Neuf, the most famous bridge of Paris and one of its most beautiful. The gay lights adorning this artery of our world made it all seem like a fairy tale.

I detected a slight commotion on the Pont des Arts, but it faded into the fantasy of the city. I drifted in and out of the conversation about Buck Birnbaum. Then three bicycle-riding policemen went by in a rush, their capes flying—and I sensed a new worry, an insecurity. I watched them stop at the Pont des Arts. They ran out to the center of the narrow wooden bridge. In a few moments, some pedestrians on their boisterous way past us were discussing something that had occurred on the bridge, and I overheard one of them talking about someone having jumped, probably not an uncommon event in such a big city. My uneasiness burst into fear. Down on the river a small boat sped by towards the bridge.

"Got to go," I said. But the others were already running with me.

We ran up the quai towards the Pont des Arts. A policeman held a passport and a pair of glasses. There was no question it was

Pam. "Oh, good God!" I cried. I was in the war again, at Monte Cassino where the grenade went off. Sally and Faith took hold of me. I don't know how long I screamed in anger out over the river.

An eternity later we spoke to the police and told them who we were. They asked us to go to the station with them. I had no sense of what was going on, but they said it took only an hour for the rescue team to recover the body. Ellen, Sally and Faith took me back to the hotel. They poured a stiff drink for me. Pam's face was before me. Sally and Faith left me alone with Ellen. She lay clothed on the bed comforting me. All night long, the bells of St. Sulpice announced every quarter hour. Pam's face would not leave me. "Now I am blind," she kept saying. At six o'clock Ellen stroked my cheek, and I passed out while Paris stirred.

There was a memorial service for Pamela in two days. Ellen continued to help me. I said very little. She fed me in the room, stayed with me like a full time nurse and took care of my needs.

"I keep seeing her face, Ellen. It won't go away."

"Think of something else—of me."

It took a great effort to attend the memorial service at the American Church, and I tried to get away from myself by notifying Pam's parents and making all the necessary arrangements for the body to be returned to Illinois. But Ellen really did it all. And all the time Pam's face was before me.

Once Faith and Sally came to visit me after the memorial service. I could see they never fully understood the guilt I felt, save once, when Faith reminded me: "Now you've been hurt three times that I know of." That evening, Ellen forced me out to dinner at a fancy restaurant on the Place St. Michel. We looked down on the Seine from the second floor of the Rôtisserie Perigourdine. The food was good but tasteless to me, even the framboises I usually relished. All the sweetness was gone. She tried to be reassuring.

"Tommy," she said several times, "why should you feel this guilt? It wasn't anything you did at all. It took two to tango—you said that. It all stemmed from the nervous breakdowns she had. A classic case."

"Easy for you to say. Whether you're right or wrong, I feel it."

"We all have to face the music a few times in our lives," she insisted, "but we aren't responsible for everything that happens…you least of all."

" But I collaborated."

"Let it slide by, like the river down there." We watched the water streaming past us.

"I guess I'll have to."

"Now," she said, staring right into my eyes. "Let's pull ourselves together. It's time for us to get the hell out of this city." I realized she had said "us," wondering if it were only a figure of speech.

Before she walked home with me, she asked if I had contacted Buck.

"I tried once the other day. I wanted to square things with him."

"Good," she said. "And what happened?"

"He was drunk, it was pointless."

"But you tried, at least. That's the point." She seemed encouraged. As we moved slowly up along the rue Christine away from the river, the theatrical lights of that old part of the 6th Arrondissement fell on us kindly from above. We held hands while we walked. Once on the rue Dauphine she put her arm around my waist, looked up at me. I began to feel more normal again. Pam's face became diffused in the familiar setting of old Paris. "Where will we go?" she said. She had said "we."

"How about tomorrow to the Loire? To lose ourselves…the castles."

"That sounds good. Fast. You need a change of scene."

"Maybe Blois."

"Never been there," she said. "Castles—sounds just right."

She didn't tell me until we left in the morning, that she had called Buck later that night. She told him about us leaving Paris and he hit the ceiling. All he could do was give her hot anger and recriminations. "Iscariot and his harlot won't get away from me!" he had threatened. "I'll follow you wherever you go." She never expected that strong a reaction and was sorry she had even mentioned it.

TWENTY-FOUR

The Simca we rented was tinny and tiny, but it had enough power to move us to the south out of the city. Circulating around the Place de la Concorde was always a hazardous experience for any American, but we made it.

We were in dense traffic along the Seine. The Eiffel Tower snapped by, and across the river to the west, the Bois de Boulogne were soon bypassed. I had no idea precisely where we were headed, but the compulsion to leave the city behind us was overpowering. I was moving southwest, an old compass point towards the Loire Valley, which Ellen thought might give me more peace of mind away from the Paris ghosts. Somehow Blois seemed a fair destination. And driving the small car in the persistent, menacing traffic was an antidote for me. Every once in a while I turned toward Ellen. She was so necessary for me to recover from the shock of Pam's death. I drew balance from her, and hope.

"You're doing fine, darling."

"Where are the butterflies these days? Haven't seen you making your little sketches."

She put her hand on my thigh and gripped me playfully. "That's where they've gone. It's all arranged."

I reached down to take her hand, but she resisted.

"Eyes on the road, please," she said. "We have lots of time for nonsense."

"My kind of nonsense." I said.

She went on: "You sound better, Tom. This is part of your therapy, and I want you to keep your eyes on the road and not talk too much."

"Okay," I said.

She began humming a tune I couldn't recognize.

As we passed Versailles, I saw the sign to Rambouillet, and when we went through the summer capital I remembered the road I last had seen from a bicycle on a trip with Irene. The countryside was familiar, too, but I told myself not to dwell on it. Ellen hummed her tune. I pressed harder on the gas.

I looked in the rear mirror to be sure of myself. Ellen turned several times to look out of the rear window. When I asked her why, she told me about Buck's words to her the night before. We plowed on. I was feeling better. The ride reinforced my sense of escape, that old feeling that had removed me from harm's way so many times before. In a few minutes the roadsign for Ablis appeared, the place Irene and I had spent overnight during the storm that pushed our bodies together. "Damn it!" I said aloud. Ellen put her hand back on my thigh...

"I've been here before. Sorry."

"Long ago?"

"No. With Irene—our trip to Chartres."

"Oh, the famous trip. I remember. What happened there? You never seemed the same afterwards."

"It affected me."

"Did she affect you, too?"

"Not as much as Chartres, but she was a vital part of it."

"Oh, I see." She looked at me. I wondered what she detected. Her hand, still on my thigh, squeezed softly in some sympathetic reaction. Then she said, "You two split the other day. I noticed it in your room when we were talking. And then the dinner. I don't want to be nosey, but was it eventful?"

"It was civilized," I said.

"No recriminations?"

"It was rather touching..."

265

"But it hurt," she said, taking her hand away.

"Yes. For both of us."

"Were you in love with her, Tom—and she with you?"

"I'm not sure, but I always react badly when I'm shoved away."

"Maybe you should have done the shoving, Tom. You're awfully passive sometimes. I've seen that."

"Please put your hand back. I love you, Ellen."

"We're talking about you and Irene."

"I wanted it to be good fun, but she wanted more…"

"Like you and Joyce—you and your harem. Tom, don't you see? You affect people, especially women. We all love you, but you hardly ever go the full round. You get hurt unnecessarily. You go all the way with us but you don't go all the way with yourself." It was a valid point, and it stopped me.

The car sped on. "So I'm a lousy lover," I said.

"You're a wonderful lover, but you withhold something. You give us pleasure but that's not enough. It wasn't enough for Pam or Irene or Joyce."

"You're talking about commitment."

"Yes, we want it. Even Joyce, who seems highly excitable. All of us want that extra mile, but you run out of gas, as you once said."

I hadn't expected this from Ellen.

"And it's not just commitment. It's loyalty. We want to be able to count on you—when we need you and even when we don't. Trite, isn't it? When we allow you into our bodies, we expect that loyalty. Otherwise, you're no different from Buck …"

I recalled Edouard's statement about loyalty, his faith in it. Although he had used the word in connection with the Maquis and his exploits during the war, it had a far larger meaning, something to do with a sense of allegiance and true interdependence—no small order.

"Is this upsetting to you?" she said. "I'm sorry, but the words about Irene started it all. She's just a kid. She idolized you. I could see it whenever we got together with the group. Her eyes shone with such an intensity when she looked at you. You had her hooked totally—except for the one thing, and she finally realized it, apparently."

"He, the new man, is somewhat shy, she tells me. She's considering marriage."

"See?" she said and smiled. I stopped the car off the road, and clutched her close. It was the longest, deepest kiss I had ever given to and received from a woman, and my heart was pumping hard with her message. All at once I realized what she had done for me, and I hadn't questioned it until I was driving a car to escape from Paris. She had been with me three days, watching over me like a nurse. Her generosity—her loyalty—had been entirely unselfish and sincere. And the lesson I might have learned from the three women leaving my life—all within a week—she now gave to me in this cheap little car carrying us away. Away from what?

Cars passed us on the road, one of them far over the speed limit. "Another crazy Frenchman," I said. Ellen followed it with a quick turn of her head.

"Maybe Buck!" she said. Time passed. She relaxed. We sat there and took each other in. Finally, she put her finger to her lips as if to silence me. "Tom, in the lake that day after we lay there on the beach and began to fall in love with each other and then consummated it like the innocents we really were, I knew. And you knew, too. You told me with your eyes, not your tongue. You gave from the goodness of your heart. You understood about the butterflies and the dark, hostile air in which they flew. That day will never leave us. You changed towards me after that, and I towards you. When I saw you again in Paris after that Spanish caper to Pamplona, I was sure. Just because of the way you looked at me—and I'm sure I couldn't hide my feelings from you. It may sound ridiculous, but it was like sitting at a Punch and Judy show, waiting for the story to unfold, and I saw all the players making good moves and bad moves. It was a spectacle, and you were there, pulling the strings. Then you needed help to pull your own string. I had to say something to tell you how much I loved you—and why."

I got out of the car and walked around to her side. I opened the door and beckoned her out. "Please," I said. Ellen had that look I had only seen twice before in my life. She stood straight and faced me. I took both her hands in mine and pulled her to me, our arms completely around each other and our heads side by side. It went on for minutes, and we were silent.

Finally, I said, "Thank you for being in my life." She began to cry and smile at the same time, and I urged her to get back into the car. The cathedral came to mind, and the light was still strong enough. Maybe we could make it. The sun would be on the windows of the west front, and we were only fifteen minutes away. I started the car and we flew along the road. Just ahead of us, as we came into the hill town of Chartres, another car was speeding up the road. Ellen became uneasy.

The narrow streets of the town weren't easy to negotiate, and it would have been disastrous if we were going too fast. We climbed while the engine moaned, moving up back streets that rose to the summit where the cathedral and its two high towers stood over the town. The light was failing now, and I urged the vehicle on, negotiating some tricky turns. I wasn't sure we would make it in time to catch the setting sun on the blue windows.

Then car brakes screeched ahead of me, and I desperately squashed down on my own brakes. We heard the crash. The car ahead had smashed into the side of a building just short of the summit. Garbage cans and glass were all over the streets. Smoke came from the car. It had hit a curb, leaped up against the wall of a building and come to rest on its side. The driver's door was open, a bleeding body thrown askew.

Just then the giant bells of the cathedral began their deafening toll. I got out of the car while the big bells boomed their message of six o'clock and ran towards the broken car and body. A police car hurtled up the street. Moments later a young gendarme was leaning over the body with me, listened to the heart while taking the man's pulse. He pronounced the body dead. He turned the victim over, while the heavy bells tolled. Ellen took one look and screamed.

"Oh, my God, it's Buck!"

"You know this man, madame?" the gendarme said. He began going through the torn jacket and pulled out his passport and wallet. He examined both carefully, and discovered a small envelope. It had French stamps used for airmail to the U.S.A. He handed it to me, and I read Buck's father's name and home address on Central Park West. He then extracted a piece of paper from the slit envelope. Ellen trembled.

"C'est en anglais," the gendarme said, and I grabbed the note. Among many words written in Buck's crabbed hand were some addressed to his father: "I will definitely not return to ruin my life."

I explained the note. "He was our friend."

"What a pity," he said.

We got back into the car and accompanied the gendarme to the police station to give our statement. The body was picked up by an emergency vehicle. Its sirens screamed in the streets. Then we left the station and drove back up to the cathedral. The bells had rung long, but now they had faded into the siren's call. Ellen put her arm around my shoulder while we looked at the statues. We walked into the church hand in hand. That was the end of it.

Epilogue

It had been a special recollection, that landmark class reunion. And it was coming to an end. We milled around in the big, lavish rooms under the high ceilings and ornate crystal chandeliers, waiting to go. After two days we had become used to these rich surroundings from another era, felt more comfortable in the unique ambiance of the place, and strangely enough tried to preserve the feeling of being there, even though our classmates' faceless shadows called into question what and whom we were recalling. Our reluctance to leave was embarrassing after awhile.

When the reunion came to an end, we stood around on the Arden House front steps, and Jack McCormick solicitously bade each of us a brief farewell. "Glad to see you all again. Make it the next time." Many weak handshakes, gestures of goodbye. There was always the unexpressed question: who would be around the next time?

Ellen and I drove south and over the George Washington Bridge back into Manhattan. Then we sped on our way east over the Triborough, past LaGuardia Airport on our way to Long Island and our beach house on the south shore. Traffic was light, and Ellen was extremely quiet beside me. There was a feeling of relief from the revival of the past we had been exposed to during the landmark reunion.

It was the end of more than an old class get-together. Like all anniversaries, digging up old memories gave us a sinking feeling.

The Street of Four Winds

It was as if we had taken a long swim in the ocean and touched strange, forgotten objects in the water around us. A weird immersion in ancient times with a mixture of pleasant and difficult recollections. One thing for sure: the tide moved in and out, like our lives. Perhaps that accounted for the silence in the car as Ellen and I drove south, a silence I tried to break by switching on an FM radio station and its soothing music.

This was self-defeating, because by chance I had tuned in on a program of old Noel Coward songs, the first of which happened to be "I'll Follow My Secret Heart." Very sentimental. Nostalgic. The music inevitably brought Pam Batterford to mind, and all of the past just revisited with Norman, Betty and Fred misted around me.

Then, strangely enough, Joyce Frost reappeared, Joyce and her bright spontaneity, her resonant love of life and vice versa. How Bill Watson's obsession with her "red" color, as he saw it, was a key to all of her Paris passions so long ago. Her ghost drifted near...

Ellen must have had second thoughts about the reunion, too.

"I was just thinking of your first words the other day, Tom, when we drove up there," she said softly.

"The irony, you mean?"

"Yes. Our many ironies, the twists of fate in our Paris cauldron."

"You make it sound like Macbeth. But you're right. It was ironical—a bunch of Americans abroad, trying to grow up and understand themselves."

"Did you ever?"

"What?"

"Grow up?"

"Never," I said.

"And the people! What a cast of characters! Remember when Joyce—out of nowhere—sent you the red painting so many years ago."

"She had a reason for that, I suppose. Amazing how she got my name from that by-lined story the *Manchester Guardian* picked up from the wire service. It was like her to do that."

"A delayed gift to her teacher," Ellen said.

"Me, a teacher? More likely she was mine."

"Or maybe her attempt to change her life and make us laugh at the same time."

"Possibly."

Now our house appeared in the headlights, and I fumbled for the garage opener.

"Please don't drive in just yet," Ellen said. "And open the windows, will you? I want to hear the sea."

"Haven't you had enough of that? If we extend it, the trip down memory lane can be a drag."

I opened both side windows of the Peugeot, admitting the sound she sought along with a light, refreshing breeze. "Brise Marine" clicked in my mind, the old Mallarmé poem Irene once read to me.

The wind came in with the distant ocean sounds, one of the four winds…the shortest street in Paris…the Hôtel des Quatre Vents, now, sadly, transformed into an office building.

"Got enough of the sea sounds?" I asked.

"No," she said. "It's so cleansing."

She shuddered, and I reached for her hand. It came alive.

We sat there in the driveway, listening to the ocean waves breaking on the shore behind the house. And the four winds sighed. They were talking to us. They always talked to us, bringing strange movement into our lives.

"Memories and possibilities," she said, suddenly romantic. I sat there, holding her lively hand, and thought of Irene and Pam, Fred and Goodie, Sally, Buck and Faith, Norman and Joyce, Bill— all of them. The whole Paris "bande," Betty used to say. Now it was like the trailer to a movie, a Fellini film running in and out of the past while the ocean breeze whispered…

Then the blue lights of the cathedral windows caught Irene's grey eyes…bright beacons of beauty. Like a dog ridding itself of rain, I shook my head and released Ellen's hand. It felt confining in the car.

The Street of Four Winds

I cleared my throat and lit a cigarette, then opened my door to get out. Once there, free, I paused, took a deep breath before a drag on my cigarette, and walked around the car to her door.

"You look like a firefly with that cigarette," Ellen said when I came around.

"Firefly or butterfly?" She laughed.

"Mere figures of speech—that's what we are," she said.

The film was still running. Another wind blowing. She came out quickly and our arms were automatically around each other again, hugging like we had so long ago. We lingered there in the darkness, close together, my ear against her faded blonde hair, as to a shell from the sea, listening. Ocean breakers continued beating the coast beyond us, sounding metaphors.

Check out these other fine titles by
Durban House at your local book store.

Exceptional Books
by
Exceptional Writers

Current Titles

BASHA   John Hamilton Lewis

DEADLY ILLUMINATION   Serena Stier

DEATH OF A HEALER   Paul Henry Young

HOUR OF THE WOLVES   Stephane Daimlen-Völs

A HOUSTON WEEKEND   Orville Palmer

JOHNNIE RAY & MISS KILGALLEN   Bonnie Hearn Hill & Larry Hill

THE MEDUSA STRAIN   Chris Holmes

MR. IRRELEVANT   Jerry Marshall

OPAL EYE DEVIL   John Hamilton Lewis

PRIVATE JUSTICE   Richard Sand

ROADHOUSE BLUES   Baron Birtcher

RUBY TUESDAY   Baron Birtcher

THE SERIAL KILLER'S DIET BOOK   Kevin Mark Postupack

THE STREET OF FOUR WINDS   Andrew Lazarus

TUNNEL RUNNER   Richard Sand

WHAT GOES AROUND   Don Goldman

Nonfiction

MIDDLE ESSENCE—WOMEN OF WONDER YEARS   Landy Reed

PROTOCOL   Mary Jane McCaffree & Pauline Innis
   For 25 years, the bible for public relations firms, corporations, embassies, governments and individuals seeking to do business with the Federal government.

BASHA   JOHN HAMILTON LEWIS

Set in the world of elite professional tennis and rooted in ancient Middle East hatreds of identity and blood loyalties, Basha is charged with the fiercely competitive nature of professional sports and the dangers of terrorism. An already simmering Middle East begins to boil and CIA Station Chief Grant Corbet must track down the highly successful terrorist, Basha. In a deadly race against time, Grant hunts the illusive killer only to see his worst nightmare realized.

DEADLY ILLUMINATION   SERENA STIER

It's summer 1890 in New York City. Florence Tod, an ebullient young woman, must challenge financier, John Pierpont Morgan, to solve a possible murder. J.P.'s librarian has ingested poison embedded in an illumination of a unique Hildegard van Bingen manuscript. Florence and her cousin, Isabella Stewart Gardner, discover the corpse. When Isabella secretly removes a gold tablet from the scene of the crime, she sets off a chain of events that will involve Florence and her in a dangerous conspiracy.

DEATH OF A HEALER   PAUL HENRY YOUNG

Diehard romanticist and surgeon extraordinaire, Jake Gibson, struggles to preserve his professional oath against the avarice and abuse of power so prevalent in present-day America. Jake's personal quest is at direct odds with a group of sinister medical and legal practitioners who plot to eliminate patient groups in order to improve the bottom line. With the lives of his family on the line, Jake must expose the darker side of the medical world.

HOUR OF THE WOLVES   STEPHANE DAIMLEN-VÖLS

After more than three centuries, the *Poisons Affair* remains one of history's great, unsolved mysteries. The worst impulses of human nature—sordid sexual perversion, murderous intrigues, witchcraft, Satanic cults—thrive within the shadows of the Sun King's absolutism and will culminate in the darkest secret of his reign: the infamous *Poisons Affair,* a remarkably complex web of horror, masked by Baroque splendor, luxury and refinement.

A HOUSTON WEEKEND   ORVILLE PALMER

Professor Edward Randall, not-yet-forty, divorced and separated from his daughters, is leading a solitary, cheerless existence in a university town. At a conference in Houston he runs into his childhood sweetheart. Then she was poverty-stricken, neglected and American Indian. Now she's elegantly attired, driving an expensive Italian car and lives in a millionaires enclave. Will their fortuitous encounter grow into anything meaningful?

JOHNNIE RAY & MISS KILGALLEN   BONNIE HEARN HILL & LARRY HILL

Johnnie Ray was a sexually conflicted wild man out of control; Dorothy Kilgallen, fifteen years his senior, was the picture of decorum as a Broadway columnist and TV personality. The last thing they needed was to fall in love—with each other. Sex, betrayal, money, drugs, drink and more drink. Together they descended into a nightmare of assassination conspiracies, bizarre suicides and government enemy lists until Dorothy dies…mysteriously. Was it suicide…or murder?

The Medusa Strain   Chris Holmes

A gripping tale of bio-terrorism that stunningly portrays the dangers of chemical warfare in ways nonfiction never could. When an Iraqi scientist full of hatred for America breeds a deadly form of anthrax and a diabolical means to initiate an epidemic, not even the First Family is immune. Will America's premier anthrax researcher devise a bio-weapon in time to save the U.S. from extinction?

Mr. Irrelevant   Jerry Marshall

Sports writer Paul Tenkiller and pro-football player Chesty Hake have been roommates for eight seasons. Paul's Choctaw background and his sports gambling, and Chesty's memories of his mother's killing are the dark forces that will ensnare Tenkiller in Hake's slide into a murderous paranoia—but Paul is behind the curve that is spinning Chesty out of his control.

Opal Eye Devil   John Hamilton Lewis

From the teeming wharves of Shanghai to the stately offices of New York and London, Robber Barons lie, steal, cheat, and kill in their quest for power. Eric Gradek will rise from the *Northern Star's* dark cargo hold to the pinnacle of high stakes gambling for unrivaled riches. Aided by his beautiful wife, Katheryn, and the devoted Tong-Po, Eric fights for his dream and for revenge against the man who left him for dead aboard *Northern Star*.

Private Justice   Richard Sand

After taking brutal revenge for the murder of his twin brother, Lucas Rook leaves the NYPD to work for others who crave justice outside the law when the system fails them. Rook's dark journey takes him on a race to find a killer whose appetite is growing. A little girl turns up dead. And then another and another. The nightmare is on him fast. The piano player has monstrous hands; the Medical Examiner is a goulish dwarf; an investigator kills himself. Betrayal and intrigue is added to the deadly mix as the story careens toward its startling end.

Roadhouse Blues   Baron Birtcher

Newly retired Homicide detective Mike Travis is torn from the comfort of his chartered yacht business into the dark, bizarre underbelly of LA's music scene by a grisly string of murders. A handsome, drug-addled psychopath has reemerged from an ancient Dionysian cult, leaving a bloody trail of seemingly unrelated victims in his wake.

Ruby Tuesday   Baron Birtcher

Mike Travis sails his yacht to Kona, Hawaii expecting to put LA Homicide behind him: to let the warm emerald sea wash years of blood from his hands. Instead, he finds his family's home ravaged by shotgun blasts, littered with bodies and trashed with drugs. Then things get worse. A rock star involved in a Wall Street deal masterminded by Travis's brother is one of the victims. Another victim is Ruby, Travis's childhood sweetheart. How was she involved?

THE SERIAL KILLER'S DIET BOOK   KEVIN MARK POSTUPACK
Fred Orbis is fat—very fat—but will soon discover the ultimate diet. Devon DeGroot is on the trail of a homicidal maniac who prowls Manhattan with meatballs, bologna and egg salad—taunting him about the body count in *Finnegans Wakean*. Darby Montana, one of the world's richest women, wants a new set of genes to alter a face and body so homely not even plastic surgery could help. Mr. Monde is the Devil in the market for a soul or two. It's a Faustian satire on God and the Devil, Heaven and Hell, beauty and the best-seller list.

THE STREET OF FOUR WINDS   ANDREW LAZARUS
Paris—just after World War II. On the Left Bank, Americans seek a way to express their dreams, delights and disappointments in a way very different from pre-war ex-patriots. Tom Cortell is a tough, intellectual journalist disarmed by three women-French, British and American. Along with him is a gallery of international characters who lead a merry and sometimes desperate chase between Pairs, Switzerland and Spain to a final, liberating and often tragic end of their European wanderings in search of themselves.

TUNNEL RUNNER   RICHARD SAND
Ashman is a denizen of a dark world where murder is committed and no one is brought to account; where loyalties exist side-by-side with lies and extreme violence. One morning he awakens to find himself paralyzed in a mental hospital. He escapes and seeks vengeance, confronting old friends, the Pentagon, the Mafia, and a mysterious general who is covering up the attack on TWA Flight 800.

WHAT GOES AROUND   DON GOLDMAN
Ten years ago, Ray Banno was vice president of a California bank when his boss, Andre Rhodes, framed him for bank fraud. Now, he has his new identity, a new face and a new life in medical research. He's on the verge of finding a cure for a deadly disease when he's chosen as a juror in the bank fraud trial of Andre Rhodes. Should he take revenge? Meanwhile, Rhodes is about to gain financial control of Banno's laboratory in order to destroy Banno's work

Nonfiction

MIDDLE ESSENCE—WOMEN OF WONDER YEARS   LANDY REED
Here is a roadmap and a companion to what can be the most profoundly significant and richest years of a woman's life. For every woman approaching, at, or beyond midlife, this guide is rich with stories of real women in real circumstances who find they have a second chance-a time when women blossom rather than fade. Gain a new understanding of how to move beyond myths of aging; address midlife transitions head on; discover new power and potential; and emerge with a stronger sense of self